# BURN UP

## JACKSON KANE

------------HOT TREE PUBLISHING------------

For information, contact the publisher, Hot Tree Publishing.
WWW.HOTTREEPUBLISHING.COM

EDITING: HOT TREE EDITING
COVER DESIGNER: BOOKSMITH DESIGN
FORMATTING: RMGRAPHX

E-book ISBN: 978-1-925853-79-7
Paperback ISBN: 978-1-925853-81-0

# Steel Veins

# Prologue

The best thing about being the baddest motherfuckers on the block is knowing that no one has the balls to say otherwise. We could walk around like king shit because people did what we told them to do. Yeah, we were still relatively new as a club, but we took this town over like a tornado.

A club like ours was still small fish in the scheme of things, but without any nearby competition and nobody to fuck with us, we seemed all that much bigger in this tiny-ass pond.

I wasn't a greedy man, but standing on a bed lined with cash and two girls on my nuts, I knew what I liked.

I was a king, and this was my throne.

"Hendrix, baby. Let me play too. Please?" I didn't know the raven-haired beauty's name. I'd paid her to strip dance for me across the room. She was just the background noise—a sexy TV show to steal glances at occasionally while the redhead and I set up different positions. I ignored her until I was ready to change the channel.

A stack of twenties tumbled from the bed as I flipped the redhead onto her back. She giggled and flailed, knocking over a half-full bottle of the most expensive tequila I'd ever seen. I didn't care as I had a case of that shit next to the bed, and we were both already pretty fucked up.

It was good to be the king.

Life was short, but I lived it to the fullest. Tonight, that meant having the craziest sex I could ever imagine in my room of our clubhouse. Tonight I was a rock star. A fucking rich-ass rock star!

"I don't mind, baby. She can play with us," the redhead invited.

"I don't care what you mind." Flexing hard and jerking abruptly, I pulled the fabric of her blouse apart, popping the buttons off one by one like buckshot. At each snap, I watched her chest sharply rise and her sullen face light up with excitement.

I snatched another bottle of tequila, twisted off the lid with my mouth, and drizzled the golden liquid over her contorting torso. I let it glisten in my room's harsh neon-sign lights while I dragged down her tight denim jeans. She giggled and wiggled for me, kicking them off toward the edge. The softly humming, black light bar above my door caught her parting lips and made her teeth glow with brilliantly white excitement.

The girl was ready and hungry. *So* hungry....

She'd wanted this for a while, but I hadn't noticed her until tonight when she was all over me at the party. I think her name was Nancy or Nicole... or Tess. She looked like a Tess.

"*Hehehe*... tickles!" the redhead gasped as I tongued the tequila out of her belly button.

"Let me get the rest of that for you." My tongue did laps over her hip bones and across her ribs.

"More, baby, more!" she cooed, trailing off in a haze. With the alcohol cleaned up, I dragged my lower teeth and bottom lip over the silky skin of her hard stomach. The slight, darkened lines and light pressure marks on her skin were faintly picked up in the hard lights. This girl liked it rough, and I liked it every way I could get it.

I then realized I was still wearing way too much clothing. I kicked my thick boots across the room and stumbled over to the slow-dancing brunette. "Get this shit off me," I growled at her, hanging my arms out to the side.

Immediately, she worked my pants down and, with firm care, reached in and guided my cock and balls out with her other hand. The thin cotton blend of my boxer briefs, the only barrier between us, tightened around my bulge in her grip. Between her massaging fingers, my cock had eagerly begun to harden. She dragged her long nails between the waistband and my coarse pubic hair before fisting my long, fleshy shaft. The brunette was all clenched, glowing teeth, parted glossy lips, pulse racing, heavy breathing…. Fuck me! She ate me up with lusty, yearning eyes. My cock was hard enough for her to swing on!

I'd seen this brunette a few times here and there but never gave her any play. She was expensive, and I never paid for sex.

The booze always slowed the process, but I never minded. I wasn't a selfish man in regard to sex. It just gave me more time to explore and play. I got off on orgasms—mine, hers…

it was all the same. I just loved pleasure. That itch wouldn't stop until it was scratched. I was never in a rush, and I've never heard any complaints. Only begging.

I peeled the brunette's fingers off my throbbing cock. Instead, my eyes were fixated on the redhead lying on my bed. Her dark form was drowned in a sea of green paper— my cut from the weapons deal. The glowing islands of her painted lips, white cotton bra, and panties were all I could make out of her features under the black and neon light. The latter was broken by a banded stack of cash that she slowly ground into her pussy.

What a sight to behold.

I smiled, riding the hot shiver that rattled my bones. I shrugged my vest to the floor and let the brunette pull my shirt off. "Stay," I commanded, so she plunked herself in the chair, pouting and looking dejected. Obviously, this was not how she thought this party would go. Unfortunately for her, I wasn't like any of her other boys or girls. I would be making her work for it.

*Make her cry and scream for it!*

I grabbed the brunette's hand as her legs parted and her fingertips disappeared behind the crushed elastic-band of her satin panties. That wasn't what I was paying her for. I shook my head, making a *tsk-tsk* sound as I watched her expression shift from longing into despair. Leaning in, I lightly bit her ear and warned, "Touch that gorgeous pussy again, and you'll be getting your rocks off at home."

I sauntered back over to my bed, throwing my vest back on. It was all I wore... well, that and a smile. "Come here,"

I beckoned the redhead. This lovely girl propped herself up and above thousands of dollars, empty or spilling glass bottles of booze, a handful of assorted pills, and a few ounces of weed and crawled over to me. My smutty little angel.

When she was close enough, I worked my fingers through her hairspray-coiffed hair then down the back of her neck. I squeezed and scooted her closer, spearing her gaping mouth with my thick cock. I was gentle at first, slowly gliding the entirety of my length past two rows of teeth and over her depressed tongue. I filled her mouth then pushed further. My mushroom tip slid down the back of her experienced throat until my balls rested on her chin.

I let her pull her head away only to drive back in again, this time faster. With her limits tested, and any sense of gentleness in her thoroughly abandoned, I let her consume every inch of me. Fast. Hot. Wet. Whole. The redhead moaned and murmured through a full mouth. My cock, rocking back and forth, robbed her of everything but the basest of primal instincts.

She jerked me out urgently, a long trail of saliva arcing off my tip, and gasped for air but only for a moment. She reached for it again like a starving baby bird, so I prodded her onto her back and ripped off those glowing white panties instead.

I needed to feel her sweet, sticky wetness on my skin. Needed to drink her all up. Her knees spread, parting that perfect pussy slightly. She either knew I needed it, or maybe she just hoped I did. Either way, she was soaked enough for a fifty-dollar bill to be plastered to her inner thigh.

*This couldn't have been more perfect,* I smirked. At the end of it all, I'd take their clothes but let them leave with any bills that were stuck to their bodies. It was horrible, I know, but they loved the game too. It was why they kept coming back. I practically had a goddamn waiting list!

Two of my fingers slid easily between those soft, wet lips and plunged into the pulsating pussy of the redhead. I curled them rhythmically while she tried to suck my soul out through the head of my cock. I thought it was working too. This girl could put a vacuum to shame.

"Take off your clothes and stand on the other side of the bed," I ordered the brunette.

She eagerly stripped off the last few bits of cloth that covered her finely curved body. "Whatever yo—"

"I didn't tell you to talk," I interrupted her, pulling my fingers from the redhead's hot, little pussy and licking them. Gods, I loved the way they tasted inside and out. "You're just here to watch. What part of that don't you understand?"

She was stunned into silence. Insulted but turned on, she complied. I could get high off her frustration. That was the trick. It was how I always got the best tail.

I never let them fuck me the first time. I never paid for sex. I paid her to watch.

The brunette wanted me now, and every time she came around after this, it'd be free pussy. Hey! A man's gotta have hobbies. These girls were just that, a hobby. Getting shot at was no fun, but hell, it was part of the job. So it took a little more for me to unplug and unwind compared to the average Joe.

I flipped the redhead onto her stomach across from the brunette so I could look directly at her while I fucked the other girl. The brunette just slowly shook her head, glowering in feigned outrage.

"Girl, you're gonna catch my dick on fire with a pussy that hot. Let me cool it down." I nibbled at the redhead's lower lips and blew some air over them.

She swooned, her whole body shivering. After slipping on a condom, I lined my cock up and slid in. A little looser than I'd have liked, but once I got going, it didn't matter. She moaned and quivered with each thrust. I speared her good, her ribbed walls contracting involuntarily around my swollen cock.

Still, it was the brunette that I was really having sex with. My eyes were locked onto only hers and hers on mine. In the shadowy light, I could see her naked tits rapidly rising and falling. She licked her bottom lip and dragged her teeth down it, the corners of her mouth straining to keep from speaking against my orders or openly panting her arousal.

I could see it in her. She wanted to speak. Wanted to plead. When she opened her mouth to do just that, I shook my head and slapped the redhead's ass.

Her back arched, her ass rising even higher. Beginning at her curled toes, I felt her whole body tense up around me. Her thighs became steel cables, her ass polished stone, her soaked pussy a vice clamping down around my insatiable shaft.

She squeezed me out like a bottle of hand lotion left out in the sun on a hot day. I leaned back but fiercely ground her hard, tight ass into me. I let my head loll from the totality of my release. If I didn't balloon my condom, I'd have liberally painted her pussy walls. Then I collapsed on the bed, my dick whipping out of her. Sweaty and satisfied, we lay on the bed. I motioned for the brunette to lay with us. To revel with a filthy, naked mass of sated, carnal flesh atop a mountain of blood money soaked through with alcohol and sweat and sex.

Could life get any better?

As if to answer my rhetorical question, the door smashed open, wood chunks from the doorframe peppering the room like shrapnel. Blinding light flooded in—-or, more accurately, flashlights and screaming flooded in.

The answer was, *no, it couldn't....*

The girls freaked and bolted from the bed. I knew what was about to go down, so I just lay there and enjoyed my throne for those last few moments.

"Freeze! On the ground now!" shouted one of the three angry, armed men.

"Evenin', Officers. What seems to be the problem?" I wasn't going anywhere under my own power as I was feeling a little drained.

"It's 10:00 a.m., asshole. What the fuck do you think the problem is? Hendrix 'Junkyard' Cedro, you're under arrest." One of the overzealous cops dragged me from the bed and kindly helped me into the standard facedown position with his knee planted painfully between my shoulder blades. They swiftly cuffed me and stood me up on my wobbly feet.

10:00 a.m.? Damn, it *had* been a long night. I wasn't

even tired, but that was probably because of the drugs. "Restraints aren't really my thing, Officer, but if you go a few doors down, Fast Eddie loves that—"

"Shut up, shithead! We got you and your whole faggot bicycle club!"

*Wishful thinking, asshole....*

Yeah, they caught me with a shitload of money, but the club had tied up all the loose ends that would've really put us away. I had made sure of that. Leaking this little party to the cops was the only way to guarantee the club got away with the rest of the money.

What a way to go out. I couldn't help but smile.

"I was acting under duress! I swear!" At this point, it was all by the numbers. Line dancing. I was going for a ride, so why not enjoy it, right?

"Yeah? Tell that to the judge."

"I'm serious, man! It was the only way into your mom's pants. She's really kinky like that—" I got to find out what one foot of polished metal Maglite tasted like. The impact cracked at least one tooth and easily brought me to my knees. These cops had no sense of humor. I coughed, spitting out a chunk of inner cheek I'd just bitten off. "Thanks for that, but it was still worth it. There's this thing she does with her tongue—"

That was when the line dance turned into a mosh pit. Just boots and flashlights leading to that deep, comatose sleep after that. Man, this was such a great plan.

As long as I survived it.

# Chapter 1
## MAYA

"Happy sweet sixteen, baby sister." I extracted the lavishly wrapped present from my bag.

"Thanks a lot, Maya! So... what'd you get me, you old hag?" Anna playfully ribbed me.

"Old hag?" I jerked the gift back away from her grasping hands. "I'm only ten years older than you, and it looks like..." I singsonged the words at her, "I just got myself a new Coach handbag."

"Really? Is it the tan and black Madison Carlyle?" Anna's amber-brown eyes lit up in excitement. She took a swipe at it, and again I yanked it away. "*Mayaaaa!*" she whined then stared at me with large, puppy-dog eyes. "I'll be your bestest friend forever…"

"I'll settle for you not being a bitch." I squinted at her and finally let her wrench it from my hands.

"It's my birthday! I get to be as horrible as I want!" Anna then squealed in delight after ripping apart the packaging. The spacious, leather bag slid onto her shoulder with ease. Having received a new pair of pink sneakers and fashionable top that she changed into earlier, Anna took the opportunity to stand up and model everything for all of us.

We hooted and cheered her on as she strutted the invisible catwalk that was the living room of our childhood home, her long, black hair swaying from her exaggerated sashay. Turning her back to us, Anna propped her hands on her curveless, beanpole hips and did her best sultry look-back stare. Her expression came across more like pouty and maybe a little constipated, but I didn't care as long as she was having fun. We all laughed with my nerdy sister and whistled catcalls at her.

At only just over five feet tall, her dreams of professional modeling had been dashed after hitting puberty. With her almost boyish physique, it was pretty easy to tell that she took more after our Korean mother than our American father.

I was a little taller than Anna but only by a few inches, so I wouldn't be seen walking any runways during Milan Fashion Week either. I was also a little fuller than Anna and didn't have the one cute dimple she had on the right side of her face when she smiled, but aside from that, we shared many similar features. Where we differed was on our own personal styles. Being *older and wiser*, at least that's how I always teased her, I had outgrown the teenage obsession for heavy eye shadow and flashy, edgy clothes. She always called me boring because I valued things like subtlety and professionalism. I tended to keep my hair cut slightly below my chin, wore pants suits and muted dresses, and generally assimilated into the law firm culture.

"Thank you so much for all of this!" With a big smile, my sister skipped back across the room. She was referring more to the modest birthday party I threw together for her than just the present. She hugged me then quietly whispered, "And thank you for hosting the party. I know how tough it is for you to be here."

I originally wanted to have the party at a restaurant, but our father, Bruce, wouldn't allow it. He didn't outright say why, but I knew he wanted it at the house so it'd be easier for him to remember to show up.

"Hey, just because Dad and I don't see eye to eye anymore doesn't mean I'll ever stop harassing you." I winked at her. Seeing eye to eye was the biggest understatement I'd ever made. We hated each other, but there was no need to belabor the point, especially on Anna's birthday. "Where is he?"

"I dunno. Club stuff, maybe? I haven't seen him yet today." Anna shrugged.

She was good at acting aloof and indifferent. It was a survival mechanism she'd developed to not let things important to her crush her... like her father missing her birthday party. I could always see through it though. I couldn't blame her for it because I did the same thing at her age right after Mom disappeared.

And almost on cue, the front door swung open with a heavy crack. Although the music continued, the various conversations petered out quickly.

Dad was home. He was drunk, and he wasn't alone.

Anna was a wonderful, smart girl, and I did everything in my power to keep her from getting hurt. I even went so far as to challenge our father for custody.

I lost.

Being that Slick, as he was known in the club, had no priors and nothing to tie him to any alleged illegal activity, the judge had to begrudgingly rule on his behalf. As far as the court was concerned, he was just a tax-paying, law-abiding carpenter.

Walking out of that courtroom was the first time he had ever threatened me. My father's words, muttered clearly through a plastic coffee cup because we were in public, still chilled me. "Your mother vanished. Hope that's not contagious."

The words struck me like an arctic breeze bending Caribbean palm trees. It was wrong and horrible to hear that from my only parent.

Since then, I kept Anna as close as possible, but it would never be enough. For the following two years, whether I liked it or not, Anna was his—a prisoner to the notorious Steel Veins motorcycle club.

When father and company swaggered in, they dragged with them an oppressive cloud of reeking cigar smoke, worn-out pussy, and old, spent motor oil. If Hell had a scent, it would be that.

At just over five and a half feet tall, Bruce was dwarfed by some of the taller men in his inner circle. But what he lacked in height, Dad made up for in presence. Stout, but not fat, he had an old bodybuilder's thick frame and the temperament of a patient rattlesnake. Although there were, of course, a few inherited commonalities, neither Anna nor myself shared Dad's remorseless blue eyes or his stony jawline.

"The fuck is all this?" Dad's temper rose with his confusion. He'd obviously already started drinking. The remaining guests took a few steps back, visibly startled at the outburst. He was an unrestrained, emotional man who was quick to anger and even quicker to violence as Mom had found out a few times.

Bruce spied the cake and decorations and slapped himself on the forehead, immediately remembering what day it was.

"Aww, shit, baby! Was that today? Fuck. Guys, it's my beautiful daughter's birthday!" He had the slumped-shoulder sag of a life's worth of bad bike posture as he sauntered over to Anna. He started singing the happy birthday song, gesturing emphatically that everyone join in. Intoxicated bikers and extremely uncomfortable teenage girls stumbled through the lyrics, offkey and out of sync. The song had all the wholesome sincerity of hostages reading off demands to a camera at gunpoint.

"Happy fucking birthday!" Dad cheered and clapped and was joined by his hollering biker minions. Anna's friends huddled a little closer together and seemed to shrink beneath the oppressive and unwelcome gaze of the intimidating middle-aged men.

"Here you go, baby." Dad thumbed out a couple hundred dollars from his wallet and gave it to her along with a kiss on her forehead. "Get yourself somethin' nice, huh?"

"Thanks, Dad." Anna offered a weak smile but couldn't hide her unease as she was already on the verge of tears at the embarrassment in front of all her remaining friends.

Our father, of course, didn't notice. He was too busy being father of the year.

I was just mad. It was one thing to forget or ignore an important date for one of your kids, but to come in and shit all over it like that? *Bravo! Fucking monster....*

"Maya." The word pierced me like a shattering icicle. I hated him so much, but what could I do that wouldn't make things worse for Anna? I lowered my eyes, my throat turning to jagged glass.

The man wasn't large or muscular, but encircled by his goons, he was bolstered with a sense of inviolable authority. It was terrifying. He'd spent so long dispensing life and death and ruling with "brotherly love" that he'd forgotten what paternal love was. He viewed Anna as a young patch member as opposed to a daughter. And me, after everything that happened with Anna…

I was a traitor.

Slick broke his gaze and, with the cock of his head, directed his boys into the pool room.

"Yer *honor*," spat a biker as he jostled passed me, clipping my shoulder and driving me back a step.

After Mom's disappearance and after what happened to me, I had started studying law, which was why I went to college. It was only within the last few years that any firm in the area would even look at me. Given my connection to the alleged "family business," I had a difficult time finding a position as a freshman lawyer at any law firm—finally being successful at some of the sleaziest out there, one of which I immediately quit after being hit on too many times on the first day. I would have had better luck if I had relocated, but as much as I wanted to, I just couldn't leave Anna alone with them.

I was all she had.

One of the other Veins sniffed my hair as they walked by. Any time they could, the Veins loved reminding me just how unwelcome I was here. They skeeved me out so badly that if I could've taken my skin off, it would have stood rigidly all by itself. But I choked it all down and pushed it away. Never letting them see how uncomfortable they made me was a skill with which I had far too much practice. I would never let them intimidate me, at least not while in front of Anna.

Despite not making it to the cake-cutting part of the party, Anna's friends all quickly made excuses to abruptly leave. I couldn't blame them now that a gang of unsavory bikers was lingering around. If it weren't for Anna being held captive here, I would have sneaked out too.

Anna was all smiles while thanking her friends for coming, apologizing for her father and half-heartedly making plans to get together soon. I offered to walk everyone to the door and closed it behind them. When I turned back, I saw Anna sitting sullenly in the middle of the room surrounded by empty chairs.

"You okay, Anna?" I asked now that it was only the two of us.

"Yeah, of course!" Her cheery words were strained through a practiced smile followed by a timid laugh that made my heart break. "You know how Dad is...."

Yeah, I knew, all right, but I decided against responding to her rationalization. Anna didn't need my anger, my doubt, or my weakness. I couldn't burden her with that, so I would be strong for her. "You wanna come over to my place for a few hours? We could marathon *Kitchen Nightmares* on Netflix and binge on cake and ice cream."

"Okay." She glanced back toward the kitchen, which was on the other side of the biker-infested entertainment room. Her face screwed into a sad half smile while her eyes watered as she turned away. She opened them as wide as possible to trap the tears, struggling to prevent them from rolling down her cheek. "I should, uh, probably go get the cake you got me."

Anna was so strong because she had to be, but everyone had their limits.

"Wait! I have a better idea!" I grabbed her arm as she hesitantly headed toward the bikers. "Instead of that crappy, store-bought cake, how 'bout we go grab ingredients and bake one from scratch?"

Anna took after our mom and fell in love with the kitchen. Despite only being sixteen, she was a phenomenal cook and an even better baker! Starting at the tender age of three, our mother had allowed Anna to help her in the kitchen, which mostly just meant washing veggies, cracking eggs, and kneading—*and eating*—a lot of dough. Every day after school, Anna would rush through her homework to help Mom make these amazing dishes for dinner and club events.

"That sounds great!" Anna's slightly puffy face lit up.

She snorted, shook her head, and held up the wad of dirty money. "The ingredients are on me, I guess."

"Put that away before you get an STD." I smirked at her then remembered something I was excited to tell her but had forgotten. "Oh! I didn't tell you! I found the recipe to Mom's famous chicken pot pies! We should make that tonight too!"

"Yeah, I'd love that." Anna sniffled, the corner of her mouth twitching, catching the cascading tears on the cuff of her sweater. She looked up at me and now smiled—a beautiful, genuine smile full of teasing snark and love. "I'll make sure you don't screw anything up."

"Hey!" I let my eyes flair at the joking insult then shoved her playfully. "Go grab your stuff, you punk."

She didn't need the reminder. Anna always packed her jacket and a backpack in the off chance she was allowed to sleep over at my place. It was a fairly slim chance because rarely did Slick ever feel so benevolent. Most of the time, our father kept us apart out of spite alone.

Anna scampered up the stairs that led to her second-story room while I sat quietly in the wreckage of the failed birthday party. I frowned when I remembered the second, small present I got her last year on her birthday… a deadbolt lock for her room to help her feel safer when she slept at night.

And that was nothing compared to the present I had to give her this year.

*I will get you out of this, Anna, I promise!* I drew a heavy breath and exhaled, trying not to cry myself.

My solemn pledge was interrupted by the rhythmic tapping of heavy, ringed hands against a marble-topped bar and the raucous laughter that followed in the entertainment room straight down the hall. I tried not to look at them, but the house had an open floor plan, and I could feel their eyes on me.

If I left the room now, it would be obvious that it was because of the bikers, and I didn't want to give Dad that satisfaction. I would endure their invasive glares until we were good and ready to leave.

God, I hated feeling pushed out of my childhood home.

I tried to recall a time when I saw him as a father and not just some thug in a leather vest. It pained me, but nothing came to mind. He did diddly squat during our childhoods that Mom didn't at least have a hand in. Birthdays and other celebratory milestones in my life were all because of her, and only *very* occasionally could she actually get Dad to make an appearance. The club always came first for him. Everything else... this family... it was all just decoration. Old Christmas lights on a long, dead pine tree.

Mom had been the soul of our family.

She could warm the house with just a wink and a smile. The aromas of her steaming chicken pot pies and her famous kitchen sink stew hung joyously in the air and somehow made the house sing for days. Minty cardamom, ginger, and cinnamon were her favorite scents, and they greeted us like a loving caress each day when we came home from school. It was no wonder Anna got into cooking at such a young age.

It smelled like an honest-to-God home.

Despite the supermarket cake and other baked goods I brought in for Anna's party, the air in the house these days was stale. Hopelessness settled thickly into the house's very foundation, and smoky ghosts and rancid memories haunted each and every room.

This place wasn't home any longer.

I didn't know what this structure was anymore. Everything, although familiar in layout, seemed so out of place, as if someone hung all our family pictures up at the neighbor's house and pretended we lived there instead. It felt like every private, cherished moment was on display in a forgotten family museum that no one ever kept up.

"The fuck do you mean Deadeye's gone? He's the one that brought me into this club and gave me the St. Louis chapter!" Dad bellowed in the other room before quieting to a low talking voice. "Is he dead?"

I couldn't hear the reply, so I walked a little closer, hugging the wall to stay out of eyesight. It was dangerous to eavesdrop on club business, but they were all so drunk that as long as I was careful, I should be all right. At least, I hoped.

"We're talking about the national president of the entire Steel Veins organization here!" Dad barked in equal parts bewildering disbelief and venomous anger. "And you're telling me that some nobody asshole traitor fuck from..."

"Leslie, Oklahoma," another biker gruffly added.

"Where in the spiky-shit is that?" Dad grumbled then immediately continued. "Doesn't matter. So what you're telling me is that some fuck from a nowhere chapter in Butt-Fuck, Oklahoma, is our new national president?" The question was punctuated by the loud crack of Dad's fist slamming into the bar.

"There's already a list of new club rules in effect now too," someone said, pausing long enough to probably look them up on his phone. "All new members with less than three years in the club were dropped back down to prospects—"

There was a roar of cursing and angry disapproval.

"So that means fucking half of us aren't even members anymore!" a different voice rang out, and more marble-top slams echoed throughout the house. "What the fuck are we going to do now, Slick? I'll be goddamned if I'm going back to being a fucking prospect!"

"Nobody's going anywhere," Dad growled, quieting down the room. "I'll tell you what we're going to do. I want you to find every Steel Vein that was loyal to Deadeye and have them contact me. Fuck it, I want every support chapter with a chip on their shoulder and lead in their belly to call me. Find me every pissed-off, disenchanted biker out there!" Dad let the words hang in the air. I could almost feel the heat steaming off the glares he must've been giving his men. "If our club don't want guys like us, fine. Fuck 'em! We won't be a motorcycle club. I'll make us a fucking army!" Dad finished to thunderous and sinister applause.

*Jesus*... an army of angry bikers sounded ominous. What was all that about? Whatever it was, it couldn't be good. I was going to have to look into some out-of-the-box ways to keep Anna safe.

I slunk back toward the front entrance and secreted Anna away when she rounded the bottom of the stairs with her backpack and light coat.

It wasn't until after we went shopping and returned to my apartment that I decided to give her this year's second present. I had it with me in my large purse the whole time but didn't dare give it to her with anyone else around.

"Hey," I said when we parked in my condo's private lot. It had become dark enough that I wasn't worried about anyone accidentally stumbling into eyeshot. "I did get you one more thing."

"Yeah?" Anna asked curiously but with a wary look on her face. My second presents were never gift certificates or clothing or really anything a well-cared-for teenager should ever have to ask for. "What is it?"

"Your *real* birthday present. It's a twenty-two semiautomatic pistol," I said flatly, extracting the safely unloaded gun from my bag and placing it into her hands.

She stared at me hard. She didn't like the club either because we had both lost so much to it. Anna deserved not to get such a dangerous present, but that was the world she was born into.

The world we both were born into.

"Take it, Anna. Just keep it on you when you're at home or near any of the bikers." I desperately needed one of these when I was sixteen. "Have any of them tried anything?"

"It's not like that now. He doesn't let them stay over anymore." Anna nervously lowered her eyes, and her voice fell to a whisper. "At least not as much."

It made me furious. What kind of parent left their children in this kind of environment? It was criminal! I sighed. Of course, it was criminal. That was the whole point.

"Let's head inside." I smiled widely, trying to lighten the mood. We'd talk about the gun a lot more at length, and maybe I'd even be able to take her down to a firing range at some point, but that was all a discussion for another day. Tonight was supposed to be a celebration, and I was determined to make it one. "That pot pie ain't gonna make itself!"

"Oh, hey! I almost forgot!" Anna plunged both arms into her backpack, fishing around for something, and she came up with a now crumpled letter. "It was addressed to Mom, but I figured I should give it to you. It looks like maybe a bill or something."

A bill? A decade after her disappearance? I tore open the envelope, only to discover it wasn't a bill. It was for a safe-deposit box out in San Francisco. What the hell was this?

*"Due to the lack of response from both Amanda Merritt of 1232 Waller Road, St. Louis, MO and Robert Merritt of 567—"*

Robert Merritt? I wondered at the oddness of seeing those two names together.

"Isn't that Dad's brother?" Anna asked inquisitively.

"I think so... but why would he share a safe-deposit box with Mom?" I vaguely remembered a horrific argument about him a long time ago but couldn't remember exactly what it was all about as I had only met him once. I scanned the rest of the document.

*"...SeaCoast Bank will be closing. Your safe-deposit box can no longer be held for you. The treasurer has declined to receive the property as abandoned. Please claim your box prior to the date posted, or your box's contents will be destroyed. It will be necessary to appear in person with your pin number."*

"Pin number? Do you know what that is?" Anna asked.

"No idea. I'm sure as hell going to find out though." Looked like I'd be tracking down our dear old Uncle Robert. I turned back to my little sister. "Are you ready to watch Gordon tear people's hopes and dreams apart while we make some amazing food?"

"While *I* make some amazing food." She smirked mischievously, then grabbed my hand and dragged me to the door. "But you can be my sidekick. Ready, Robin?"

"Like hell I'm going to be Robin! Whenever there's a situation where one of us is Batman...." I pointed to myself and nodded confidently.

This pseudo-argument would set the tone for the whole evening as we poked fun and tried to one-up each other. As fun as everything with Anna was, in the back of my mind, I couldn't help but wonder about that letter. I'd better start looking into it tomorrow.

Maybe a family reunion with Uncle Robert was long overdue.

# Chapter 2
## MAYA

"Yeah?" a gruff voice picked up.

It had taken me two days to build up the courage to finally make this call since getting the letter from Anna. "Hi. I'm looking for Robert," I announced cautiously into one of my burner cell phones. I had witnessed too many failings in the legal system firsthand to trust in it completely. I didn't own anything technically illegal, but I made sure to have as many resources at my disposable as possible.

"Who's this?"

"My name's Maya. Is this Robert Merritt?"

There was a long pause.

"No," the man replied begrudgingly. "You got the wrong number—"

"Don't hang up!" I blurted, hoping to stop him before he killed the call. "Please! I think I'm your niece!"

Another pause, but the line was still open.

I continued on, filling the silence with anything I thought might get this man to talk to me. "My name is Maya Merritt. I think you knew my mother, Amanda. Am I talking to the right person?"

Silence. I knew I'd said what I needed to. This time it was his turn to reply if he was going to at all. It had taken countless hours to track this number down as I had started with nothing else on this man. No current address, place of employment, medical history, anything. "Robert Merritt" was a ghost, but this man, whoever he was, was very much alive. If he hung up now, I knew I'd never get this chance again.

"Little Mai Tai?" the gruff voice on the other line asked in more of a fatherly tone than anything I had heard in years.

I was struck by the tinge of sadness that saturated his words.

"Mai Tai..." That nickname... I was engulfed by one of those blurry memories that orbited the periphery of my mind since I was a little girl. A remembrance that, for years, was completely gone until it suddenly, pressingly wasn't. It languished on the tip of my brain for days at a time then silently floated away like driftwood atop a dark bay in twilight.

For some reason, I had convinced myself over the years that it was a classmate in elementary school who had given it to me, but that never made any sense. How would nine-year-olds know about tiki mixed drinks? I *knew* I had reached the right man; I was talking to my Uncle Robbie.

"Y-yeah, that's me," I stammered, surprised at the flood of buried emotion that swelled in me. I didn't know him for long, but I remembered Robbie always treating me well.

"How in the hell did you find my number?"

"I, well... It wasn't easy." I had to call in a few favors to get the access I needed just to start searching. After several hours of calling around and dealing with discontinued lines and unhelpful people, I just got lucky. Either way, the why was more important than the how right now. "I need help, Uncle Robbie."

I heard a deep, regretful sigh, and I could only imagine what was running through his head other than he had no reason to believe or trust me. "I'm sorry, Maya. I can't help you. Don't tell anyone you contacted me. It's for your own good, I promise you. Take care, Mai Tai."

"No! Wait! Please! I wouldn't have called you for my sake or even for Mom's. It's for my little sister."

"Anna?" His voice now was a whisper. Was I speaking with a ghost after all? "Is she okay?"

"Yes… uh, sort of... I mean...." My brain was jumbling up all my words, so I stopped, took a breath, and continued. "Anna lives with our father, your brother, and things are getting bad. I don't think she's safe there anymore."

"Angel, I can't help her. If I come back there, everything will get worse for everyone. You gotta find another way. I'm sorry."

"There is no other way! She's just a girl, and she needs help!" With everything that had happened, I couldn't control myself. This conversation was slipping away from me, and with it went the last hope I had to save my sister. I couldn't let that happen. "I need you to give a shit!"

"I do care, goddammit!" His distant, sad voice burned; I definitely had hit a nerve. He then paused to calm himself.

"I want to help... but I—You gotta go to the cops if she's in danger."

"The cops?" I scoffed, typing furiously into my laptop keyboard. "You, of all people, should know better than that. Bruce has them all in his pocket!"

"I'm sorry, Maya."

Robbie was a heartbeat away from hanging up the phone, and as much I needed to know everything about everything, it was obvious that these revelations would come in their own time if I was able to get close to him. I had to choose my next words *very* carefully.

"Wait! I don't want you to come here." I blurted to keep him on the phone a little longer. "I need to know about the safe-deposit box, and then I'll let you disappear again."

"Heh, that damn box. Ya know, I forgot all 'bout that thing. I'll tell you right now I have no idea what your mom put in there. I can't even remember where the damn thing is."

"It's in San Francisco."

"That's right!" Robbie chuckled to himself. "Near her sister's place, right? Call your Aunt Gina. I'm sure she can help you out."

"I have and she will, but...." I sighed nervously, ungluing my eyes from my laptop. There was nothing I could do to help the program run faster, so I set it aside and just waited for it to be done.

*And now came the fun part....*

"Mom registered the box in your name too," I added. "And being that I can't prove you're legally dead, it won't pass to the next of kin, which is Dad. You need to come with me. I can't pick it up without you."

"*Aww*... shit!"

"Yeah." I transferred my laptop to the coffee table and flopped onto my small couch, my head falling back onto the pillow. "So stop being a selfish prick and take some damn responsibility!"

The older man grunted with surprise at my outburst. "It'll have to wait a few weeks. Something big came up that I have to take care of first."

"That's the other thing. The bank is permanently closing its doors in one week. If we're not there by then, whatever is in that box will be destroyed." There was a long pause, and after a while, I hoped he hadn't hung up. "Are you still there? Uncle Robbie?"

"All right, all right. I'm here. Fly out to your Aunt Gina's place and wait for me. I'm leaving in two days, so I should be in Cali by...." I heard him mumbling to himself. "By the end of the week. So five, six days at the latest. It'll be cutting it close, but I promise we'll get 'er done."

I wanted to believe Robbie. I really did. I had been about sixteen when Dad and Robbie had their falling out and he disappeared. But before that, I remember really liking him. Mom always talked about him fondly but only when Dad wasn't around. Unfortunately, the cold truth of it was that I didn't know him well enough anymore. He seemed honest and sincere, but I couldn't put all my faith in a child's foggy recollections. I had to do a little more digging. If it was just for me, then maybe I wouldn't be so cautious, but this was for Anna.

"Did my mom give you a passcode or a key for her safety deposit box? Anything you could either tell me or overnight to me, maybe?"

Robbie thought for a moment.

"No, I don't think so…. I'm sorry. Nothing I can remember. Mandy… your mom… she was a lifetime ago," he corrected himself. There were subtle hints of mourning in his voice.

I should've known it wouldn't be that easy. Life had a way of overcomplicating things. But how much did he know about Mom's disappearance?

"I'll need to come with you to California then," I said, mustering up all my resolve.

"Abso-fucking-lutely not!" Robbie was so taken by surprise at the request that he nearly yelled out the reply. "No! That's not possible!"

"Robbie, if something happens to you on the way, I'll never get that box. The box could be nothing, but if there's even a chance that something in there helps me get my sister away from Dad and the Steel Veins, I have to try."

If I spent enough time with him, maybe I could help jog his memory for that pin number. I was always good at problem-solving and quick thinking. It was a long shot, but I didn't have any other options.

"Maya, listen to me. You can't come with me," he said with absolute finality. "Something goes bad on the road… I can't protect you. I promised your mom that I'd do whatever I could to keep you safe. For the longest time that meant staying away from you and Anna. Now it means stopping you from coming with us. Take a plane, and I'll be there soon. I promise."

"Okay," I relented. I hated the idea of taking the word of a long-lost relative on something as important as this, but what else could I do? Besides, if the *us* he was referring to was who I thought they were, I was experienced enough to know how dangerous tagging along would be.

"Mai Tai?" Robbie asked with unexpected tenderness.

"Yeah, Uncle Robbie?" I responded, feeling like garbage that I didn't have more control over the situation.

"It was real good to hear your voice, angel. Don't worry. I'll see you soon." Then he hung up.

I dropped the phone on the couch and ran my hands over my face, feeling a little defeated at how the whole conversation went. I wanted so much more from that call.

When I finally looked up, I noticed the trace I'd been running on the phone call through my laptop to triangulate his location had finished and was blinking. It looked like Uncle Robbie was in Topeka, Kansas, these days. Given Robbie's military background, criminal record, and the fact that he'd been off the grid for....

*Jesus!* While not being declared legally dead, Robbie Merritt had disappeared about ten years ago. How had he been flying under the radar for so long? That meant cash jobs and off-the-books deals. After some more searching, I landed on the one thing that seemed to make sense, especially if he was handling vague *big things* that were coming up.

Robbie had to be a member of the Coffin Eaters motorcycle club.

I'd spent my whole life on the periphery of the Steel Veins; it's what made me work hard to become a lawyer. After Mom disappeared, my eyes were truly opened to the horrible things my father was doing in the name of the club. Despite only being a lowly fledging in the hierarchy of attorneys at the moment, I had picked up a lot of useful skills when dealing with outlaws and criminals.

I browsed through town documents and police records, but I couldn't find much on Robbie specifically. He must have been fairly careful, but the club as a whole...

The Coffin Eaters had suffered multiple attacks from rival gangs in the last few years. Several members had disappeared under mysterious circumstances, and the town itself had filed a lawsuit against the club for public endangerment. After looking into their history—what little I could find outside news of arrests and deaths—it looked like they were pretty much a small-time club. They were nothing like the Steel Veins or even Los Lobos, and the C.E. didn't have any other chapters.

With all that trouble surrounding them and their club on the verge of collapse, they were going all the way up to California for side work? *Now?* It had to be a big job, which meant that whatever it was, it had to be extremely illegal.

I just sat there, thinking and staring at the blinking cursor in the navigation bar. It mocked me with its impatience. Meanwhile, my laptop was softly humming, awaiting commands.

Online, I was a digital lioness in data crunching. I could find and tear through countless research and backlogs with ease. Though outside in the real world, what was I? I'd done my best to pull Anna away from our father once and failed miserably. The realization that I just wasn't strong enough or smart enough made my hands tremble slightly. I was just another scared girl caught in the silky yet sticky MC web, like a fly waiting to be devoured.

Now my sister's only salvation was completely out of my hands. It hinged upon a man who probably never even met her in person. Never saw the naïve hope that twinkled in Anna's beautifully innocent, brown eyes.

I covered my eyes to hide myself from my living room window and the shame it reflected back at me from not being able to help Anna more. I could no longer see the glowing laptop screen, the portal that held boundless possibilities, but I could still feel the crushing weight of that defeat all the same. Twisting me from the inside out. At any moment, I would snap and burn away like kindling in a fire.

My phone lit up and vibrated with a text message. I heard it but was too lost to move. Then it vibrated and lit up again. Then again. Then it rang. It was Anna.

"Hello? Anna?" I asked, trying to keep the worry from entering the sound of my voice.

"Hi. Can I come over?" she asked through stifled breathing.

I could immediately tell that she'd been crying. That kindling inside me began to catch, but it turned out to be anger, not shame, that was the flame.

"Yeah, of course." I cleared my head and focused on the logistics of picking her up.

"Can you pick me up *now*?" Her urgency stoked that budding flame within me. I could only imagine what had happened to her this time.

"I'm on my way." I sprang up from my stupor and grabbed my wallet and keys. "Is everything okay? What's going on?"

"Dad's really drunk, and he…. I didn't get out of the way quick enough. It really was my fault."

"Fucking Christ!" I snarled. That flame in me became a fire. "Are you all right?"

"I'm okay. It's just a few little cuts from his rings." Her voice sounded strained, and I could hear her biting back more tears. "I'm sorry. I know you're probably busy—"

*That bastard backhanded her!*

"Anna, I'm leaving now. Give me five minutes. Get your stuff and wait for me outside. This wasn't your fault. Listen to me. *It wasn't your fault!*"

"Thank you, Maya."

"Always." I hung up and raced to my car. I could feel all my self-pity melting away. Anger had a way of laying things bare.

This was serious. I was going to have to take drastic measures now that Anna's safety was at risk. I couldn't bring her to my apartment. She might be safe tonight, but tomorrow he'd demand that she come back home after school so he could give her an empty apology and probably some money for reparations. That's how he operated. He did whatever he wanted to whomever and bought off the repercussions.

And then what would stop him from doing it again?

*Bruce, you fucking bastard!*

How many more phone calls like this did Anna have in her? One day, it would be a police officer that called me, apologizing and asking me to come identify a body, a murder they would never pin on our father. Or worse, there would be no call at all.

She would just be gone.

The chilling thought shook me to the core. Putting my cowardice aside, I knew what needed to be done. I had to take Anna to the one place I knew she would be all right. With Dad so connected with the police here, traditional safe houses were out of the question. He'd just show up and pull her out of there. I needed to take her to an organization I knew that took in abused women and children outside the purview of the law. These places weren't strictly legal. They were more like underground railroads to keep victims away from their abusers when the system had failed them.

Anna wasn't going to like it, but at least she'd be safe. Hopefully she wouldn't have to stay there for long. If there was any incriminating evidence in that safe-deposit box, then I could use that to legally remove her from our father's custody. Until then…

I guess I'd have to get used to operating outside the law.

I no longer cared what my Uncle Robbie said about staying out of this. There was too much on the line. I needed to ensure that he made it to that safe-deposit box. He'd have to figure something out because come hell or high water, I was going with him to California.

My chest tightened a little. Growing up around the Steel Veins made me apprehensive of bikers in general, and the thought of spending almost a week with a motorcycle club scared the shit out of me, especially one that didn't want me there in the first place. I guess I was used to that though.

I didn't care anymore. I didn't care if I was caught with the Coffin Eaters by the police. I didn't care that I was jeopardizing my career, my freedom, my life for a box that might only have some baby pictures and maybe some old love letters. I wouldn't be able to live with myself if I didn't at least try.

I couldn't trust my sister's fate to be in anyone's hands but mine. After I dropped Anna off at the underground depot as directed by my contact, I would leave for Kansas and ride out with Robbie's club somehow.

# Chapter 3
## HENDRIX

I knew it was coming.

Toward the end, all you can do is count. The minutes. The seconds. The white-painted bricks that make up the six-by-eight cell walls. This was my second stretch in county. The longest by far.

The original case against us fell apart. It was some paperwork error mixed with the fact that the jury wasn't a big fan of the cops' piñata approach to bringing in perps. At least that's what they told me a few days later when I woke up from the coma.

Everyone was released but me. It turned out that I didn't fill out some paperwork on one of my guns and I had some drugs kicking around my room that I probably shouldn't have.

I was invincible back then. A big, swinging dick that could do no wrong. I was in my late twenties with more money and women than I knew what to do with. I was arrogant and reckless. I guess it was bound to come crashing down eventually.

Eighteen months turned into five years awfully quickly. Prison had a way of taking the fun out of things. Shit that happened outside sometimes needed retaliation inside. Just the way it was. I knew they were going to add time to my sentence when my club needed me to send a "message" to some newly incarcerated Russians about a bad deal.

Just because I wasn't wearing my cut, my club's vest with patches, didn't mean I couldn't still feel the weight of the leather on my shoulders. It was a heavy, angry weight that I wasn't sure I wanted anymore. All that "changed man" shit was just so much parole board review hot air. I knew who I was. Who I'd always be. With so much time to think, I began to wonder if it was all really worth it.

Lately, it felt like I was jogging up sand dunes. Every step I took was on shifting alliances. It was the same in prison. Make a deal with black, then brown wanted to gut you. Smooth shit over with the Chinese, and you had problems with the Puerto Ricans. It took a fuck ton of maneuvering and effort to stay roughly in the same place.

Yeah, I was good enough at the game, but I didn't need it like some of the other guys. I had skills and connections that went beyond the club. I went down this road originally because I loved the thrill of it all. We were bangers. The killings were part of it, a tool like a needle for a junkie, but that wasn't what got me off. It was everything else. The power. The speed of it all. Fucking heroin to me. Of all the drugs that were available in prison, that wasn't one of them. And five years was a hell of a detox.

I coped mostly by reading and working out. I'd packed

on a bunch of muscle since getting here. I was stronger, meaner, and way more connected than I'd ever been on the outside. I'd become a monster, a force to be reckoned with. Our prison system at work.

"Cedro! It's your lucky day. Let's go!" The guard stood in the doorway, impatient and pissed off. I paused then finished my last set of pushups. "Before I change my mind!" he spat. Half these sadistic fucks would be on the other side of the bars if they hadn't been hired as guards.

Fuck him. I'd waited five years for this. I'd take as long as I damn well pleased. Don't get it twisted. It wasn't that I wanted to stay. I was beyond ready to get the fuck out. The thing that no one tells you is that it's not the confinement that's the worst part. It's the lack of control. All the power I had before coming in... it was hard not to feel like that was a different guy. For half a decade, I jumped when they said jump, moved when they said move, ate, slept, bathed, and shit when someone else told me to.

When that door swung open for me to leave, my sentence fully served, goddamn... that feeling was indescribable. I felt a little like the old me. Like I just woke up from another coma. I was free! Not just from this windowless iron box but free from other people telling me what to do and how to live every second of the day. It was *my* time now. I was in control. I would always be in control from now on.

"Later, Junkyard. Be seeing you, man." My cellmate saluted me lazily from his bunk.

I looked around the cage one last time at all my worldly possessions. I had a couple books, an additional blanket, and some other odds and ends. I wouldn't take anything I didn't have to. My hand absently drifted over my stomach to the three raised scars. I had enough things to remember prison by.

"Nope." I cracked a long-overdue smile and lazily saluted back to my roomie.

With every step down the long, concrete hallways and stairwells, the weight of my obligation became lighter and lighter. I didn't mind furthering the club's agenda while inside. I didn't even mind the added time or the three shivs to the gut that came in retaliation for what I had done. The eye-for-an-eye shit never ended. What killed me was that I was out of the loop completely. Despite all the sacrifices I made, I rarely had visitors to let me know what was up with the club. Not that I was sentimental, but when you got soldiers inside, they gotta know what they're fighting for.

I didn't know if I was ready to hang up my colors for good. Though after this last stint, I was certainly ready to have that conversation. If I decided it was time to leave, it wouldn't be easy. My lifestyle wasn't one I could just bounce from without consequences. I knew too much about all the crimes we'd committed. As with everything we did, there would need to be a vote. They could force me to stay.

The guard had to stop at every pod door, show his credentials, and have me look up at the camera before the buzzer would sound and the door unlocked. With every thick-ass metal door that slammed behind me, my resolve doubled.

All in all, it took a few hours to go through out-processing and listen to the various threats disguised as encouragement to not come back. They were preaching to the choir. Motherfuckers would see me dead before they saw me in a cell again.

They threw me some clothes that I'd never seen before. I tried to remember what I was wearing when they picked me up. I remembered and laughed. I was naked. I thought of the two girls, and my balls ached. That *was* a fun night.

The door to the control building finally slammed shut behind me. I could see my club brother, Skids, through the two razor-wire topped fences, sitting on his bike, struggling to figure out what looked like a new phone. He had these shitty flip phones for as long as I had known him. Guess he finally joined the twenty-first century.

I stepped through the side door of the front gate, the last barrier between me and the rest of the world, and beelined for my friend. A sunbeam split the overcast sky and caught me square in the face, stopping me dead in my tracks. Skids was distracted so I took a moment to take it all in, my first deep breath not surrounded by walls or a fence of any kind.

I howled as loud as I could! Skids was caught so off guard by my yell that he juggled the phone clumsily before it slipped from his hands and smashed onto the ground. He shot up off his bike and cursed like only an old man with a vocabulary coming from years of experience could. Then he realized what had happened and that it was me who had hollered. His dark, wrinkled face lit up into the biggest grin that I'd seen in as long as I could remember.

"Junk, my boy!" The old man threw me my vest. I barely

had time to catch it before he caught up and crushed me in a big, ol' bear hug. "Jesus, boy! You're enormous! What the hell were they feeding you all this time? Smaller inmates?"

"Skids, you beautiful sonofabitch!" I clapped him a few times hard on the back. "Maybe. I was too afraid to ask what the fuck was in that Salisbury steak, man."

Seeing my vest again actually made my heart skip a beat. In prison late at night, I often wondered what this moment would feel like. It was the longest I had ever spent without it since the cut was given to me. The top rocker was a white patch with black letters that read "Coffin Eaters." I'd given so much for those two words and the crossed pine boxes pictured below it. I honestly hoped I wouldn't feel anything when I saw it again. It was a part of me though, like a limb. I sighed. Sometimes limbs had to be amputated.

Still, it was damn good to see Skids. He was one of my closest friends in the club. He vouched for me and mentored me all throughout my prospect days. He was old, "always right," and ornery as a sonofabitch when crossed, but he always had my back.

"Where's my bike?" I asked him while looking around. Riding was an addiction I could never kick. It was up there with blinking—it was just something I did. Hardwired into my DNA.

"You're riding bitch because you just broke my brand-new phone!" Skids picked up the gadget and shook it at me.

"Fuck you, old man. I'm bigger than you are." I smiled and brought my arms up in a flex, showing off my biceps.

"Put the guns away. We're still in front of a prison, and

we're two hours late." Skids checked an antique pocket watch he'd always carried in his vest. "They couldn't bear to see you go, huh?"

"Don't know what you're talking about. I was a model inmate." I slapped my hands together in mock prayer. "Pray to Jay-sus!"

"Oh, I'm sure the Mikhailov brothers would've disagreed with you. Put your hands down. Don't go getting yourself struck by lightnin' till you buy me a new phone."

"I'll buy you a dozen phones with my cut of the deal with the Russians." It'd be nice to have a little spending money again. Or a lot. We made a lot of money off that deal, and I was definitely looking forward to my portion. "When we get back to the clubhouse—" I stopped, seeing Skids jovial face turn regretful. Something was wrong. I could feel it in my gut. "Robbie... please tell me we didn't get burned on this. Not after everything that's happened."

"It all fell apart after your scuffle with the Russians on the inside."

"What? Tex told me Miles ordered that hit because the Russians were threatening to back out of the deal." He told me it was a power play to show them that we weren't messing around."

"Yeah, well something got lost in translation." Skids pulled out a pack of smokes, packed it, and offered me one. "There was a beef between us and them because of it, and things got bad for a while. We lost some good men."

"No.... Who?" I waved it away.

"J-Rock, Trainwreck, and Smokey." All three of those

guys were in favor of the guns deal we'd put together.

"Fuck...." I'd keep my suspicions to myself, at least until I was absolutely sure. The word "betrayal" was a loaded gun, one you'd better be damn sure was aimed at the right person.

"The C.E. is a skeleton crew now. We're looking to get affiliated with the Iron Legion *as a support club!*" Skids barked the last few words with no small amount of disdain as he lit the cigarette. He didn't like the idea at all, and neither did I. The Coffin Eaters came together as a charter because we didn't want to be anyone's bitch.

"Why would Miles let that happen?"

"It ain't Miles's show anymore. Tex forced him out after the deal soured."

Skids's words dropped in my gut like I'd swallowed a fishing hook. "Tex is running shit now? Fuck me."

"He saved us. As much as I hate it, his connection with the Legion is the only thing that can pull our asses out of this fire—"

"The fire everyone thinks I lit...." My mind reeled. Everything seemed to fall into place. There was no message from Miles. I struck first. It explained why I lost my protection inside. It also explained the Russians' retaliation that landed me in medical for a month.

*Tex, you set me up, you slimy fuck.*

The old man sighed. "Nah, we all knew it was self-defense. Shit just happens in prison. A man's gotta do whatever it takes to stay alive in there. That's why we never pulled your patch."

"Yeah." That's why no one but Skids came to visit. They didn't trust me. Skids's usually sharp blue eyes looked a little distant like something else was bothering him. "Something else on your mind?"

"No more bad news with the club, I promise." He chuckled, putting his hands up. "Just reconnected with some family recently. Got a lot on my mind is all."

"You good?" I gave him a look that said I was listening if he needed to vent.

"I'm all right, son. It's nothing but ghosts." He exhaled smoke from the side of his mouth.

"Okay," I replied somewhat hesitantly as I clasped him on the shoulder.

"It's good to have someone I trust back on the outside."

"About that, Skids. I did a lot of thinking inside, and I need a favor from you. I'm looking for a way out of the C.E." I watched his expression carefully.

"What? Junkyboy—" He choked on a cloud of smoke, the cigarette nearly falling from his lip in surprise.

"I know, I know. I've given the Coffins more than my fair share, and I'm young enough that I can still make it work as a civvy."

He stared hard at me but didn't say anything.

"Robbie, I need to know, man. Will you back me if I bring it to a vote?"

"You're breaking my heart, son, y'know that, right?" He put a hand on my shoulder, but he could see my resolve. There was no changing my mind. "Yeah. I'll back you."

"Thanks, Skids. Tell me there's at least a homecoming

party tonight. They don't hate me that much, do they?" I cracked a light smile, trying to lighten the mood.

Shit might be fucked up back home, really fucked up, but I was wearing real clothes outside in the sun as a free man! That was a powerful feeling. I would have plenty of time later to work out the Tex thing completely. Right now, all I wanted to do was go home and live. Regardless of what state the club was in, today was a damn good day, and I felt like celebrating.

"Like they need a reason to get loaded and make a lot of noise? Of course, there's a party." His gruff voice started slow and stern, but quickly his demeanor cheered up. A brother getting out of jail, no matter the circumstances, was always a win.

He tossed me my keys with a grin. "Your bike's around back, I had Moll drop it off. You need to stop anywhere before we hit the clubhouse?"

"You're kidding, right?" I called back to him on my way to the parking lot. "I just spent five years in a little box with a bunch of guys, and there's a party tonight. Take me to a place that sells condoms by the case. I am fucking murdering me some pussy tonight!"

And there she was. The girl of my dreams. Black and red and chrome and rubber. Heaven on two wheels and manufactured by Harley. I couldn't stop myself from breaking into a run toward her.

"Oh Nikki...." I kissed the cool, metal gas tank of my Harley. "Oh, baby, I missed you as much as I missed pussy." I kissed the tank again and lovingly rubbed a hand over the leather seat. I slid the key in the ignition. My girl eagerly started right up and purred for me.

"Unhhh! That's my girl!" I yelled again and kicked the stand back, letting the shocks take my full weight, then revved the engine, making my bike talk to me. "I know, baby, I know. Daddy missed you too."

Skids nodded to me, making sure I was good before he took off.

I threw it in first gear, jacked up on the clutch and brake, and did a burnout with the back tire. The smoke show coming off my rear tire forced a few guards to run out of the control building and yell at me. Maybe that old reckless me wasn't completely gone after all.

Before they reached me, I eased off the breaks and clutch, twisted the throttle, and brought the old girl up on just the back tire for a second as I took off.

"Thanks for everything, Pondville!" I flipped them the bird.

Today was a good day.

* * *

The familiar compound was setting up when we pulled in, and the party looked like it was just about to kick off. The prospects and hang arounds were filling the coolers and prepping the grills, which were old, metal, oil drum barrels sawed in half with legs welded to them. There were mamas, a few old ladies, and friends of the club already here or pouring in behind us. Despite the lack of familiar faces, as a lot had changed since I was gone, I still missed the hell out of the atmosphere.

"Junkyard! Back from the dead! Lookin' good, killer," Miles called out while he was outside smoking a cigarette when we parked the bikes. He was about ten years older than me, stocky with a light beard and salt-and-pepper hair. He bumped fists with Skids, and we exchanged hugs.

"Good to be out, Miles."

A Toyota Corolla pulled in the lot, idling indecisively as if not sure where or how to park as each club was organized differently and had their own lot rules. It always made it easy to spot someone who'd never been here before. When it finally parked, a conservatively dressed girl, at least for this crowd, stepped out.

"I'll catch you boys inside. I'm gonna enlighten the lady as to where she can park her cage. Will be inside inna minute," Skids quickly excused himself and rushed off to the girl, waving off the hang around that had approached the car.

"You're too old to fall for jailbait, Skids," Miles jokingly ribbed the man, getting only a middle finger in reply.

"Who the hell is that?" I asked. It was hard to make her out in the low light, but as she drew a little closer, I could tell she was cute—*very cute*.

"No idea." Miles offered a light smile then shook his head. "But nothin' that pretty comes around that ain't trouble."

Radically different than the townie, junkie girls that hung out at the clubhouse, this new girl was something else entirely. Dark hair, light olive features, big almond-shaped eyes, and a tame but exotic flare. She wore a loose, white, silk blouse over a pair of tight jeans that showed off the small curves of her hips.

She wasn't a knockout in the traditional sense—all big tits and curves that went on for days. She was compact, tight, and toned like a runner and had an air of confidence that was hot as fuck. I couldn't contain my budding smile.

I was looking forward to meeting this girl.

"Don't worry. I'll card her when I get her back to my room."

Miles chuckled scurrilously. "Took us a week to clean that room the last time you brought friends home."

"I hope you used fire. Otherwise...." I shook my head in feigned fright. "Hey! Speaking of rooms, do I still have one here? What's the climate like for me these days?"

"Hate to say it, but you don't have a lot of friends around here right now."

"Figured as much. Tex told me that the order to take out the Russians in prison came from you. After all that we went through putting that together, I'd have never set fire to it intentionally. I'm sorry about how it all went down. I had no idea."

"I don't doubt it." Miles didn't appear surprised. "It was tense for a few months after the new blood was patched in. When Tex got their support, it was only a matter of time till somethin' popped up so that he could challenge me. I was pushed out right before you were put in medical. I don't hold any of it against you. You've always done right by me."

"Appreciate that." I looked down, nodding. Miles was

always one of the good ones. Sucked that they found a way to cut him out as prez. The crossed coffins on my arm—the symbol of our club—strangely seemed to itch. "Looks like Tex bent both of us over the pine boxes. Where's everybody? I don't see any actual members anywhere."

"Inside. We got a logistics meeting for the run tomorrow." Miles checked his phone. "Actually, it looks like it just started. Let's head in."

"Charity ride?" I asked.

"I wish." The thought of what was coming made Miles grimace. "It's the pine boxes that got bent over this time." A statement like that coming from the ex-president didn't bode well at all.

"Iron Legion?" I asked covertly.

He nodded.

"Shit...."

I glanced back at Skids to let him know we were heading in, but it looked like he was in the middle of a heated argument with the girl who had just arrived. My guess was that it wasn't over the parking situation. We all had our battles to fight, and that looked like one he wanted to handle alone. I might've been looking at one myself when I sat down at the table, so I pushed open the clubhouse doors.

For a brief moment, I thought I was in the wrong building. The place was so radically different, I barely recognized it.

"Fucking hell. Love what you've done with the place. It's got that Satan's man-cave vibe to it," I muttered to Miles. The real question was where did Tex get the money to turn our humble little community hall into a goddamn heavy metal ski resort.

Miles just shook his head. I could tell he didn't care for its excessive nature either.

Expensive wood panels paved the walls while checkered tiles and carpeting covered the floor, supporting a host of new leather furniture, large-screen plasma TVs, and pool, foosball, and card tables. Toward the back was an elevated mini stripper stage accompanied with a tricked-out liquor bar with an LED-backlit backbar. Then there was an entire new wing for our personal rooms.

I could only imagine what they looked like!

Gone were the days of drunkenly collapsing against the tagged-up drywall or fucking some bitch's brains out on the concrete floors. That last part I didn't miss all that much. Concrete was cold as hell and hard on the knees. I tried to avoid it whenever possible, but, hey, sometimes you just made the most of what you had.

I threw open the doors to the war room, the name for our private meeting room where all club business was discussed. The room itself appeared at least similar to how I remembered it. The walls and floor were uniformly renovated to match the rest of the club's aesthetics, but the spirit of the room was still intact somehow. That had to be the work of Miles and Skids. Neither of them liked change and I was glad for that. It was the first thing in the entire clubhouse that actually felt like home. Where everything outside this room had been replaced with shiny and new shit, in here, it just looked like it was updated, which I was all right with. The incorporation paperwork was still framed above a cascade of old pictures. The death's-head symbol over the club's crossed-coffins logo hung ominously on the far wall above portraits of fallen members. That gray wall, however, was far more cluttered with pictures of the dead than when I left five years ago. J-Rock, Trainwreck, and Smokey—all good men and loyal brothers—were now just squares of photos behind a thin layer of ash-smeared plexiglass.

Under Tex's rule, the number of photos would be increasing dramatically, and that wouldn't be slowing down any time soon.

The three men that sat around the table—all new members—stood up to greet me. I made the rounds and did the introductions, but I didn't feel like a returning brother. They regarded me as a nomad, a friend of the club that was just passing through.

I was now a stranger in my own home.

Skids showed up as I was bullshitting, and Miles and he took their assigned seats. Their presence was encouraging, reminding me that for however long I was staying, I did have allies here. It looked like everyone was accounted for except President Tex, who hadn't shown up yet.

After a few more minutes, which felt a little too much like a power play, the new Coffin Eaters' president shoved the doors open. He was a little shorter than I was and a few years younger, which put him in his late twenties. His long hair was neatly pulled back, and he wore a beard. Beneath his nice, new leather jacket, Tex's stomach had grown a bit since the last time I saw him. The king eats the best, after all.

Clasping all his guys on the shoulder as he passed, Tex took his place at the head of the table. The gavel came down with a loud *bang*, and everyone else took their seats. It was still weird seeing Tex, of all people, in the big seat. That squirrelly prick must have had to do some serious maneuvering to get the club's majority vote for president.

It was all new to me, but the changing of leadership was ancient history to these guys. Life in the club typically went at such a breakneck speed that if I wanted to survive, I had to form new alliances constantly. Memories had to be short, and I got that. However, I was still pissed, not that I could show it, of course. I couldn't let the past sidetrack me from getting out. I had to focus on my future. Nothing else mattered.

"First things first. Welcome back, Junk. We missed you, brother." It was custom for the president to publicly welcome returning brothers, even if he wasn't hoping I'd return. Coming from Tex, it was an empty gesture. Either way, it was followed by a renewed round of cheering by the other guys. "I'll keep this brief because we got ourselves some celebrating to do. The truck will be here tomorrow at ten, and we leave at noon. Road captain, we good with the route and motels?"

"Yep," Loopy answered him. "No sweat."

"Hold on," I interjected. "I've been underground for a while, so would someone wanna fill me in on what we're doing exactly?"

"My bad, Junk. We're muling fifty kilos of coke to Cali for the Iron Legion. That going to be a problem for you?"

Tex informed me casually, astutely studying my reaction.

"Jesus, fuck! Seriously? Yes, that's a goddamn problem for me. I was in prison six hours ago! I'm not all that eager for the free ride back!" Tex was out of his mind if he thought I'd just hop on this like nothing had ever happened. I was on parole. If I sneezed in the wrong direction, my ass would get busted.

"All right, I'll level with you, Junk. After your stretch, you deserve at least that much." Tex paused, sizing me up. "The club isn't going to make it on our own anymore. We need the Legion, and we need their money if we're going to keep our turf. This run will net us over a hundred K. This isn't even a real decision. It's just some shit that we have to do, and it's already been voted. This *is* happening. It's the life, brother. Fast or dead, you know how it goes."

The room was tense, and it was obvious now to me what was really going on here. The new guys were fresh and judged me without even wanting to know me or my loyalties. The old guys were in it too deep. They might not have liked the direction Tex was taking them, but the club was all they had left. They were in it for life, regardless of who was the president.

Not me. I was done drinking the fucking Kool-Aid.

"Well, in that case, I wish you fellas the best of luck. You let me know how all that shit works out." I pushed my chair back from the table.

"It's no secret you want out, Junk. I can imagine you're pretty pissed about the Russian thing." Tex took a deep breath and regarded me like a concerned parent would chastise a kid who reached for the cookies right before dinner. "Truth is, we got too many guys down or dead. I can't spare you right now. If you call a vote to leave, I'll make sure you'll lose. And if you run, well... you know what happens. No one wants that."

"Goddammit, Tex." Skids was quick to get my back. "He doesn't need your fucking threats."

"Our boy here has been out of the loop, old man." Tex stood up and planted both hands onto the table so that he could look us over from a position of dominance. "I'm just bringing him up to speed to how things run around here now. These are hard times for the C.E., and I gotta make sure everyone here's on the same page."

I glanced around and realized I was up against a wall. I had, at most, two guys whom I knew I could count on but not the rest. Not these new guys. Tex was the club, at least for now.

"But hey, it's not all doom and gloom. We're brothers, right?" Tex announced loudly, lightening some of the tension in the room. "There's no reason we can't be reasonable. Junk, you do this for us, and you're square. I'll get you what's owed for your trip to county plus your cut from this gig, and you walk away free and clear to start your new life."

I studied Tex but couldn't find any words that my fists couldn't say for me better. I was really pissed now. I shouldn't have to do *one last job*. Being out wasn't good enough. I wanted my freedom. I deserved it. I bled for it. I earned it.

*Real freedom.*

But here I was, a prisoner all over again, but just of a different system and a bigger cage. Now I was sure I wanted out of the MC.

"Why?" I asked but continued before Tex could try to decode the vague question. "Why get in bed with the Legion? Clubhouse got a nice overhaul, and it doesn't look like you boys are on the breadline."

"The C.E. is dying, brother. We got no foothold here anymore. There's pushback on every side by the other crews. If we don't get brought into a larger club and soon, this MC is done and over."

I ran my hand over my face and took a minute to contemplate. Tex and I never saw eye to eye, but I understood what he was saying. Even with the prospect push, the club was hurting for members. Topeka itself was a dying city on more than one level. There just wasn't enough love or interest in the club here anymore.

The Coffin Eaters were being taken into the Iron Legion family, a much bigger club. If anything, being in the Legion before I walked away meant that I had a much larger support network if I needed help on the outside. If a member left on good terms, he was still protected. Yeah, I understood the advantages, but I just didn't like it. It meant that they would own us.

And I was no one's bitch.

"All right, so get some Legion down here to help with the ride. I'll hang home and protect the clubhouse and families."

"This is the rite of passage—*our* initiation. We all gotta do this. Word's already gotten out to the surrounding clubs and gangs that if anyone tries anything against us and ours while we're gone, the Legion will crush them. We don't need you home. We need you with us."

*Fuck!* Tex had me by the balls, and there was no getting out of it. I was on the hook for one last ride.

"All right," I replied, trying not to sound sullen. "If I'm gonna skip out on parole, I might as well have a good story to tell the guys when I go back to prison." Through the joke and dark smile, Tex could plainly see my anger at him for forcing me to do this as well as my burning eyes that told him to watch his fucking back when this was all over.

"Like I said, Junk, it's good to have you back." He returned the look. Obviously, there was no love lost between us. "That's it for official business so—"

"I got somethin'. Kinda fell into my lap." Skids interrupted, all eyes falling on him. Tex motioned for him to continue. "I got us some side work for us to vote on. A girl needs a protected ride to Cali. She's offering twenty thousand, but it's gotta be now."

Conversation and dissenting opinions exploded as a result of the last-minute bomb Skids dropped on us all. Now I wondered if his ghosts and this girl who showed up at the clubhouse today was what he was referring to back at the prison.

The rest of the guys sounded off in a cacophony of questions and objections.

"Who is this gash?"

"That's a lot of cash for a ride!"

"Right now? We can't split ranks!"

"It's on the way. Fuck it!"

"We don't know her! Turn it down!"

The gavel came crashing down, bringing all arguing to a halt. "We'll have to put it up for a vote, but I don't think this is a good time for it, Skids." Tex glowered in exasperation, but as the subject had been duly brought up at the table, it had to be voted on.

"It's good money for somethin' we're doing anyways!" Skids hollered, rising to his feet.

I didn't know if the other guys picked up on it, but something was up with this job. Skids was too invested in it for some unknown reason, and it couldn't just be the money. I knew him better than that. The old bastard was accustomed to living light and detached from his military days.

"What if this bitch is a narc? I'm not willing to risk the coke money and our cred with the Legion over a girl we don't know." Tex was talking a lot of sense, and based on how he was showcasing his opinion, I could tell the club was going to side with him on this. "Let's put it to a vote."

Skids saw it too. His eyes flashed in panic, and then he abruptly added, "Her name is Maya. She's the daughter of the Hangers' prez."

Everyone stared at each other for confirmation on what they all were thinking.

"You're telling me she's the daughter of the Iron Legion's biggest rival? How do you know this girl?" Tex demanded skeptically.

"What matters is that we have an opportunity to hurt the rivals of the club we're trying to get in bed with. Right now, if we do the coke mule gig, the Legion will just be making us a support chapter. We'll be sucking their dick for what? They'll kick us some jobs here and there, but we'll be connected to them in name only. If we show them we can hurt their enemies too, we'll get a full patch over. That means voting rights, a bigger presence here, and help dealing with those pushing in on Topeka." Skids sat back down and gauged the group once again.

The old man made a compelling argument. Even Tex had to think that over. "Let's vote. Bring the mystery girl with us? Nay," he kicked it off then let everyone else weighed in.

"No!"

"Yay!"

"Nay!"

"Yeah..."

"Of course!" Skids grunted, his frustration clearly apparent. I knew he was lying and was trying to play the bluff like he was indignant that they'd question his wisdom.

Skids turned to me expectantly, an inkling of growing doubt hinted in his weary features about whether or not I had been able to see through him.

I thought it over. Suddenly introducing an extremely unpredictable variable into a dangerous run that could potentially get us all a few decades behind bars? Not to mention drawing some crazy heat from the Hangers if they found out the girl was gone and with us? Assuming, of course, if I believed Skids's story in the first place.

Desperate men will say anything.

Any way I sliced it, I thought it was a fucking terrible idea.

"Yay," I decided, pushing down that doubt. For some reason, I could see that this really mattered to Skids. I trusted him. I had to. Despite everything, he had my back, and I needed to have his. That was how this worked. Otherwise, what was the point of it all?

"Motion passes," Tex grumbled with a disapproving shake of his head, obviously displeased. "Make sure she's here on time. I'll be goddamned if I hold us up on her account. Any more business before the gavel falls? No? Good. Let's get the fuck outta here! We've gotta party to attend!"

"That was close, old man," I muttered as I leaned in toward Skids.

"Yeah, it's a good thing you're back home—for however long that lasts." He headed for the door before turning back for me. "I'll keep my end of the bargain." Then he left, phone in hand, about to make a call.

Skids was still sore about me leaving the club.

Through the open door, I could see the main room filling up with old and new faces as the party kicked off.

"Junk. A minute?" Tex asked as everyone else shuffled out. "What was that with Skids?"

"Just hashing out the end game, man."

"Fair enough. Not all that happy about the way you voted. You just tipped the scales in a very unpredictable way. I thought you were smarter than that."

"What can I say? I get a little unpredictable when blackmail gets thrown around." Only half the reason I voted against him was spite. The other half was loyalty. Intelligence had to take a back seat this time around.

"Things are a little crazy right now. Lotta moving parts. I need to make sure prison didn't... I don't know... twist you all up, you know? Gotta make sure that the Junkyard I remember is still in there and thinking about what's best for the club in this... sensitive time." Tex was fishing for info so hard, I wanted to check myself for hooks.

"That Junkyard bled out on the floor in a prison shower because his club turned their backs on him. Or maybe it was just the new C.E. president who turned his back."

"Careful...," Tex rumbled in a deep tone, eyeing me menacingly.

I swung around to address him directly. "From where I'm sitting, Prez, 'What's best for the club' seems to be... open to interpretation these days."

"You missed a lot, brother. A little gun-running money never would've sustained us. I'm looking at the long haul here. The Coffin Eaters wouldn't have survived without me stepping up."

"That line of bullshit tuck you in at night? Does it 'finish you off' before bed too?" I made a jerking-off gesture at him, then walked over to his chair and sat on the table so I could speak more privately. "I noticed there are a few more pictures on that wall that shouldn't be there. All of them were real supporters of that Russian deal we set up. What happened, Tex? Some convenient accidents? I also found out that you had me kill those two Russians before the deal was off. You used me to help sabotage our relationship with them, then you left me to die by their retaliation. The leadership under Miles looked weak as a result, making it real easy for you to challenge him, especially when you had a new connection to our saviors, the Iron Legion, in your pocket. Really, a brilliant plan. Gotta say, I'm impressed." I finished with a deliberately slow, mock clap.

Tex mulled it over, wondering how I'd connected all the pieces. It was all I could think of since I got out of prison. I just needed my suspicions confirmed. Sitting on that kind of betrayal and not knowing would've eaten me alive. I might be a big bastard, but I sure as hell wasn't an idiot.

"I love a good fairy tale as much as my kids, Junk." Tex eyed me. "Good luck proving any of that."

"Legion leadership, that's what's in this for you?" I accused. "You bring us in to the I.L. fold, they get a presence in Kansas, and you get... what? They gonna make you a cabinet member?"

"V.P. of the mother chapter. The C.E. has always been a dead-end club, a minor stepping stone. That's it."

"You sonofabitch."

Tex excelled at making connections, but not even I thought that he'd be able to swing that kind of sweetheart deal for himself. That's how he got the money for all these clubhouse upgrades. The Iron Legion must've fronted Tex a ton of cash.

"You can't prove any of that, and bringing it to the table right after you get home will make you look spiteful and untrustworthy like a prison bitch... or a snitch." Tex shifted tones like other people swapped hats. That kind of manipulation just came naturally to him. "Besides," he said, lightening up considerably, "despite what you think, this is better for everyone. Miles… Skids… the others… they'll finally get to see what the big time is all about."

"The big time...." The words sat distastefully in my mouth. "That's not why we started all this. When this is over, you just keep your promise and let me walk. Don't make me bust out the coloring book and connect your dots for everyone to see."

Tex got up and whispered to me, his tone shifting again to something dark and lethal. "Who the fuck do you think you are, Hendrix? You think you can threaten me? Look around! Your club is dead! New members, prospects, and hang arounds—I outnumber you now. You live and die on my say so! You're one convenient accident away from being mounted on that wall. You remember that." He shoved passed me, his shoulder squarely smacking mine. "Welcome home, Junkyard. Don't outstay it." He spat on the floor near me then slammed the door behind him.

I sat there an extra half an hour, taking everything in before joining the rest of the party. He was right. Even with Skids and Miles, my support network had evaporated these last few years. I didn't have much in the way of blood relatives. The ones I did have weren't local. So I walked out of the war room to join Miles and Skids for a beer, but neither were anywhere in sight. Already there was a mama whipping her top around. The party was gearing up to be a loud, sloppy night. Just the way I liked it.

Today, so far, was shit, but I'd be damned if I couldn't make it a good night. I picked out the cutest girl around and sidled up next to her at the bar. The blonde smiled as I playfully bumped into her and introduced myself. But before any conversation could start, I heard this unwelcome voice from behind.

It was Loopy, the road captain, interrupting our tête-à-tête. "I'd heard stories about you. How you got picked up on the way to county. Girls on your dick, swimming in money. Who'da thought a little jail time would've turned you into such a little bitch?"

I let my head drop. There was only one way this exchange was going to end, and I wanted no part of that. It was exhausting, and it had already been such a long day. I stole a long breath then lifted my head to face him. Then I raised it a little more. Fuck me, he was a tall bastard.

The sides of his head were shaved into an extreme mullet, his long hair pulled back into a ponytail. His arms crossed over a new vest with fresh patches. He was a brand-new prospect into the club within the last year or so. I missed every part of this guy coming up, yet he looked like the kind of guy I would've voted down.

"Funny, I haven't heard anything about you. Guess you must be nobody," I replied with a touch of boredom, opening my first glorious beer in half a decade. "Fuck off, new blood."

The wafting scent of the long-lost cold brew nearly lifted me out of my chair—such a stark opposite to pruno prison wine that was brewed in a toilet with smuggled ingredients from the cafeteria. That shit tasted like gasoline had sex with hot vomit. I tried it once and nearly went blind, so that was the end of that. But that didn't stop me from dreaming about that one day I would have an actual beer again.

Today was that day. *This* was that beer. And I pitied the human that came between us.

"Don't go fucking ignore me!" He slapped the beer out of my hand. I longingly watched it rocket across the room and spin out on the carpet like someone kicked my puppy. "We're on the same level. New or not, I'm as much of a C.E. as you are!"

At first, I was furious. I wanted to mangle this big, dumb bastard. Then I realized that in the free world, beer grew on trees. I leaned against the bar, dropped my head back, and laughed at the absurdity of it. This was just Tex being petty, so he put Loopy up to this. He was pissed that I voted against him and wanted to show me that the old days were over, that he was in charge now, and that I'd better get in line if I knew what was good for me.

"Prospect! I seemed to have spilled my beer. Clean that up!" I calmly ordered the portly kid who appeared to be fresh out of high school. I whistled to the hang around working the bar and had him toss me another beer, then I eyed my discontented, new-blood brother. "Go ahead, whip it out. You put yours on the bar, I'll put mine on the bar, and this pretty little thing can judge who has the biggest." I squeezed the blonde next to me. "What do you say, darlin? You up for a cock-off?"

"Fuck you!" Loopy firmly pressed an index finger into my chest, which only proved my thoughts about Napoleonic complexes.

"You don't have to be embarrassed. I can go first," I offered as I deftly removed his finger.

He stood there awkwardly, not entirely understanding how to fight on this level.

"How 'bout this instead? Walk away or be carried away." I popped the beer open, tipped my head to him, and added, "Your call."

"Fuckin' tough guy. You did a stretch? So what?" He yanked down his collar to reveal some faded prison tats. "You're just a punk. We all know you sabotaged the deal with the Russians. You don't give a fuck about the C.E.! You helped start this club, and now you're gonna turn your back on us like a pussy!"

The room's conversations lulled toward a halt as people began to take notice of us. This wasn't about me at all. It was for everyone else who probably didn't like the direction Tex was taking the club, but he was using me as a reminder at how it was before with Miles. I was being set up as a warning. This was supposed to go down regardless of what I said.

I shrugged it off dismissively. "Never meet your heroes, asshole."

If I couldn't get out of it, I could at least play it my way. I turned back to the blonde and smiled. Loopy's face turned beet red, either at the insult or the blow off. Probably both. He was itching for that fight that I wouldn't give him.

Loopy slapped the second beer out of my hand, and it sailed over the head of the prospect as he'd just finished cleaning up the first. The poor kid sighed and trudged over to the second mess. All conversations in the room now abruptly ended as they turned to see what happened and, more importantly, what was about to happen.

The blonde arose to her feet and excused herself as she realized it was getting too hot around here for her. I grabbed her thigh before she could escape and whispered for her to join me afterward. She smiled and nodded then stealthily disappeared into the crowd.

I spotted Tex who was watching casually. He tipped his beer to me as a feigned cheers as his smug smile ate half his goddamn face. I debated relocating it to his ass but then chose a more theatrical route.

"You know why they call me Junkyard?" I turned to face Loopy. He was a good half a foot taller than me, which didn't bother me. Quite the opposite, in fact. I loved dealing with tall guys because they were always overconfident. Big guys relied on their size for intimidation and wound up actually fighting a lot less effectively than the rest of us.

"Yeah, you used a junkyard car shredder to dispose of the club's bodies. Ain't no shredder here, man." Loopy searched around, garnering support from his friends.

"Nah, we never did have a shredder." I signaled the hang around behind the bar to toss me a third beer. "You know how expensive those things are…."

My train of thought blurred when *she* walked in—the girl Skids was arguing with outside. She wore sheer determination across her features like a mask that only barely covered her fright and unease at being in a room full of degenerate bikers. A woman who was here only because she needed to be, not because she wanted to be.

I didn't know who she was, but I knew *what* she was—a woman from another world. A better one. One that didn't kill you as hard or try to trap you in a box and peel years off your life. A world where my soul wasn't ground into a fine paste. A lifestyle I'd been so far removed from that I wasn't completely convinced it was still real. I wanted to be a part of that. *Her* world.

She was gorgeous in an exotic way that didn't exist here. Obviously of Asian descent. Slender build. Long, soft face under a dark, chin-length, bob-style haircut. Her white blouse comfortably hung over her tight, sexy jeans.

In a throng of black leather, jeans, long hair, and metal, she wasn't at all what I was expecting to see tonight. She was the first spring breeze through the pried-open window of a forgotten, dusty room long stagnant. The only thing was that this window didn't like to be opened. This girl didn't belong here. I needed to meet her before she realized that and left. *Or was removed.*

I abandoned the argument with Loopy. I was looking to get laid, not get into another fight. Tex could keep his posturing. I didn't feel like playing his game before, and now it was even less appealing.

Her almond eyes flitted across the room, probably searching for Skids, but there was still no sign of him. She saw that I was the crowd's current focal point and took me in as I sauntered over to her. The light skipped off her reddish-brown eyes like sunbeams over black water, making them shine darkly with each approaching step I took. She was cautious but curious.

My favorite combination on a beautiful girl.

Her body language was mostly closed off to new conversations, but I could squeeze a little wiggle room out of her lack of a frown that made her approachable but only to a man with the right mix of courage and crazy. I let the hands in my mind trace down her every supple, golden curve. I smiled. I was that man.

I needed to meet Robbie's ghost.

Her subtly narrowing eyes suddenly shot open in surprise as her gaze slipped passed me. I immediately knew what that meant. It wasn't good.

"Hey, I'm not done—" The moment I felt fingertips come down on my shoulder, I was on. A switch in my head flipped. I was back in prison. Loopy would need to turn me around to hit me, or else he'd look like a coward in front of everyone.

I pivoted toward him, flipping the beer bottle around in my hand so that I was holding it by the neck like a club, and ducked a predictable left cross. Continuing the quick, fluid motion, I whipped the bottle hard against his knee. It was followed by a grunt as the big man hobbled, then fell hard into a kneeling position. It was like chopping down a tree.

Trapped in a cage with nowhere to run for five years, "fight or flight" turned into "fight or die." My brain was on autopilot. I moved instinctively. If there was an advantage available, I instantly took it without thinking. That's all there was to it. My backhand with the bottle pinged off that sweet spot on his jaw, and Loopy was unconscious before he hit that lovely, checkered tile work. He didn't look so tall now.

"Tex, you remember, right?" I sardonically called out to the man in the audience. His confident expression withered at being dragged into this now failed display of authority. "We sure as hell wanted one of those shredders. What they could do to a car... such beautiful machines," I lamented, holding everyone's attention.

The beer bottle was unbroken, the beaded condensation along the chilled glass being too slick for any of Loopy's spattered blood to stick to it. A tooth must have shattered when I hit him, and his jagged grin mangled his lower lip when he had hit the floor. The black-and-white tile rapidly filled with pooling red.

I twisted the cap off and finally had my first, long-denied sip. Cool and crisp as time froze, allowing me to appreciate each and every nuance. It really did hit that old itch. *So* much better than I even remembered. Fuck, I *loved* a good IPA.

"We had to make do with an old car crusher," I resumed while Tex seethed, his eyes narrowed. He shook his head, hoping I'd stop, but he awoke something in me that couldn't be slowed... let alone stopped.

I strategically stomped down on Loopy's throttle hand. Through my heavy boots, I could feel the bones in the big man's hand crunch like old candy canes under a tire.

God, hands were so very sensitive due to their function—to *feel*. The pain was enough to wake Loopy up and double him over.

The room was crypt-silent except for the rising swell of his screams.

*You sonofabitch,* Tex mouthed the words at me. I knew I'd have to watch my back, but I'd have to do that anyway. This wasn't my club any longer—his previous words sank in my head and heart like tossed stones in a lake. He was right, and I was angry, but with the seventh member down, it looked like this new club was an even split. Tex and his two guys and me with mine. I liked those odds a little better.

"I think your boy might have trouble riding tomorrow. Might have to take a sick day." I cocked half a smile to match the prez's scowl as I imagined how staggeringly easy it was to let that brutal side of me take over.

I was greeted with disgust and horror when I turned my attention back to the girl who didn't belong here, the outsider that I found so intriguing. Violence came so naturally that it took me a moment to even register what I had done had upset her. It was hard not to associate this out-of-place girl with a "fresh start." In two steps, that fresh start turned her back on me and disappeared.

Now it unnerved me at how easy it was to slip back into the MC mindset and physically tear someone apart. Yeah, it had the mamas and a few old ladies bathing me in lusty glances. I'd get my cock wet tonight, no doubt. Hell, I should've been thrilled. Satisfied on every level. I was still *the fucking man*!

Past the bravado, the victory felt hollow. I'd divided the club, alienating myself further in the process. Worse still, I had this oppressive feeling that the civilian world had also rejected me as well. I wore the colors of a brotherhood that didn't believe in me and had the heart from a regular world that could never accept me. I was an outsider on every level.

With all eyes on me, I had never felt more alone.

# Chapter 4
## MAYA

"Van's here! Who's driving Miss Daisy?" the voice rang out, and I realized they were talking about me.

The men had their bikes lined up and were loading them when I strode over with my duffel bag. I would have immediately gone over to Robbie, but he'd told me last night to keep our connection a secret. I had to assume it was for my own good.

"I'll take her in the van," Robbie's voice was quick to intervene. He tossed a worn, canvas military sack toward the driver's side door to load when he eventually got in to leave.

After the fight last night between Hendrix and the other biker, if you could call something as brutally one-sided as that a fight, I found Robbie outside. He was smoking out by my car, waiting to scold me some more, no doubt. I had so many questions for him, but I was also exhausted. He had told me that I'd be riding with him in the van for the trip and that we'd be able to catch up on everything then.

"No. She rides. Cargo is too valuable. Skids, you're

taking the prospect. So who wants her?" Tex offered me up like I was a raincoat on a sunny day.

My heart fell a little as there were still so many questions I needed to ask Robbie. I wasn't too worried though. Being that I was stuck with them for a few days, I should be able to find some time to spend with just Robbie and out of earshot from everyone else.

"I have a car. I can just follow—"

"I'll take her when we get to the motel!" someone shouted. The other bikers laughed, but it didn't sound like a joke.

*If I even made it that long.* The thought arced in me like black lightning. The staggering realization of where I was and what I was trying to do filled my lungs with sand. This was all frighteningly *real*.

"Where the hell is Junk? Skids! What's the girl's name? Maya, right?" Tex's expression darkened at the mention of Hendrix as he asked Robbie about me like I wasn't even there though I was almost directly in front of him. It was amazing how condescending this man was, and of everyone here, I thought I liked him the least so far.

"Go wake him up! Tell him we leave in ten!" When Tex finally addressed me personally, it was only to issue orders. I obeyed immediately and left. The more distance I put between him and me, the better.

Robbie had assured me that Hendrix was a good man, the brother he trusted most here. The man that, from what I saw, wore violence as comfortably as most people wore vintage T-shirts. A nagging part of me wondered if I could actually trust Robbie, let alone Hendrix?

The human wreckage mixed with the party debris created a morning-after war zone in the clubhouse. I gingerly picked my way across the minefield to the bikers' rooms where all the doors were open except for one. It had to be Hendrix's.

I touched the door but was hesitant at first about opening it. It felt like I had spent the whole night trying not to think about him, and failed miserably. Hendrix was the quintessential opposite of my type. I liked the quiet, nice boys with the small smiles that, for the most part, had their lives together. Netflix-wine-and-takeout-on-the-couch kind of boys. This man was not that... in spades.

Instead, I knocked. No answer. I knocked harder this time. "Hendrix?" I called out. No answer.

*Dammit.*

I was an adult, I'd convinced myself, garnering the courage to open the door.

The mattress was completely off its box spring. A naked, blonde woman was asleep facedown on the carpeting surrounded by a few liquor bottles. The scent of sex had settled but was still thick enough to paint a pretty vivid picture of what kind of night it had been.

"Hendrix?" I repeated, half expecting him to crawl out from under a pile of clothing or to flip over the bed and be covered in vomit.

"Yeah, yeah... I'm coming," a deep voice boomed from the bathroom. Sounds of cascading water stopped, followed by a burst of steam as the shower door was flung open. He strolled out of the bathroom, drying his face and near shoulder-length, dark brown hair with a towel, and... he wore nothing else.

I gasped inaudibly. In the morning light, I could see him *very* distinctly. *All* of him—a dark-haired version of Chris Hemsworth with a few weeks' worth of beard over a fierce jawline. Hot water droplets cascaded down his steamy, tattooed form, colliding and speeding through the valleys of his chiseled ridges. My gaze was hijacked. I could only follow the droplets down the deep grooves of his chest, abs, and hip bones as they trapped themselves in the dark, matted patch of hair that hung over his cock.

*Jesus! Unless they just had sex, he couldn't be that large at rest... could he?*

"You're pretty when your mouth hangs open like that," he remarked as the towel dropped to his wide, tattoo-painted shoulders. Between the cut slabs of beef that made up his chest and his massively defined arms, which looked like they swallowed soccer balls, Hendrix exuded an incredible, primal strength that sent a thrill through my whole body.

He wasn't as bulky or swollen as a bodybuilder, but with his rugged, working-man nicks and scars and his overall brusque yet confident demeanor, Hendrix looked like a man who could easily kick the crap out of someone. Seeing him naked with all his corded, well-used muscles ready to fire at the drop of a hat really put last night's fight in perspective. That other biker never stood a chance.

He was lucky Hendrix hadn't killed him.

"Ten minutes," I stammered, screwing my eyes shut and whirling around. I was so mortified that he caught me staring! My face flushed with heat that I wrote off the whole interaction as embarrassment, not attraction. I felt like such a creep.

Again, I reminded myself I didn't like filthy, disgusting bikers or tattoos or muscles.

"Um, Tex said..." Goddammit! I was trying to spit out the message, but to do so, did I have to be in the same room as Hendrix... while he was naked? If he was ugly, I think it would've been easier, not that I thought he was attractive.

"Go on. What did Tex say?"

In my mind, I could see him grinning at my discomfort. I was sure he already knew what I had to say, but he was forcing me to stay and finish the message just because it was making me uncomfortable! I tried imagining him as being really ugly. Like with a potbelly and too much body hair. Though when I opened my eyes, I could see his reflection in a mirror behind the partially closed door.

I felt the universe betray me. That silly image of him in my mind chipped away like bad nail polish. There was only this naked, mind-blowingly handsome, scarred monster of a man who stared at me with a knowing smile. His eyes trapped mine while he dragged the towel over the rest of his body, making no attempt to cover himself in any way.

I swallowed then blurted out, "Ten minutes. They're leaving for the thing." My job officially done, I fled from his room. "Probably less than that now actually," I shouted from the hallway as I sprinted away from whatever mess I had just stumbled into.

*Yeah, that went well,* I thought sarcastically as I tried

to push the palm of my hand through my forehead. Ugh! I figured I'd have to formally meet Hendrix at some point, but that was not how I'd imagined it would go.

"He's coming," I reported to the pack of bikers when I arrived outside, not knowing who in particular needed to know.

"I'm sure he was!" one of the bikers interrupted me, noting with amusement how flushed I was. The rest of them laughed.

"He's on his way, I mean!" I scowled, ignoring the comedian. I hated bikers.

Everyone was on his bike and was ready when Hendrix finally came strolling out of the clubhouse, buttoning up his pants.

"You well-rested? We've got a fucking schedule to keep, shithead! Move your motherfucking ass!" Tex was barely keeping it together, but everyone could tell how pissed he was.

Hendrix smiled and started his bike. "Are you saying we don't have time to stop for coffee? I'm already looking forward to prison." He did what looked like a visual check over his bike, trying various connections and listening for anything that might be slightly off. In other words, he was delaying the ride even further.

Despite myself, I couldn't resist thinking that his personal chaos was a little charming. His boots untied and his clothing disheveled, he made no apologies and no attempt to rush. This was a man living at his own speed.

I reminded myself that I had been around vulgar, asshole

bikers my whole life and wasn't interested in guys like him. But just as quickly, my brain sabotaged my resolve by adding that I'd never seen a biker quite like Hendrix.

Violence came easy to men like Hendrix; that part resounded loudly in me. It came easy to my father too. Finally clearheaded, I thought of Anna and what I needed to do.

"The fuck do you think? Mount up! Your bike's fine! You're taking Princess. No more delays!" Tex's tone was so bitter that it was barely a shade removed from an outright growl.

"Safety first," Hendrix snapped coldly. These two men really didn't like each other.

It wasn't until they started riding off that Tex's words pierced through my cloud of thought. I was riding with Hendrix? Crap. After this morning, I would have rather ridden with almost anyone else. I made such a fool of myself around him.

Hate I understood. I was prepared to feel a lot of that on this trip, but what I felt toward Hendrix was already more complicated than I cared to think about. I was already at a disadvantage somehow with him, and I didn't like it.

"Don't worry," he nonchalantly spoke, snatching my duffel bag from my shoulder and stashing it in one of his bike's side compartments. He then packed the rest of his stuff and got on his bike. Hendrix tapped the seat behind him, the part I would be riding on, beckoning me to join him, and winked at me. "I bite even less with my clothes on." He then tossed me his helmet.

"Can I just follow you in my car?" I insisted once again. There *had* to be some way out of this.

"You paid us twenty thousand dollars to drive unprotected in your own car?"

*What? Twenty thousand dollars!* My eyes almost shot out of my head. Panic set in as I tried to figure out what he was talking about. I didn't have anywhere close to that much money. Oh shit! It must have been Robbie! My God... did he give them that much money just to convince them to take me? A million more questions sprang to mind, but now Hendrix's expression was shifting from amused disbelief to outright suspicion. If I blew our cover, would Robbie have wasted all that money?

"Ah... yeah, *obviously*. Of course, that makes sense. I just, uh... meant that maybe we could take my car instead. It would be more comfortable." Jesus, I may not be that experienced at being a lawyer, but I needed to become better at lying under pressure!

Hendrix studied me a moment longer before finally breaking the tension by saying, "I've been in a cage for five years. If you think I'm crawling back into another one just for carting you around, you are out of your pretty little mind."

"Hey... yeah. Sorry." I tried not to look at him as I jammed the helmet on and cautiously attempted to mount the bike. Immediately I tried to change the subject. "Is there anything I should... Dammit! Fuck! *Ow!*"

When I swung my leg over the side, the exposed skin of my calf slapped against something extremely hot. It was going to be a warm day, and I thought I'd be in a van for most of it, so I made the mistake of wearing shorts. I jerked my leg away before any serious burns could set, but it still hurt like hell, and the quick recoil tipped me hard to one side. My weight shifted dramatically as my reaction threatened to throw me off the bike completely. I was so terrified to touch anything else on the motorcycle that all I could do was tense up and brace for the inevitable impact onto the pavement.

Without looking, his large, rough hand snapped down on my thigh and steadied me. The unexpected thrill of his hand grabbing me sent a surge of adrenaline within me that immediately dulled the sting of my leg. I was shocked at how strong and quick he was. I had almost killed myself, and we hadn't even moved an inch yet. First, the pitiful lie then this.... What the hell was I thinking? I wasn't up to this. I was so screwed.

In all the years growing up with and around the Steel Veins, I had never actually ridden a motorcycle. I had stayed away from all that to the degree that I knew very little about motorcycles and which parts to avoid, apparently.

I didn't notice his hand sliding down my thigh until I felt the sandpaper of his palm on the flesh above my knee and down to my calf. My heart raced again as he twisted my leg slightly to examine the burn, which was now only a red spot. I suppressed the image of his naked form, struggling to put it far out of my mind, but I could feel the flush brighten and singe my cheeks.

"You're okay?" he asked as his clamp-like fingers released one at a time then slid off me entirely.

"Uh… yeah." I felt stupid in every way possible, but I was so glad that my slipup about the money seemed to fall off his radar… I thought.

"See those pegs?" he had to yell over the super-loud engine while he pointed them out to me. "Step on them! Your ass and your feet are the only things that touch this bike."

"What about leaning and all that? What do I do with my legs and arms?" I had heard that there was a proper way to sit and move your body so that you didn't endanger or hinder the driver, but I never paid any attention to it because I had never thought I'd be on the back of a bike.

"Have you ever had rough sex?" he asked, completely straight-faced, any hint of suspicion gone.

"What?" Surely I couldn't have heard him correctly.

"Have you ever had rough sex?" he repeated loudly.

I didn't want to answer him, but he was treating it as a legitimate question.

"Yes," I replied, probably coming off more bashful than I would've liked.

"Speak up! The engine's pretty loud!"

*"Yes! Yes! I've had rough sex!"*

A few of the girls who were leaving the clubhouse turned to him and either smiled or blew kisses. I couldn't believe I just screamed that statement to the entire parking lot. My face lit up like a Christmas tree. I hated how easy it was for me to blush. It betrayed all the emotions I'd rather not display, but, hell, I might as well have been wearing a flashing LED sign.

"It's a lot like that. Smash your hips into me as close as you can." He palmed my lower back and did just that.

His belt and thick denim ground the thin cotton-blend of my shorts into my pussy. A hot shiver ran up my stomach at the impact, snapping my eyes shut. I silently gasped for air and bit my lip, desperately trying to kill the steamy image of him stepping out of the shower, wearing a towel in all the wrong places.

"Then hold on for dear life." The side of his head was cocked toward me when I opened my eyes. Oh God, how much of my daydream had he seen on my face? Too much, I decided when I saw a creeping smile crease his lips. "And pray that I get off before you do."

With a roar of an already obscenely loud engine, he jerked the bike forward, startling the hell out of me. Worried I might fall off again, I clamped my thighs and arms around him as tightly as I could. I couldn't hear it, but I could feel his laughter through my death grip around his chest.

I was beginning to understand that Hendrix was such a special kind of bastard.

Within seconds, he'd put more speed and wind behind us than I'd been prepared to expect. I had to screw my eyes shut just to get my breathing under control. After a few minutes, feeling comfortable that I wouldn't fly off into the stratosphere, I finally opened my eyes. The helmet was extremely inefficient as it only covered the top of my head. Strictly to protect myself from the wind and Hendrix's whipping hair, I buried the side of my face into his shoulder and watched the patched, asphalt road blur by.

Downtown Topeka stretched out before us like the weathered skeleton of a downed dinosaur, its dusty stone-and-brick rib cage enveloping us as we rode through.

Riding through Topeka made me remember why I loved St. Louis so much. Every city I had been to had their own, unique pulses. Some beat faster than others. The heart of St. Louis pumped hot, passionate blood with a quickened rhythm that, for me, was the epitome of diversity and change. Granted, not all of that change was good, but it was always interesting. It was alive and had something to say, whether you wanted to hear it or not.

Topeka, on the other hand, felt as if it courted life support like a jilted, resentful lover. Nothing here was new or invigorating, only repaired, tired, and waiting for either innovation that would never arrive or death. A city that once might have had a purpose was only standing for its own sake as to keep an otherwise empty stretch of highway filled with at least something.

It was a sad, pathetic place that I never wanted to return to.

Once we hit the highway, Hendrix sped up to join with the rest of his MC. Cars we passed bled by so quickly that it looked like they were driving in reverse. I was surprised at what little change I felt on the bike as he pushed us up to speeds I'd been too timid to try in my own car. The engine roared a little louder, the wailing wind pitched a little higher, and we bent forward a little more, but that was about it.

We passed Robbie in the van and fell in rank with the dozen or so other bikers then slowed to match their speed, which was surprisingly tame in comparison. Speed was the only thing about the menacing pack of riders that was tame. They owned the road. Cars and other riders changed lanes to let them pass for fear of being crushed beneath the gasoline-fueled landslide of these Vikings rampaging into battle.

The heat radiating from both the engine and, of course, the man in front of me cut the chill and edge of the wind to make for kind of a relaxing ride. Having edged beyond my motorcycle biases, I could begin to understand why people enjoyed them. I would have understood it even more if the vibrations of the road and bike didn't make me have to pee.

The day melted away into blurred pavement and countless miles. I never knew which city we were currently in because it was all just one limitless road that I barely registered the shift from Kansas into Colorado. Our few stops for food and bathroom breaks were so quick that I couldn't steal any time with Robbie without looking too conspicuous.

I was trapped in my head at seventy miles an hour. I tried to stay focused on piecing things together with Robbie and rechecking the list of all the questions I wanted to ask him. What happened to my mom? What was his relationship with her? Why had he disappeared?

Those cyclical thoughts and fears were interrupted constantly by simply being in the moment. As hard as I tried, I couldn't completely push Hendrix out of my mind. It was impossible. Amidst the ebb and flow of the endless ride, my face pressed into his black vest and my arms and legs folded around his leather and denim-wrapped, steel form. I couldn't help but breathe him into me.

Unconsciously, I lined myself up with the rhythmic, soothing rise and fall of his chest as he took in air. For hours, as the taillights became headlights, we breathed and moved as one person. I *wore* him on every level.

Despite how much I tried to drown it with rationality or experience, a crippling urge kept floating lazily to the surface. It wasn't enough. I cursed it, but still I wanted more.

There was little denying it now. I yearned for it. For him.

Hendrix was an ex-con. No, he was currently a criminal, having violated his parole. I didn't know what they were transporting, but I was pretty sure it wasn't teddy bears. Hendrix personified everything I had spent my entire life trying to avoid—the seductive nature of that dark, edgy lifestyle. It was easy to write off my father and the rest of his thugs because they were horrible in almost every way imaginable. Corruption and selfish greed incarnate. Of course, I didn't want my sister or me around that kind of cancer.

Hendrix scared me. Not just because of his strength and the horrors that were part of his potential. No, he scared me because I couldn't write him off like the rest of them. It was obvious he didn't want to be a part of whatever this illegal run was, and he'd showed me an inkling of concern when I burned myself on the bike. If I was being honest with myself, I even had to acknowledge that he was walking away from that fight last night. Yes, he did take it way too far, but he didn't throw the first punch.

I knew that at least part of me was vilifying him to protect myself from giving him a chance. Was that wrong? No. I needed to. If I let myself fall for him, I'd be jeopardizing my future. It was hard enough finding work in the legal system in a prolonged recession, especially given my family history, which was something I spent years distancing myself from. No, actually running away from. My reputation would be destroyed if people found out that I surrounded myself with the criminal element.

What would Anna think?

Finally, Denver came into sight like a dream. The blended swatches of stubborn, blue sky slowly drowned in the celestial blood of dusk where skyscrapers stood on end like massive, broken dominoes before the equally silhouetted mountain range. Rocketing toward the brilliant glass giant, the evening lights of cars, streets, and buildings spread like wildfire, transforming the city's look into a glowing volcano of life in the growing darkness. I was lost in a sense of awe, feeling appropriately microscopic in the scope of things.

I'd never been to Colorado before, and for the life of me, I couldn't figure out why. It was the most beautiful place I'd ever seen in person.

# Chapter 5
## HENDRIX

The Lost Wild Boys opened their gate for us, and we flooded in. I was surprised we were here as I didn't think we had any connections in Denver and just figured we'd be crashing at a motel. Miles filled me in that Loopy was originally from this club, and since we patched him in, the two clubs had been working with each other a little more.

The whole thing made me a little uneasy, but I assumed most of that was because of my dislike of Loopy. Honestly, I didn't know these guys from a hole in the wall. They could be on the level, but I'd have to feel them out to know for sure.

"We're here. Hop off," I told Maya.

"But you said when we left today that—" She yawned, groggily protesting. The girl had been a trooper. That was a tough ride for anyone, let alone a passenger. "That 'I should pray that you got off before me.'"

"I was just fucking with you, darlin'." I winked at her. "Hop off."

Her face soured as she peeled herself off the seat. I put a

hand out for her to use as a counterweight as it would help when she swung her leg over to dismount, yet she spitefully didn't accept it.

The girl was proud. I liked that.

"I need my bag," she murmured as she stretched her muscles then patted down the front of her wrinkled clothes.

I stepped down and stretched myself too. I loved riding, especially after my court-mandated hiatus, but that first dismount and stretch afterward were almost as exquisite as the ride itself. Every time I got off my bike after a long ride, it felt like a day well spent regardless of where I was heading or what I was doing.

I opened one of the saddlebags and handed Maya her stuff. "Hey," I complimented after she grabbed the bag but before I let it go, "you did great today. That was a hell of a first ride." I gave her what I hoped was a small, honest smile and released my grasp.

She examined me cautiously, clutching her property close to her as she attempted to gauge how genuine the smile and my kind words were.

"Look," I added so that we weren't just awkwardly gawking at each other, "I just saw Skids go inside. He'll take care of you."

"Thanks," she replied, wearily heading toward the clubhouse.

I could understand her confusion, but I meant it. It was a hell of a ride, and, to be honest, I wasn't exactly on my best behavior to begin with. I was still pissed and angry at the way everything went down that dragged me into this mess, but that wasn't her fault. Being in prison for so long might have made me even rougher around the edges than I already was. Hey, at this rate, soon I'd be foaming at the mouth and pissing on shit to mark my territory.

From that lie she told earlier to cover up her surprise about the money she gave the club for the protection ride, I was certain she mattered to Skids in some big way. I was sure I could press either of them for details, but I trusted Skids. If he wanted me to know, he would have told me.

I found myself watching Maya work out a cramp in her right calf muscle on her way to the front entrance. She bent at the waist, and I traced her thoroughly with my eyes before I'd realized I was even doing it. There was something about that girl... because I could watch her for hours.

Riding for hours on end like that always put me in a familiar trance—what meditation must be like since I never felt the need to waste my time doing that kind of new-age shit. It was a feeling that didn't exist anywhere else in my life. Anytime I needed to clear my head, I always took off for a few hours and lost my troubles in burning rubber, billowing smoke, and biting wind. When I arrived back home, I was an empty cup, ready to be filled anew.

However, this ride with her was different. All my pent-up pain and rage were drained away like always, though underneath all that were unrelenting thoughts of Maya. Having her wrapped around me, I couldn't get her out of my head. A few times I'd repositioned her hands, not because I was uncomfortable or because it was making it difficult to ride but because I just wanted to touch her, to feel her silky skin not marred by scarred track marks or shitty tattoos.

Maybe prison did make me soft. Soft with rough edges, I chuckled. My hypocrisy knew no bounds. My eyes were riveted on her as Maya dropped her bag and bent over to retie a loosened shoe. Her shorts matted invitingly against her ass, and her shirt rode up just enough for the clubhouse's harsh exterior lights to shine off the bare, golden skin of her back. The muscles in my lower stomach clenched. I squeezed my bike's handlebar to force some of my blood from shunting preferentially to my cock. At least prison didn't make me want to fuck any less.

"Junk? Man, you all right?" Miles asked as he passed me on his way in.

I watched her slowly arch her spine, exposing more skin, then glance back at me. She knew I wanted her. That I wanted her warm, wet softness wrapped around me, wrapped around my cock. I wanted it so bad I could taste her. I wanted her sweaty and screaming. I wanted to rip those clothes off her and slam her up against the clubhouse wall.

"I'm good." I had to think about broken bike parts and rancid trash just to clear my head enough to finish my sentence. "Just a long ride. Little rusty, I guess."

She turned back and disappeared inside.

"I hear that, man." Miles nodded and headed in as well. He was completely oblivious to my distraction, and I was thankful for that.

I grunted, grabbing and squeezing my raging hard-on through my pants. I'd given myself an extra minute to get it under control and adjusted my cock so it was a little more manageable before heading inside the clubhouse. I had forgotten how much hugging there was when meeting new clubs. Shit, I was so glad I took the extra minute outside to relax. The last thing I wanted was some sword-fighting action.

All the members shuffled into the meeting room, which left the main room empty except for a few mamas who were waiting around for us to be finished plus a few sketchy-looking hang arounds who were eyeing our van and whispering. Never a good sign, but something I'd have to deal with later if it was anything but innocent curiosity.

A dark-haired Latina dragged her arm across my shoulder and eye-fucked me as I walked by. She was pretty for club property. Exotic, young, and with a smile that screamed *I like it rough!* I enjoyed exotic, but she didn't hold a candle to Maya.

Goddammit! This shit had to stop! *Right. the. fuck. now.* I didn't do hang-ups or comparisons. Pussy was pussy. That was it. I just needed some easy pussy to set my head straight. I was sure the Wild Boys wouldn't mind sharing their stock in the name of hospitality and all that. I had to put this Maya shit behind me.

"Hey," I grabbed Tex, stopping him from entering their meeting room. He ripped his arm away but reluctantly stayed to hear me out. "This shit. This animosity we have. It needs to stop, at least until we get this Legion run done. We both want the same thing—me gone."

"Agreed." His anger at me begrudgingly subsided, but

only a little.

This whole thing would be temporary, of course. If I could tie him directly to the murder of my brothers, the ones that supported the deal with the Russians, there would be a reckoning. I'd nail him to the fucking wall. For now, that had to wait as we both needed to focus on the task at hand.

I leaned in closer so as to minimize any eavesdropping. "How well do you know these guys? I'm picking up some weird vibes."

"Well enough. Loopy vouched for them. We should be all right here."

I raised an eyebrow at him in skepticism and cocked my head to the shady hang arounds.

Tex followed my gesture and spotted them. "Yeah, all right. We'll post a watch with just our guys till we leave tomorrow," he added reluctantly.

I nodded. The additional eyes on our van was the right call. For a change.

"One more thing." I stopped him again from heading in. "Maya, that Hangers' girl. You gotta cage her. She's a wreck waiting to happen. There's no way she'll make it on a bike another day without falling off or killing the rider. Let her ride in the van with Skids. She doesn't know what we're hauling. Besides, everything is locked up, right? She couldn't get in if she wanted to."

Tex rolled it around in his head then dismissively agreed.

What I said was all a lie. She was probably the best passenger I'd ever had, but the lie was for the best. This girl was a thunderstorm of distraction for me. I didn't have a lot of faith in what the C.E. was doing right now, so that was even more reason to stay focused. I was probably headed back to jail or, more likely, an unmarked grave off a highway somewhere. This muling business was risky. With this amount of drugs on us, we wouldn't be flying under the radar for long.

For as much as I wanted to tear Maya's pussy apart and devour every inch of her, I had to put some distance between us. She wasn't tainted like I was. She wasn't a part of our world. I knew that one taste of her would never be enough. Once I dipped into that well, that pure pussy, I wouldn't be able to stop.

When this run goes up in flames like I knew it would, if I was tapping that ass on the regular, then she'd be more likely to get dragged into the fire. Maya seemed like a decent chick who didn't need that grief. I didn't want to see this life take its toll on her like it did all the girls inside the clubhouse.

The meeting was quick, mostly logistics and sleeping arrangements. There was a lingering uneasiness coming off the Wild Boys, but we were all at their bar before long, and by then, it didn't seem to matter as much.

Pyramids of liquor shots were being carted around by completely nude mamas. The bar was snowy with lines of coke as they challenged C.E. members to blow races. I had to wonder if we just stumbled into a celebration.

With the first leg of the trip down and with a lot more to go, no one was in the mood to get annihilated. It seemed like no one told the Wild Boys that because within the hour, the place was near bursting with drugs and girls that went way beyond good house manners. Tex seemed wary of the craziness of it too, but he went along with it, albeit at a much slower pace.

Skids had taken first watch, no doubt to talk to Maya about whatever the hell they had going on. I was glad she was out there with him as I scanned around at the ass-grabbing and the girls who were passed around like party favors. Nothing good was going to happen to her in here tonight.

Miles was right at home. He didn't have to worry about the burden of command, so he was already a mess. I, on the other hand, nursed a beer and observed the mayhem, turning down attempt after attempt by their members and girls at stepping up my party game. As much as I wanted to get my dick sucked, the whole thing put me off a bit.

That's when I spotted the hang arounds in the back, the same group of guys who were scoping out the van earlier. They were chilling on the far end of the bar with no drinks of any kind. They just watched. No one bothered them or even really acknowledged them. If this was an out-of-control high school dance, then they were the chaperones. It felt *very* out of place.

I didn't know what was up, but something didn't feel right. I headed back out to my bike to grab my gun just in case. When I stepped out, I found two of the chaperones outside closing the main gate.

"What's up, brother? You all right?" one of them, dressed in a hoodie and with no cut or colors, asked me while clicking the lock in place.

*Brother.* That word was awfully forward for a nonmember to be throwing around. I could see the bump of a gun in his waistband. That was another odd thing for a nonmember to have on the premises.

"Just grabbing something out of the bike. What's up with the gate? You expecting trouble?" I asked lightly, playing down my suspicions as I shook the closest one's hand.

"Nah, just a thing we do at the end of the day," the other man spoke up. He was bald with a handlebar mustache. "Keeps our guys safe. Cops are dicks around here."

"Yeah, it's cool. We're just looking out for everyone," Hoodie smiled disarmingly and shook my hand.

I noticed the letters *TLWB* were tattooed under his knuckles, each finger getting its own letter in the acronym. *The Lost Wild Boys.* Only members were allowed to get club ink.

These guys were members masquerading as hang arounds. They were sober, armed, and locking up the only way out of the compound. Right then, I knew it was on. Whatever it was, some shit was about to go down, and, with the C.E. in the shape they were in, it would be a fucking massacre.

Hoodie saw me notice the letters and squeezed my hand, preventing me from letting go as he reached for his gun. I didn't bother going for my knife on the opposite side of my free hand—I'd never reach it in time. I twisted, ducked low, and slammed forward, simultaneously jerking my hand behind me and throwing my shoulder into his rib cage. I rammed him into his friend, which bodily threw us into the gate.

Hoodie let go immediately as we all hit the ground in a heap. Being on top, I was the first one up. Hoodie went for his gun, but I kicked it into him before he got it out of his pants. He screamed as the impact set the firearm off. The bullet most likely tore through his thigh and must've hit a major artery because blood poured out of the bottom of his pant leg and over his shoe like someone left the tap wide open. He'd be unconscious in seconds and dead in minutes.

In any other situation, I might've felt bad, but fuck every one of these assholes for what they had planned for my friends.

The bald man squirmed to get his dying friend off him. He already had his gun out, but his arm was pinned against the fence. I palmed the side of Hoodie's face and shoved him out of the way, pulling my knife with my other hand.

"Whoa! Whoa! Take it easy!" Handlebar Mustache tossed his gun when he realized he wouldn't be able to get a bead on me before I gutted him.

"You know what I'm going to ask you. Don't fuck this up." I slid the edge of the blade under his nose. One quick slice and that hunk of flesh and cartilage would be a vivid memory.

"Yeah! Okay! Okay! The drugs in the van. We were going to steal them and replace the drugs with bags of sugar. Relax that thing, huh?"

"How'd you *know* about the drugs?" I let my anger seep through each syllable. I angled the blade up and slowly slid it across his flesh. The sharp edge sliced the skin beneath his nostrils and began parting it from the underlying tissue, blood spurting over his lips and chin. This was going to get real messy real quick.

I was so damn pissed because, had these fuckers succeeded in making the switch without us knowing, that would've been a death sentence for us when we made the drop with the Iron Legion. If I hadn't gotten to them first, these fucks would have killed me and the rest of us, either here and now, or indirectly by way of the Legion at the drop site once they found out all we had was fucking sugar.

"Loopy! It was Loopy! For fuck's sake, stop! He told us when, where, and what it was. Stop!" the man screamed in a real panic. I almost didn't hear him over the thrumming rage in my ears, and I was surprised at my restraint. In prison, I'd be finishing the conversation with the knife embedded in this asshole's eye.

"Gate combination," I seethed. What little patience I had was fading fast. I'd have to get the damn thing open to get our bikes out if we had any hope of surviving tonight.

"It was just changed! Only Saul knew it." He looked down at his dying partner, now completely unconscious.

"Then why the fuck am I keeping you alive?" I growled, locking eyes with the man, my face within an inch of his face.

I could usually see it in a person when he was resolved to end my life. It was something in his face, an intensity of either of rage, expediency, a perverted excitement, or just plain self-preservation. My eyes burned holes through him as I tried to figure out which one it was for him.

He whimpered at the intensity of my resolve he saw in my face. He knew he was dead.

*Fuck!* My face soured. I had to turn away. I didn't want to be that guy anymore! I pulled the knife away, leaving the man's face intact.

I wanted out, not further back in. Hoodie killed himself when he went for his gun. That wasn't on me. I didn't want to rack up a body count tonight. I didn't want *any* of this.

*I just wanted to fucking get laid!*

"Thank you, broth—" Mustache started before I turned the knife over and smashed the side of his head with the pommel, knocking him out.

"You're no brother of mine." I spat on him, then stuffed both of their guns into the back of my pants, checking to make sure the safeties were on first. I wasn't going to repeat Hoodie's mistake. I grabbed my pistol from my bike and jogged around the corner where I discovered the van to be fine. The Wild Boys were probably waiting for the gate to be closed first. Skids and Maya sat inside and had the doors open for cross ventilation. I could've run and warned them, but they were both sober and would know when shit went sideways. The rest of the C.E. inside were fucked.

I wasn't ten steps back around the corner to the main door when the man at the gate was beginning to come to. No one can ever tell how long someone is going to be out, but I was desperately hoping it would be a little longer in this case. I could either leave him and rush into the clubhouse like a cowboy before he woke up enough to warn his MC brothers for backup, or I could guarantee his silence, run back to the gate, and slit his throat. That move would give me a few more minutes to plan our escape.

I hesitated for a moment before I knowingly made the wrong, less practical decision. "Yee-haw...," I muttered to myself sarcastically and swung open the clubhouse door like Clint Eastwood in a spaghetti western. No killing for me tonight, I'd decided, just a whole lot of maiming. For now, I was all smoke and no fire.

*Let's see how long that lasts,* I skeptically thought as I stepped into bedlam. I fired a round into the ceiling, drawing a sea of dull, startled faces toward me. "Coffin Eaters! Mount up!" My words reverberated loudly through the din of confused and soon-to-be frightened people.

One of our sober "chaperones" in front of me pulled his gun and began to rise from his chair. I kicked his face with the heel of my boot with such force that it sent him reeling over the small table where he had been sitting. Then I drew down on the other fake hang arounds on the far side of the room.

"Loopy set us up! They're trying to hijack the van!" I yelled to Tex, tossing him and our sergeant-at-arms the two pistols I'd taken off the Wild Boys in the parking lot.

A bullet whizzed by my head, catching one of the girls in the throat. I drew down on the shooter and screamed for him to stop. He did. For an eternity, Tex, the sergeant, and I had a tenuous bead on all the chaperones. It was a standoff with no easy way out without killing a whole lot of people.

Although everyone had heard the gunfire, no one knew

for sure if it was actually a gunshot because of the music, the shouting, or the drugs. It wasn't until the girl dropped to the floor when the place froze. She twisted on the ground, writhing, gurgling up as much blood as air.

It was horrible. I wanted to help her, but I knew the second I put my gun away, we'd be outgunned by the Wild Boys. The wide-eyed girl gasped and pleaded wordlessly as she weakly flailed her arms, slowly dying on a loud yet empty dance floor. Dozens of people stupidly looked on, too paralyzed with fear to move.

When the girl lay motionless, it all became deadly real.

Another armed Wild Boy emerged from the bathroom, and now we had lost the balance. The second he fired, it was like someone pressed the play button. Everyone lost their fucking minds. The place exploded in screaming, running, and, of course, more gunfire.

I threw myself toward Miles, toppling him like an upended bowling pin, then rolled over and put a round in the leg and arm of the guy who shot at me. Miles vomited everywhere when he hit the ground as he was obliterated on all sorts of shit. I grabbed him and started dragging him out the side door because he would have to go in the van as there was no way he could ride.

*"Everyone! Side door! Go! Go! Go!"* Tex screamed, licking off gunshots almost indiscriminately.

The gunfire filled the air, reminding me of a child stomping on a roll of bubble wrap. What followed was the hideous combination of pops, screams, and the sound of meat slapping against the wooden floor. I realized it would be a twisted medley that would be lodged in the back of my brain for a long while.

Miles and I crashed into the parking lot outside just before the rest of our guys. The music was still so loud inside, effectively masking the gunfire, that the parking lot was starkly serene in comparison. I quickly hauled Miles to the van, which was located all by itself toward the middle of the parking lot. When we drew close enough, I overheard some of Skids's and Maya's conversation.

"...my fault. During the year I spent as a prospect, your mom and I got very close. When she was pregnant with your sister, we..." Skids was speaking softly, but I could still hear him through the van's open windows.

Skids had always been tight-lipped about his past so I never could get a solid read on him about his family. It sounded like he was just starting to open up to Maya about the kind of connection the two of them had shared. I wished I could've given them more time to talk, but it was about to get very loud and deadly out here. They would have to catch up when—if—we all got out of this alive.

"Skids! Get Miles in the cab! Shit's gone sideways!" I interrupted emphatically.

The old man emerged from the van. "What's going on?" he demanded as he helped me carry Miles to the passenger side door where Maya was sitting.

"Loopy set us up! He was a former Wild Boy. Must've given them the heads-up about the coke. Take Miles and Maya and go." I yanked Maya's door open, and she hurriedly jumped out, clutching her purse, and gave us some room to work.

"Coke? Is that what's in this van? What's happening?" She didn't look like she had any idea about what was coming. I couldn't even imagine what that kind of innocence felt like.

A pair of our guys, half holding and half dragging another two wounded, shoved open the side door and yelled out for us to wait.

"The inevitable...," I exhaled through gritted teeth. I grabbed Maya's shoulders, captured her complete attention, and warned her, "Keep your head down and trust no one but Skids and Miles."

Her eyes widened as the gravity of the situation began to set in. She was in real danger here. That first step away from her was the most difficult for me. She so obviously needed protection, but I reminded myself that Skids had her and that he'd keep her safe.

It was the rest of my club who needed me now.

"That motherfucking rat. Fuck! Maya, get down behind the wheel well," Skids shouted when he saw the Wild Boys kick open the side door of the clubhouse and start stumbling out into the parking lot.

The van was out in the open, so there was nothing for Skids to hide behind. Fortunately, everyone that flooded out of that door was so fucked up that their initial volley of gunfire miraculously missed him. The bullets punched through the side of the van all around Skids so closely that if his breaths were tangible entities, they would have been bleeding.

I was about to have our guys open the back doors and load the wounded in with the coke, but a few of the sober Wild Boys in disguise came around the side of the building and had a clear line of sight on the rear. Out in the open like that, we'd be dead before we had it unlocked. I tucked away my pistol and stacked our wounded into the cab like fucking cordwood.

That left no room for Maya.

Skids climbed into the driver's seat and stared at me hard once he realized how full the cab was, and now he was faced with the real possibility that he would have to make a fatal decision one way or another. There was no way he wanted to leave her here like this, and he was only a second away from getting out of the van and trying something really stupid like going toe to toe with the entire damn biker army.

We couldn't survive a gunfight now with our members messed up. It would be a slaughter. If Skids had his bike here, he could have taken her out on that, but he had been driving the van. With more Wild Boys streaming out of the clubhouse by the second and the gate still closed, we didn't have time to switch my bike for his van. He needed to leave now, so that left me to be the one to get her out as it was the only way any of us could survive tonight. Save the girl to save the club… but so much distance between Maya and me.

"No!" I shouted to Skids after slamming the passenger side door. "Use the van to punch through that gate. I'll get her out. I promise." I didn't yet know exactly how I was going to pull that off, but that was on me. I'd do it somehow as long as he got that fucking gate open.

Skids grimaced harshly but understood.

"Move!" I grabbed Maya's arm when the van took off, using it as a cover on our way to my bike until it quickly outpaced us and crashed through the gate. Now we were about halfway to our exit to freedom, standing out in the open, surrounded and outnumbered.

Oddly enough, it was the whores who saved us.

What was left of the strippers, mamas, and WB support network—hang arounds, prospects, and the like—ran out into the parking lot, fleeing the firefight inside the clubhouse. We would have been dead if there weren't dozens of scared and confused distractions now running aimlessly around like a flock of headless chickens in a slaughterhouse yard. With all the hammered, angry men trying to line up shots, it was a hard reprieve to swallow because I knew how this was going to play out. There wasn't enough time to make it to my bike before everything went tits up. We needed to find cover fast.

It was a Coffin Eater who shot first as he fumbled his way atop his bike. The shot sailed right passed the Wild Boy he was aiming at and caught a fleeing girl between the shoulder blades. The girl's terrified, continuous scream at what she had seen inside cut off into a deathly quiet when the round caught her as if someone had instantaneously crushed her voice box. She hadn't even hit the ground before the parking lot erupted into chaos. Dangerous, armed men from both clubs, half crazed from betrayal and drugs, fired at anything that moved.

That was the second bloodbath tonight.

I dragged Maya away and had to throw us both behind a parked car as a Wild Boy, in pursuit of Skids, sprayed bullets at us on his way by. Maya screamed, but I had her by the shoulders as we both fell onto the pavement on the far side of the bullet-riddled sedan, so we'd be a harder target to hit.

Behind cover of his own, I spied a Wild Boy clip one of our guys who was riding out, drilling a round into his chest and one in the side of his head before blowing out his front tire. Brain matter and bone chips burst out of the back of the man's skull like pink, jellied chunks of calf sweetbreads. He collapsed over his bike, jackknifing it. The whole gruesome mess flipped headlong into a row of lined-up bikes—both ours and theirs—right by the front gate. Several gas tanks ruptured, dumping glossy fuel all over the blacktop.

"Shit! *Nikki!*" I recognized my bike's handlebar bent awkwardly, jutting out of the jagged metal scrap pile that was all that remained of the collision. I was absolutely devastated. I fucking just got her back yesterday. Nikki was a passion project for me, handed down from my old man. She had been in rough shape back when he gave her to me, but after several long months, I had her purring like a sinuous cat.

Now I was *really* pissed.

Maya had a few superficial cuts from hitting the ground but was otherwise physically fine. Amid all the gunshots, screaming, and crashes, she forced herself to regain control of her frantic breathing. The girl was terrified, but I could tell right then that she was strong enough to do what it took to make it through this. That was admirable.

That was also when I noticed her clutching a nine-millimeter pistol. Reflexively, I almost demanded that she tell me where the hell she'd got that, but this wasn't the time nor the place. I had to keep my promise to Skids and get Maya out of here safely.

Using this car as a shelter was apparently a popular idea as one of the Wild Boys decided to follow suit. When he rounded the car, I reached for my gun, but it wasn't there. Perhaps our impact against the ground popped it out of my waistband? The Wild Boy saw my cut and immediately recognized that I was C.E.; then he brought his shotgun around to fire on us.

I rolled over on top of Maya, attempting to shield her, as I waited for the end, praying my body would have enough stopping power to prevent Maya from getting killed too. If the biker was using a double-ought buck or slug ammo in his shotgun, it wouldn't have mattered as the round would have punched through both of us like paper targets.

*Click!*

"Goddammit!" I heard the man cry out in frustration. His gun had either jammed or was empty. Our luck was so thick right then, I could carve a piece off and eat it.

Maya's almond eyes became saucers as she pointed her gun at the man. She was trying to muster the courage to shoot him, but after her initial hesitation, all three of us knew that she couldn't do it. The biker wasted no time in breaking his shotgun in half to clear the jam and reload.

Maya was on the verge of tears. She closed her eyes, her gun arm still locked and shaking as she realized we were both about to die.

I couldn't let that happen. It was time to take the kid gloves off, and, if nothing else, this motherfucker would pay for what happened to my bike.

I didn't have time to wrestle the gun away from her fear-induced, iron grip, being that he'd almost finished reloading. She didn't cry out or protest when I wrapped my hand around hers and the gun, which I pointed clumsily at the man's center mass. In the end, we were just a little too quick for him.

Using her finger, I fired several shots.

I cautiously stood up as the biker's corpse hit the ground and surveyed the carnage. Coffin Eaters escaped in ones and twos or not at all. There were so many bodies on the ground that some of the fleeing men were getting thrown off their bikes as they tried to avoid them or ride over them. I was struck by all the butchery.

*How the fuck did Tex not see this coming?*

I'd been out of the game for years, and I could smell trouble the second we arrived here. He should've known better! It only reinforced what a shitty plan this was from the get-go.

I couldn't help but be a little frustrated in myself too. I was so caught up in Maya that I was blind to what was all around me. The old me wouldn't have just noticed that something was off. He would've immediately been able to recognize it as a trap. More people died tonight because I wasn't paying enough attention to what was important, a mistake I could not make again. That was if we made it out alive.

Most of the C.E. who could leave were already gone. Without a ride, we were trapped. Without distractions, we were dead. It was only a matter of time before someone spotted Maya and me. That was when the beam of a downed motorcycle's headlight skipping off the spreading, shimmery river of gasoline gave me an insane idea.

I thumbed out a shitty, plastic lighter from my pocket, flicked it on, locked it in an open flame position, and hurled it at the glistening gasoline pool that led to the heap of bikes. The lighter hit one of the leaking tanks and broke apart into a glowing ripple of blue flame as the gas vapor went up. The resulting fire rapidly spread across the parking lot in an ever-expanding circle. More screams and curses erupted as people ran, throwing themselves out of the way, as if expecting some massive explosion.

There wouldn't be one, at least not right away. It gave us some breathing room for me to come up with the next part of the plan. The fire and smoke opened the path for us by creating a lull in the gunfire. Now I had to convince one of our hosts to let me borrow his bike.

I scanned the ground and quickly found my gun by the car's back tire. The shotgun biker's corpse had almost landed on it when the bullets and gravity took him. I gazed up and spotted a Wild Boy who had just fired up his bike, obviously heading after Skids and the van full of drugs.

"Stay here and keep your head down," I ordered Maya.

"Where are you going?" Maya frantically grabbed my arm and pleaded, so terrified of me abandoning her.

"Valet's here with our ride," I explained, peeling her hand off me. I snatched my pistol and dove for the passing Wild Boy, spearing him off his bike. The motorcycle tipped over and skidded out with no major damage as it wasn't going that fast to begin with. We both hit the ground like a sack filled with leather-wrapped rocks. The Wild Boy wheezed as the pavement stole his breath from the impact, making it easy for me to get on top of him. I grabbed his collar and shot point-blank through his forehead.

I had been lying to myself about all the "new leaf" crap and about playing it straight to stay out of jail. There might have been a time and a place for that, but here in this parking lot? Hell, there was no room for the passive, the weak, or the restrained.

It was a place for only the killers and the dead.

And I was a killer.

"Maya!" I straightened his bike up, hopped on, then motioned for her to follow.

Heads started bobbing up, and guns resumed popping off after the explosion looked like it was just going to be an intense motorcycle fire instead. With all our guys dead or gone, we were now the only target.

Once she was close enough, I jerked her over my lap and the gas tank like a naughty girl about to get her ass paddled and took off as there was no time to let her get on the bike properly. Bullets zeroed in on us from every angle, every shot getting that much closer. One of them took my mirror clean off as I weaved the bike around bodies and other downed bikes. The pileup wreckage I'd lit earlier coughed up pillars of black smoke that choked the night air. Orange rivers of flaming gasoline coalesced with the oily runoff from other wrecks to extend out over the blacktop like deadly fingers, the largest of which crossed our only exit, creating a fiery barrier between us and freedom.

If any gasoline had splashed on us, those deadly fingers would crush us in a flaming fist, and we'd have gone up like a roman candle if the gas tank had been punctured. The vapor would have caught, and we'd be riding an active Harley-shaped grenade. There was no time to think or pray or even change my mind. There was only out or die.

"Hold your breath and cover your face!" I screamed to Maya just before we plunged through the yellow wall of death.

The heat crashed into us as fire licked up the smooth, metal sides of the bike and across every fold of our clothing. It searched for purchase, for anything flammable that would allow it to consume us like an angry, searing hitchhiker desperately grasping to hang on as we slammed through.

A quick twist of the throttle, and both the fire and the Wild Boys clubhouse were behind us. The only thing brave enough to chase us was the blind, sporadic hail of bullets.

I drove us several hundred yards down nearly deserted streets, looking for a quiet alley so I could make sure neither of us were burned too badly. With all this adrenaline, I could be missing an arm and have no idea what had happened.

Behind us from the clubhouse, there was a rapid series

of loud popping noises, possibly the bikes' metal gas tanks superheating, straining against the fire. I checked my remaining mirror and caught a flash of light followed immediately by the boom. The motorcycle pile finally exploded.

We could see the brilliant plume of flame, the light catching the raining shrapnel as I pulled into a side street. There wasn't much time to hang out here as we were still way too close. Once the cops arrived, everything within a mile's radius would be stopped, searched, and questioned.

"Maya?" I dismounted and manipulated her body into a better position to check her over for oozing cuts, gunshots, or burns.

"I'm okay, I think...." She was shaking and hyperventilating as she slid off the bike while reaching out for something to stabilize her. Her soft form would've appeared pale had it not been darkened with soot and blood, and her hair singed by the fire. "Oh God... I'm not okay." Her eyes rolled up at the same rate that the blood drained from her face, and she dropped like a sandbag.

"Hey! Hey!" Despite already having my hands on her, I had to lunge to catch her before her head slapped off the brick alley wall. "Stay with me!"

She was completely unconscious when she collapsed in my arms. I kicked away some broken glass and unidentifiable brown filth and laid her softly down to the cracked ground near a wall. Again, I searched her over but with greater attention to detail to make sure she truly wasn't injured. Aside from the same few scratches and bruises, I couldn't find anything more.

Now that she was completely on her back, I carefully brushed the dark hair from her face then gently palmed the side of her head so that I could thumb open her eyelids. Her reddish-brown eyes were dilated, dark, and watery, but still stunningly beautiful.

Confusion set in when she woke up, having trouble focusing on anything. I touched the back of my hand to her forehead. Her sooty skin was clammy. I had to get her to a safe place soon, or this would only get worse.

I eased my hand away from her face, letting her eyes loll and close back into unconsciousness. As my shadow receded, the streetlight caught her fully, and for the first time all night, I saw her without distraction. She was plain with slight and simple features. I was so used to hooking up with worn-out whores and druggies that Maya, being so far out of my realm of experience, might as well have been a Disney princess.

My sleeping beauty.

I brushed her cheek, not because there was anything more to remove but just so I could feel her softness across the rough crags of my skin. It was infuriating how often she was on my mind. Thoughts of her had burrowed into my brain and poisoned my focus for everything else. It felt like I was endlessly talking myself out of being near her, but every time I turned around, there she was. I just couldn't stop myself from wanting her.

I understood the lust. I wore that as easily as my cut. It was all the other emotions that came with it this time like longing and yearning that had me worried. Maya was the catchy hook of a song that I didn't know the lyrics to and was afraid to sing along with.

Flashing lights and sirens blurred passed us, robbing us of the kiss that would wake her, or however the fuck that worked. She'd have to settle for a hard ride at eighty miles an hour instead and maybe some coffee.

"C'mon, darlin'. It's time to go," I urged her softly, picking her up off the ground. Even keeping the speed down, there was no way she'd be able to hold on behind me. How the hell was I going to get her out of here?

It came to me as her near limp body collapsed against mine. Neither of us were going to enjoy what came next.

I mounted up onto my bike and picked her up, having her straddle my lap and facing me in a hug. It was probably the most difficult and uncomfortable way to ride for both her and me, but with my arms on either side of her, holding onto the handlebars, at least I knew that I could keep her from falling off.

"Oh God... Hendrix?" Maya could barely mumble. Through her disorientation, I could tell she was scared and confused. Surviving something like an assassination attempt tended to unravel people.

"That's the first time outside of sex that I've heard that combination of words in the same sentence," I stupidly tried to lighten the mood in the hopes that she'd find it comforting. Getting no real reaction, I tried sincerity. "We made it, Maya. You're all right now. Don't worry."

We *had* made it somehow, just like I had promised.

The "how" was so fast and visceral that I would never be able to explain it to Skids if he asked. Shit, Skids... I hoped he got away. I stopped one of his tails, but he had at least two more on him before I set the world on fire.

I should not have survived that massacre. Neither of us should have. Part of me knew that if I didn't have a good reason to, I probably wouldn't have. Keeping Maya safe gave me back this lost sense of purpose that I thought was truly gone.

She let me rest her head on my shoulder as I got us moving. As uncomfortable as it was, I couldn't deny how nice it was to have Maya so close. Through the cocktail of sweat, smoke, and blood, there were hints of lilacs in her stained, silky skin. The remnants of shampoo or lotion maybe? That didn't matter. I knew, until my last moment on Earth, whether that be in a week or a lifetime, whenever I smelled lilacs, I would be brought back to this moment. With her.

This girl was something else. A balm for my ugly, burnt soul. It was an oddly comforting feeling.

I had initially kept us slow at twenty-five miles per hour. I told myself it was so I could adjust and account for the additional awkward weight, but I knew that the real reason was just to hold onto that moment, the scent of her invading my senses, for as long as possible. I chuckled to myself. I was going soft after all. Still, it was a warm thought, something I'd be sure to cherish on those long, lonely nights back in prison when the cops eventually carted my daydreaming ass back there.

Once we hit the highway, I had to bring us up to cruising speed. The wind cruelly stole my lilacs as I knew it would. The bright cone beaming off my headlight burned the darkness off the rolling blacktop before me, melting it into the inky pools of night that made up the tree line to either side. With no highway lights, the nighttide robbed me of the landscape. There was only the vanishing stretch of road in front of me now. A road that, under the blanket of darkness, looked like countless others I'd traveled on errands for the club.

I sighed.

It filled me with all the ramifications and consequences of what went down tonight, and it reminded me of who I was. First and foremost, I was a biker, a criminal, and above all, at least until I got out, a Coffin Eater.

Thoughts of Maya and flowers finally faded from my mind.

# Chapter 6
## MAYA

I startled awake, gasping for air. I was drowning in a broiling sea of blood and bones and bullets... an intense and horrible night terror.

*It wasn't real,* I repeated to myself over and over. *Just a dream.*

Was it though? Had I woken up yet, or was this still that same dream?

I blinked, rousing slowly from the initial shock, but I still couldn't see anything at all. Oh God, had I gone blind? My heart started racing again. My chest tightened. Air seemed to flee the room, making it harder to breathe. I felt sick to my stomach.

No, I wasn't blind. The room was pitch-black, but there was a little glow under a door on the far side of... wherever the hell I was.

I was on a bed. I quickly ran my hands down my sides. I was wearing all my clothes except for my shoes. Where the fuck were my shoes? Irrational anxiety skyrocketed. I couldn't remember anything about what had happened, why

I was here, or even where "here" was, and I'm losing my shit over my shoes? *Get a grip, Maya. Be glad you weren't raped or shot!*

"Calm down." I had to hear the sound of my own voice even though I only dared to whisper it. I took in short, quick, shallow breaths at first, gradually easing out of my hyperventilation.

I let myself think for a second and rationalize my surroundings. I was on top of a large, tightly made bed with far too many pillows. This had to be a motel room. There were no other sounds in the room. No snoring, shuffling, or breathing. From what I could tell, there was no one else here.

I smelled terrible, like smoke and sweat and death, but there was another scent in the air. It was definitely food. Eggs and meat?

I carefully walked my fingers around me, quietly searching, just in case there was someone else in the room. I spread my arms and legs to explore the rest of the bed. There was a loud, crinkly noise as I accidentally kicked something. It hit the floor with a crackling whomp. A plastic bag? It must've been full something soft… perhaps clothes?

Okay, if this was a motel, then that meant there was usually a nightstand with a clock and a phone on it. Nothing on my side. I slowly crawled over and found the clock on the other side facedown, so I rotated it over to see the time.

"Ah!" I stupidly looked right at it. The red LED digits were so bright to my light-sensitive eyes that I immediately slapped it facedown again. Once my eyes didn't feel like they were going to explode, I slowly flipped it back up. Now I knew why it was facedown to begin with.

*Three in the morning? Okay... now where the hell was I?*

I used the clock to scan the room. It yielded extremely low light, but my eyes could pick up that this was a one-bedroom and I was the only one here. I found the switch to the bedside lamp, covered my face with my hand, and bravely clicked it on.

Through the slit between my fingers, I took in the rest of the room. It was a moderately decent-looking place. Nothing fancy but far from shitty, and it was mostly empty. There was a pile of dirty clothes in a corner, the plastic bag I'd kicked off the bed that looked like it was filled with women's clothes, and a tray of food placed in front of the flat-screen TV perched on top of the chest of drawers. I was right. It was eggs.

It wasn't until I got up that I realized how famished I was. On the way to the food, I nearly tripped over my shoes, which were placed on the floor off the foot of the bed right next to my purse. Some of that anxiety lifted, and I didn't feel as vulnerable now that I had my stuff.

There was sausage, scrambled eggs, toast, fruit, and water. The food was cold, but I was too hungry to care. I sucked it all down, wondering how the hell this was even here. No motels I'd ever stayed at served breakfast this early in the morning.

Under the tray was a piece of paper that I'd mistaken as a napkin. On the back of it, a note read:

*"Don't freak out, Maya. You're safe. I'm on the roof if*

*you need me."*

Who was on the roof? Hendrix? Then the memories came back to me slowly. He brought me here after what felt like a heart attack in that gross alley. Why were we in the alley? We were fleeing some—

My eyes drifted to the pile of filthy clothes again. Red spots and splotches stained everything. Then it hit me like a hammer to the chest.

Oh God... the memories became a flipbook of images. The first few were slow and unreal; then they flipped faster and faster, recreating the entire scene—all the horrible events of the shootout in the Wild Boys' parking lot. A blur of hell that made the nightmare I had woken up from seem all the more real. The blood that dripped on my shoes from all the wounded bikers loaded into Robbie's van. That one guy's head exploding as he rode by.... I shuddered at the thought of the biker with the shotgun.

Someone actually tried to kill me....

*Jesus Christ! I actually killed a man!*

The noise. The bleeding oil and gasoline from the mangled motorcycles that made the parking lot itself appear wounded. The fire. All that black smoke. The bullets. Screaming. All those bodies dropping.... The hellish symphony of death reached a crescendo in my head, transitioning to the overwhelming clash of its diabolical coda.

Nauseous, I stumbled quickly to the bathroom to lift the lid of the toilet, but I didn't make it in time and projectile vomited my early morning breakfast into the shower stall.

I collapsed onto the cold floor tiling, breathing heavily and unsuccessfully fighting back the torrents of food then bile that escaped me.

I wanted it to stop. I wanted to die.

After a while, the vividness of the memories settled, as did my stomach. I'd seen some bad stuff with the Steel Veins—drugs, nonconsensual sex, and a dead body or two—but nothing like that. No one ever tried to kill me before!

Wait a minute. It was Hendrix. *He* killed that biker, not me. I was just holding the gun. I felt him slide his finger over mine over the thin, metal trigger, depressing it, and the gun recoiled. *That's right. Hendrix shot him, not me,* I reminded myself.

Jesus... I had given Anna a gun and just expected her to be able to do that? To kill with it? What the hell was I thinking? She'd never be able to kill anyone. Not even to save her own life... just like her older sister.

I'd be dead right now if Hendrix hadn't pulled my trigger.

It was a sobering thought. I couldn't do this shit anymore. I was wrong to come here. I had to get the fuck out of here, away from these psychopaths. I needed to go back home before this got even crazier. Before I was killed!

I cleaned myself and the floor then ran the shower to take care of the rest of the puke. I was filthy, and the steam looked too inviting, refreshing, and relaxing to pass up. I bottom-locked the motel room door. No one was getting in without kicking it. Finally I felt safe enough to undress and get in.

The water washed away the grime and the sin of it all,

and when I was done, I felt like a new person. I was resolved to put all this madness behind me. No more. Period.

The bag had the most ridiculous mix of clothes, half of which were too big and all of it was hideous. I put on the plainest thing I could find, which was a collared plaid shirt obviously meant for a boy and a pair of ripped, faded jeans. There was nothing in the way of underwear so I hand-washed mine in the sink and dried them with the hairdryer.

I grabbed my purse and readied myself to leave this place behind me. Unlocking and opening the door, I thought about Hendrix's note. Could I really just leave without thanking him for saving my life? Or without asking about Robbie to see whether he was even still alive?

I mulled it over. My anxiety spiked at the thought of it, but I breathed deeply and got it under control. I had to distance myself from the violence, the cocaine, *all of it!* If I stayed, I don't know.... I was so terrified that if I saw Hendrix again, it might make everything that happened feel even more real. Instead, I'd call Robbie once I was in a cab and ask him to send my thanks to Hendrix.

That thought made me feel so cowardly.

As I was about to make the call, 2 percent flashed on the cell's screen. Dammit! Riding all of yesterday and after everything else that happened, I hadn't had time to charge my phone. Shit!

So much for the coward's way out.

I sighed, dropped my bag on the bed, and plugged in my phone. Was I really that shitty of a person to think that I could hide until my phone was charged then run away? I wouldn't be able to live with myself. I would poke my head up, thank him, and leave. Five minutes tops.

He was on the roof? I chuckled. He wasn't going to make this easy for me, was he? How was I even supposed to get up there?

It turned out that the motel we were at wasn't all that big. Fifteen or twenty rooms max, maybe, which meant the hallway to the roof hatch was actually pretty easy to find.

Hendrix had torn the faux leather cover off a Bible—probably the one that came in the room—and used it to prop the door open. Classy. What else would I expect from a biker, really?

The egress room that led to the roof was just big enough for a ladder and some hanging tools. The hatch at the top was wide open, a window to the brilliant starry sky. The front part of the roof that overlooked the parking lot was steeply pitched, probably to help with piled-up snowfall, while the back part was flat and ended in a waist-high wall. Hendrix lay on the uneven, black tar of a small, flat maintenance area. He gazed up at the stars, wearing jeans and a half-unzipped blue hoodie with no undershirt, and sipped at a large bottle of wine.

*Where did he get a bottle of wine?*

"Watch your step," he warned, not bothering to glance over at me.

"Where are we?" I rubbed my eyes, having the feeling I was going to either need more sleep or some coffee to get the last of the tiredness out of them.

"A few hours north."

"Did you talk to Robbie?" I blurted out. The last time I saw him, he was being chased by a few of those awful bikers. "Is he all right?"

"Haven't heard from him." Hendrix seemed quite distant, as if I had somehow interrupted him. Prayer or reflection or… something… I didn't know.

"Jesus... I hope he's okay."

"He's a hard man to kill."

"How can you be so calm about it? He's your friend, right?" That really bothered me. Robbie could be hurt or worse, and we had no idea.

"I have to believe he's all right." Hendrix finally tossed a look in my direction through a sip from the bottle. "Tex texted me. We're meeting up with whatever's left of the C.E. tomorrow, so we'll find out then."

I turned away and walked to the ledge that bordered the perimeter of the roof. I couldn't look at him when I told him what I'd been practicing over and over in my head on the short walk to the roof hatch. "I can't." The words were small and pitiful. I swallowed and began again. My determination kicked in, bolstering the words with more volume. "I can't come with you tomorrow."

"You're leaving?" His tone had a hint of incredulity to it like he was surprised that I would want to go.

"Yes. I mean, all this is just too insane for me. I was almost...." I stopped to swallow the stress of hearing the words out loud. Taking a deep breath, I continued, "I was almost killed because of cocaine. I just can't do this anymore. I don't know what I was thinking."

"I see." The disappointment in his voice really threw me off.

I had convinced myself that whatever fleeting connection we might have had when we arrived at the Wild Boys clubhouse was only imagined. Did he want me to stay? Here with him? I had to push it from my mind. It was too dangerous a thought. Hendrix was a biker. I didn't fall for bikers. That was the end of it. It had to be.

"So, thank you for everything. I hope you make—"

I turned my head at the sound of Hendrix chuckling. Why the hell was he laughing?

"You're leaving right now? At 4:00 a.m.? In Laramie, Wyoming?" He gestured broadly across the horizon. "I'm gonna go out on a limb and say that taxi services probably aren't running right now."

Dammit! I hadn't even thought of that. Between the attempted murder, fainting earlier, and my PTSD moment, I obviously wasn't thinking straight. I glanced passed Hendrix. Only one unlit highway broke the endless plains in every direction. Not even distant headlights dotted the edges of the twinkling black sky. He was right. I wasn't going anywhere for a few hours.

"Well... shit."

He smirked at my oversight and patted the area next to him. I felt silly, but at least the tension seemed to have lessened, so I took my seat.

"Consolation prize?" Hendrix sloshed the bottle of wine lightly.

"Oh God, yes!" I snatched it away, not bothering to look

for glasses that I knew wouldn't exist, and just took a long swig. I needed that. I needed a hundred of those after what we've been through. I hoped the obviously cheap, ultra-sweet wine would dull some of that horror.

"Thanks for the food. I wish I could've kept it down."

Hendrix nodded his acknowledgment.

"By the way, how'd you get that? I mean, there can't be a restaurant or a store or, hell, anything for miles that's open right now."

He cocked his head at me and smirked. "Motel kitchen was unlocked. Eventually."

"Hendrix! That's stealing!" The creases in my smile betrayed my mock righteous indignation.

"What can I say? Prison turned me into a monster." He shrugged.

"Our justice system hard at work. I'll have to write my congressman. And these?" I tugged at my poorly fitting clothes.

"The latest in fashion courtesy of Lost and Found. I think most of them are even clean." He sniffed at the shoulder of his hoodie and gave me a look that said "close enough."

I giggled softly. Annoying thoughts of how charming he was kept popping up, so I blamed it on the wine.

My eyes returned upward. I'd never seen so many stars shine so brightly before. There was almost no light pollution, minus the big, glowing "vacant" sign, which was mostly hidden where we were sitting. It was incredibly calming, and it made all of my problems and everything we'd been through feel so small and insignificant.

"It's beautiful. The stars. Is that why you're up here?" I barely whispered, turning toward him.

He heard me but didn't answer. His eyes were transfixed upward, sparkling in the low light. His hair was swept back so that the auxiliary lighting from the building and the deep night sky could fully paint his rugged features in cool, dreamy tones.

God, this man was handsome in a way I'd never allowed myself to recognize before.

We watched the stars together for a while in silence, passing the bottle of wine back and forth. My senses blissfully dulled and diluted some of the horror that, although still seemed so fresh, now felt at least manageable.

It was peaceful on that roof with him and countless billions of pinpricks above us. It was something I never would have made time for in my regular life, but it was exactly what I needed right then. I probably could have sat there all night... next to him.

"I grew up just outside of Topeka," Hendrix abruptly broke the silence. His words were soft and distant at first, like he was remembering a dream. "Small house with a big yard and plenty of cottonwood trees. As long as I could remember, I always wanted a treehouse. Some of my friends had them, and it always made me insanely jealous.

"My father worked a lot and never had the time or patience to put one together for me, so I used to sneak onto our roof instead. I'd imagine it was my treehouse. I even brought a trunk up there that—" He chuckled, tossing me a disarming smile before continuing. "—that wasn't very waterproof. It held, or rather, destroyed all of my important kid shit. A flashlight, some candy and soda, a few old comics, and even this raunchy porno mag I'd lifted from... I can't remember.

"Then on a clear night like this, I stopped looking down and started looking up. I saw the stars for the first time. *Really* looked at just them. Unhindered by tree branches and buildings, the massive scope of it... felt like I could see forever. It made me feel connected to something much larger, something more important than just myself.

"So when my parents divorced and everything else in my life got all fucked up, that roof on a clear night used to put me at ease. Pussy, my bike, my brothers... lying awake in prison in the middle of the night on that shitty cot, listening to my bunkmate get ass-fucked... it was the stars that I missed the most. All the vastness of the universe couldn't penetrate my six-by-eight cell."

I looked at him in mild awe. "That might be the worst and saddest description of a place I've ever heard."

"Yeah, if you thought the DMV was bad...." He cocked an eyebrow at me.

Hendrix was a dangerous, mysterious criminal, but he was also charming and surprisingly funny. He was a difficult man to figure out.

"What's your story? How'd you get wrapped up with a bunch of outlaws like us?"

"I've been asking myself that same question." I knew I really shouldn't be sharing anything with him. "I guess I'm doing all this for my sister. She's having some trouble at home." After everything he'd already done for me, the least I could do was not be rude. I couldn't help but like the man a little. He did attempt to shield me from a shotgun blast, so as long as I kept the conversation light and vague, it should be fine.

"So you're riding cross-country with a bunch of murderous, drug-running bikers… to improve your sister's home life?" Hendrix asked, confused, but accepted it in a *"sure why not?"* sort of way. He went to take another sip before realizing the bottle was empty, so he set it down.

"When you say it like that... it does sound ridiculous." I laughed. "It's more complicated than that."

"It always is." He smiled then stood up and stretched. A moment later, there was a new bottle in his hand. I shook my head at his ingenuity. What else did he have hidden away up here? "How are you related to Skids?"

"What?" That caught me off guard. I didn't know what to say, but I wasn't about to go into the specifics, and that seemed pretty damn specific right now. How did he find out that we were related anyway?

"C'mon. Skids is one of the most detached, old-school, military types I've known. We've been friends for a long time, and the only time I can get him to say anything about his past is with a top shelf's worth of alcohol." Hendrix paused long enough to take a few long pulls of the wine. "Ever since you showed up, he's been bending over backward for you."

"I… uh… I don't," I stammered, trying to buy time.

"Can't be his daughter. Hangers are a Latino MC, so

your dad's Mexican and your mom's... Asian."

"Korean!" I snapped back and pretended to be insulted. After a lifetime of people screwing that up, it didn't bother me now. My mom was born in St. Louis. I was third generation. I couldn't be any more American than most people here in the States.

All right, perhaps I doth protest too much, but that's because Hendrix was working out the connections and I was trying to distract him. Jesus, he was sharp for a biker. *Stop exceeding my expectations... like now!*

My disdain didn't even faze him.

When this all started, Robbie told me that secrecy was a matter of life and death. No one could know who I was or what I was trying to do. It could tie Robbie to a rival MC, and he'd be kicked out or worse. I needed to change the subject before he figured everything out. Dammit! I couldn't think of anything. Why did I drink so much wine?

"Hey!" I touched his knee. "Uh... tell me more about the stars?" *Tell me about the stars?* That was the best I could come up with? Seriously? I was *so* screwed.

He glanced over at me but ignored my stupid request. "You're his niece, that's gotta be it. It still doesn't make sense that he'd be mixed up with the Hangers. Where did you say you were from?"

I panicked, stole away the bottle of wine, and took a big sip. Now I was really worried. If the Coffin Eaters knew who I really was, they'd kill me or use me for leverage somehow. I'd seen the Veins do it to people before, and I refuse to be anyone's bartering chip.

Instead, I kissed Hendrix.

He tasted like grapes. His prickly beard was rough, but I… I didn't mind it. Hendrix was so different from the safe, clean-shaven boys that I had always dated. Even through the haze of alcohol, I could feel the heat surge to my face as we pulled away. My heart was beating faster, and my breath quickened. Boy, was I thankful it was too dark for him to see me blush.

*I did it to distract him,* I immediately reassured myself. That was it. What startled and worried me most was that I didn't hate it. It was so wrong to have kissed him.

I closed my eyes. *I hate bikers.* I tried to remind myself what they did to me and Mom and what they were. My father's face immediately came to mind, and I shuddered away from a two-fingered caress down my cheek.

When I opened my eyes, it wasn't one of Slick's thugs this time—only Hendrix. I'd never allowed myself to look at him this close before. His strong jawline, thick eyebrows, and long lashes were strikingly handsome.

Hendrix looked at me. Was he trying to read me, to figure out what I was thinking? Maybe he was trying to justify whatever was going on inside of his own head as he was searching my eyes for something. I'd seen him watching me when we'd stop to rest on the ride to Colorado. I wasn't so naïve that I couldn't tell when someone was interested in me.

"You don't have to be afraid of me." His words were deceptively smooth but also had the ring of honesty about them. I desperately wanted to believe him.

I was such a liar and a bigot.

I needed to believe that all bikers were the same to protect myself from ever being hurt again. I hadn't known Robbie or Hendrix long, but they'd both shown me more character in the last twenty-four hours than I'd seen in a lifetime around the Steel Veins.

Not all bikers were the same.

The raw truth of it was that I wanted Hendrix. I wanted to feel what a real man was like, and the lies I told myself couldn't convince me otherwise. I felt it the second he stepped out of that shower. Now here he was. There were no more distractions or pretense. He was looking directly and only at me.

He found what he was looking for and kissed me. This time, it wasn't the reaction of a surprise. He meant it. Every soft twist, nibble, and press. I fell into it, letting it happen. I was alive because of him, and I was leaving in the morning. I would never see him again. Could I really pass this up?

Countless, easy excuses came to mind to let this happen. At the heart of it, I just couldn't get the thought of him out of my mind. This went against everything I'd ever allowed myself to believe in. With each passing second, all my hang-ups and resistance became smaller and less important.

Hendrix wasn't like the rest. I had no doubt that he could turn me to ash, but I was less and less convinced that he would. If it was all a lie, one that would come back to burn me in the ass, then I would at least revel in the warmth for now.

His face in mine, I blindly pulled at his hoodie, clumsily

wrenching it off him. I had imagined what his naked skin felt like during the whole ride to the Wild Boys clubhouse to the point that I had to chastise myself for it. My fingers explored every rippling muscle of his broad back, brushing over every minute, raised ink mark or scar tissue. That man's back alone could tell dozens of stories.

With a heavy shrug, he pulled me against him. My dulled senses, tingling and heating up, smoldered. My nipples hardened into little marbles and rubbed against his stiff pecs. His lips finally peeled away from mine, finding purchase on my cheek, chin, then neck. I rolled my head back and embraced it all.

How long had it been since the last time I had sex? Six months... a year maybe? My last boyfriend was such a wet-as-cardboard wimp, even by my safe standards. I always initiated. I always set the tone. Jesus, it was borderline masturbation.

Hendrix was the polar opposite. His touch was strong and definite, his confidence radiating off him. His every jerk and twist unabashedly told me how much he wanted this too, and all I had to do was breathe it all in and hold on.

We crashed against the ledge that ran along the back of the roof. I leaned back and slipped my hideous, collared shirt over my head. Hendrix snatched it from my hands and threw it behind him. He tucked up behind me to undo my bra... or rather he *tried* to unclasp it.

"Having trouble?" I teased, giggling.

He halted, raised an eyebrow at me, and snapped the clasp, breaking it off completely. "Nope."

"Aww, do you know how expensive a good bra is?"

"Bill me." He licked down my neck and sucked on my collar bone. His tongue skated between my tits then ringed my areola. My chest heaved when he tugged at my nipple— first with his pursed lips, then with a hint of pain as his teeth bit down and nipped the tiny pink nub, tenting the entire breast away from my chest wall.

That sent a ripple from my chest down my stomach to my hips. The motion gyrated my crotch into the thick, rough folds of his jeans, and I could feel the bulge of his stiffening cock. Having seen him at half-mast, I was curious, excited, and terrified at what he had in his pants.

His hand slid over my ass and squeezed so tightly that I let out a squeak. My eyes widened, blushing embarrassment marring my face.

"You gonna make it?" he asked, lightening the pressure on my ass but burying his face into my other breast. He didn't bother looking up as it was obvious that Hendrix didn't mind my erupting, weird noises.

It was a really nice feeling. The flushness faded, and I was able to relax a little more. All that wine made it happen a little quicker than I'd ever thought possible, but even still, he wasn't judging me. There were no expectations. Whatever this was, it just was.

"I'll survive," I cooed, watching him work and dragging my nails down his back.

The playing suddenly felt extremely real when I felt his fingers crest the band of my sort of stolen jeans. They slid around back and easily dragged the fabric over my ass.

Part of me became nervous for a second, and I grabbed two handfuls of his long hair and tried stopping him from going any lower. I was more than a little intimidated as old anxieties flared up from my subconscious. *He's a vicious biker!*

It was like... I didn't expect it to go this far. Was that a bad thing, though? I wanted it… him. I'd probably wrapped my brain around every inch of his hard body, but it just didn't feel right. When he pulled against my grip and inched my pants lower worry crept in. What if he wouldn't stop? He was so much stronger than me, there was no way I could force him to do anything.

Thankfully, Hendrix sensed something was off and gazed up at me. My expression must have said it all because he let go right away and stood up. He brushed the hair from my face and smiled. "What was that about, surviving?" Hendrix leaned back and ran his hands over his head.

"I-I'm sorry. I just...." I had to take a deep breath, exhaled, and buried my face in my hands. I felt so crappy letting it get that far just to stop.

He retrieved my shirt and pried one of my hands from my face. "Hey, don't worry about it." He handed the shirt to me and waited as I shimmied into it.

Bikers aside, I hadn't known many men that could take something like this in stride.

*Goddammit, Hendrix! You make it impossible to hate you!*

I looked up at him, feeling guilty, and quickly exhaled in a defeated, breathy laugh. "Growing up in an MC household kinda screwed me up big-time. I'm sorry."

"I just got off a five-year dry spell. Another night isn't going to kill me."

Hendrix ground his teeth and adjusted the bulge in his pants to something more comfortable now that it wasn't coming out to play. Getting anxious and nervous didn't make me want him any less. My panties were still wet; it was so infuriating! I wanted every thick inch of his cock. I wanted to feel everything he could give me, to wrap myself in him, but my stupid brain just had other plans.

"You should rethink leaving," Hendrix abruptly changed the mood.

I struggled just to face him.

"I don't know what happened to you at your father's club or why it was bad enough to bring you to us, but... whatever it is that you started is worth seeing through to the end."

"How could you possibly know that?" How could he? He was surprisingly quick, but not even he could know what growing up on the outside of a club was like.

"Look at you. The impact they had on you is still deciding what and how you deal with things. You said you're doing this for your sister, right?" he asked.

"Yeah."

"Would you want her to have the same life you had?"

"Of course not, but I work in a law firm now. I'm not an outlaw!"

"You're a lawyer?" Hendrix visibly tensed, and a look of worry flashed across his face. His posture straightened and hands tightened. He probably didn't know he was even doing it.

"I'm just a freshman lawyer, but I'm really nothing more than a research assistant to the firm," I quickly clarified, hoping to put him a little more at ease. "Don't worry. I'm not going to turn you in for anything."

How could I? Even from a practical setting.

I hadn't actually seen Hendrix do anything outside the realm of self-defense. Aside from my Uncle Robbie trusting him with his life, I didn't really know all that much about the man. The one thing I did know about him was that he didn't hesitate for a moment when bullets started firing.

"And that's exactly my point. This is your world, not mine. I'm not fit for this kind of life. I mean, my God! Only a few hours ago, I was nearly killed!"

"We all gotta die sometime." Hendrix shrugged.

"I'm not… I can't just decide to be something I'm not."

"If you stay and finish this, it won't matter what kind of woman you think you are. You'll get to die as the woman you always wanted to be." He grabbed his hoodie and bottle and headed for the hatch that would take him back inside the motel.

I was speechless.

I had lost sight of the bigger picture. Anna needed me as much as I needed to help her. This whole thing wasn't just for Mom and Anna—it was for me too. I didn't have to live in the gray shadow of the Steel Veins anymore. I didn't have to be scared anymore.

Hendrix was right.

Just like that, running away seemed so foreign to me that

I couldn't believe I had even considered it.

"I'm his niece." That definitely stopped Hendrix's descent, and he craned his neck up at me curiously. I didn't know why I was telling him this, but it felt like the right thing to do. "Robbie is my uncle. I just found out that my mother had a safe-deposit box in California, and he's trying to help me get there. I'm hoping it has something I can use to get Anna away from our father and his club or something that might explain my mother's disappearance ten years ago."

Hendrix gave me that same searching look he had done right before he kissed me... like he was looking for something inside of me.

"I'll stay," I announced, slowly coming to peace with my newly found resolve. No doubt I was still terrified at what might happen to me or at what I might have to do, but I felt like I had a purpose again. What a spectacular feeling.

Hendrix grinned then climbed down the ladder.

"Hey!" I sprinted over to the hatch and gazed down at him. "Thanks for all… uh.... Thanks. Oh, and seriously, you owe me a bra." At last, a smile crept onto my face.

"That's what you get for tangling with outlaws. You should know better, Lawyer Lady." Hendrix glanced up at me before stepping out of the small room into the hall.

"Where are you going?" My real question should have been *Why are you leaving?* I didn't know what I wanted, but whatever it was, I wanted it to be with him.

"I'll be in the room." He poked his head back up, grinning. "I find determination sexy. That hot, little, half-

Korean body of yours got me too wound up to not get off, so don't interrupt unless you're willing to join in." He winked and disappeared.

He made my smile almost eat my whole face. I felt compelled to chase after him because after that dirty talk, I found him even sexier, if that was even possible. Just the thought of him, cock in hand below me, made me flush with heat again. I sighed and slumped against the half wall that held the hatch door then gazed up at the stars again. Tonight wasn't the right time. I would feel absolutely horrible if I made him stop again. "I think one major, life-changing affirmation was enough for one evening," I muttered aloud to myself.

Another benefit of seeing this through was that I'd be stuck with Hendrix, at least for a little while. I had a sneaky suspicion that I might be able to steal away some time with him at some point. God, I hoped so.

Hendrix would be my crucible. If I could survive him, I'd be tough enough for anything. Maybe even strong enough to rescue my sister permanently.

# Chapter 7
## HENDRIX

The sun was at its highest when we arrived at the abandoned railway station on the outskirts of town the following afternoon. Concrete platforms ran along on either side with intervals of riveted, iron columns suspending the thick, curved latticework of steel that hung defiantly above our heads. Harsh, seasonal shifts eroded the paneling on the ceiling, stripping the structure of its function. The bubbled yellow caution paint was mostly eaten away by a plague of rain, rust, and ruin.

Hazy, pollen-filled sunlight filtered through the spiderweb mockery of the station's ceiling, sending crisscrossing square, shadow patterns before us as my bike stamped down the tall weeds that had reclaimed the buried tracks. The labyrinth of oxidized metal made the place smell like old blood. There was definitely an ominous sense of dread and inevitability in this place.

Maya felt it too and squeezed me a little tighter.

I perpetually scanned for anything that appeared suspicious and kept the bike at a low roar to focus on our surroundings.

Last thing I wanted was to ride into another trap, but there was nothing here but ghosts and echoes.

I followed the grooved tire tracks of the other bikes that arrived before us. Why would Tex have us meet in a place like this? Between the manmade and natural barriers, it was tough enough to get two wheels out here, let alone a van. How the hell would Skids get the van—

"Goddammit." I frowned, suddenly piecing it all together. Skids didn't have the van... and that meant no coke, which meant that we were completely fucked.

The platforms all funneled into a central hub. I couldn't imagine what it looked like when it was operational, but now it was just like any other derelict inner-city park. And over there, a row of Coffin Eater's bikes sat where I would've expected a broken swing set would have been.

Of the nearly two dozen members and friends of the Coffin Eaters that left our clubhouse yesterday, only six made it out of last night's slaughter. To think, I was one shotgun misfire away from missing this little get-together. It reaffirmed my need to get out of all this MC bullshit before my luck gave out.

The greeting hugs were somber. Tex was already on the phone with the Iron Legion, explaining what had happened. Everyone else waited for the only news we could get because there was only one way that phone call would end. To be honest, I was surprised Tex even bothered contacting the Legion at all. In this game, there was no forgiveness or second chances.

In the Legion's eyes, it would be our fault for trusting

that club. That coke was our responsibility regardless of the circumstances. We fucked up and would pay a heavy price for it. I didn't know yet what happened with Skids or why he didn't have the van, but none of that mattered right now. This was all on Tex. Running drugs for protection was his deal to begin with, and it was his guy that flipped on us and set us up with his old crew. If this deal collapsed, I would make damn sure Tex was crushed beneath it.

I spied Skids and Miles leaning against an ages-old ticket booth as we made our way to them when Tex snapped his phone shut.

"Any luck with the Legion?" one of Tex's guys asked.

Tex answered the man with a dour look and a shake of his head. Then he stared at us, or rather, just at Maya. It was a curious, intense look that Tex had, which put me on edge. "I have one more lead to shake down."

The hair on the back of my neck tingled the same way when I caught the Wild Boys locking the gate. Something didn't sit right here.

"I was beginning to worry." Skids picked up on Tex's stare at Maya. He checked his pocket watch, snapped it shut, then toyed with it in his hand for a moment, his casually hooded eyes boring at Tex with a stern mask on his face.

I wondered if he thought Tex blamed him for wrecking the van. Tex was a mean, manipulative son of a bitch, but he'd never be able to convince the other members that it was Skids's fault. Skids should be safe from the backlash, at least within the club.

"Had to stop. Little lady needed a few... articles of clothing."

I winked at Maya, who immediately scowled and began to glow a beautiful shade redder.

I loved making her blush. There was an innocence there that I found intoxicating.

"I don't want to know." Skids shook his head and replaced his watch back into his pocket. I hugged him then Miles, which was always customary when greeting after a tragedy.

"Why the hell didn't you pick up your phone, old man?"

"Lost it in the shuffle," he replied as he smirked, clamping down on Miles's shoulder. "I was too busy keeping this knucklehead alive."

"Don't drag me into your lover's quarrel." Miles abstained, throwing his hands up. He was obviously still recovering from a bad hangover. "Hi, Maya."

"Hi." Maya gave him a genuine smile. By now, she'd heard it from both Skids and me that Miles was the only other person in the club worth his damn salt. "How did you two escape?"

"It was messy," Skids replied, the shift in tone almost palpable. He squeezed her tight and kissed her on the cheek.

I drew a deep breath and asked, "The coke?"

"All over the interstate. Wild Boys took out one of our wheels. The van flipped, and all the coke that didn't burn became snow. It was one hell of a sight," Miles recalled, wide-eyed, and stared off into the far distance, almost completely lost in the memory.

I figured as much, but I had to know for sure.

"The wounded guys?" My eyes flicked over at the bikes,

two of them I didn't recognize. They must have been Wild Boys' bikes. Those must've been how Skids and Miles made it here.

"Ratchet died in the crash, but we got everyone else out." Skids pulled out a pack of smokes and offered them up. I was all set, but Miles snatched one up. When he saw that Maya wasn't smoking, Skids slid his own cigarette back into the pack and put it away. Apparently, he wasn't planning to smoke around her if she wasn't a smoker.

So Skids really did care about this girl. My guess that they were related had been correct, so why not come out with it then?

"They were in too rough of shape to take with us once we got rid of the Wild Boys. Had to leave them. Must've been picked up by the cops by now." Skids shook his head like a humiliated soldier forced to abandon his comrades. After a momentous pause, he then asked, "Give me a minute with the girl?" He then grabbed my arm before I could get too far away, leaned in, and whispered, "Thanks for getting her outta there." He patted me on the shoulder and returned to Maya.

I joined Miles and the others to give the estranged family some room. Obviously, Skids and Maya probably had a lot to talk about. After everything she had gone through so far, she deserved some answers.

That initial feeling of dread I had when we arrived lingered no matter how I tried to rationalize it away. By now, it had burrowed into my bones and was screaming like a klaxon in my head. Something was very wrong, but I didn't know what it was. I scanned the area with my thumb behind me, casually hanging off my waistband right next to my gun. No one else appeared nervous or shady, and there was no sign that we were being watched or had been followed. Maya was with Skids, and they both seemed fine.

"We're good with the Legion," Tex bellowed, walking back toward us.

*We're good?* That was a death row pardon, and we didn't know any governors. A massive weight was lifted off everyone, and they visibly began to relax. Everyone except for Skids, and that made me concerned.

*What weren't Maya and Skids telling me?*

"How'd you swing that?" I kept as much skepticism from my tone as possible. What I really wanted to know was whose bed we were in now and how much did they want to fuck us?

"I told them about our other cargo." Tex cocked his head toward Maya.

"You fucking did what?" I growled.

"It was the only real play we had." Tex put his hands up in an appeal to the rest of the club. "Maya's club, the Hangers, is the Iron Legion's chief rival. It would look good that we could hurt the Hangers by escorting their president's daughter away from their club to turn evidence against them."

"That was icing when the job was done for additional leverage," Miles, nursing a headache, was quick to chime in. "A protection run, even the Hanger's daughter wouldn't have enough weight to offset the loss of a small fortune in drugs."

That had to be what Skids was worried about, but why? Hangers didn't have the reach to retaliate all the way out to Topeka. It had to be something else. There was a pit in my stomach as I waited for the other shoe to drop.

"Yeah, well, it's a damn good thing I made the call," Tex bitterly spat back. "It turns out the girl isn't who we thought she was. Turns out she's Maya *Merritt,* daughter of Bruce 'Slick' Merritt, the president of the St. Louis Steel Veins MC chapter."

*Oh shit! Dammit, Maya! Why didn't you tell me?*

The Steel Veins was one of the biggest MCs in the country, dwarfing both the Iron Legion and Hangers combined. They were One Percenters, some seriously bad news. I had heard that their old national president Deadeye was ousted by an even meaner bastard. Everyone had heard the rumors of the new SV national president, Remy Daniels. Los Lobos, the Steel Veins' main rival, claimed they killed him, but I guess it didn't take because Remy came back and shattered their whole club.

They said the guy was fucking unkillable.

If this Bruce Merritt guy was anything like Remy, Tex just made a deal with the fucking devil.

A lot of other things started falling into place like how she and Skids could actually be related. That's why Maya was so guarded about her family. I could only imagine how rough she and her sister had it growing up. No wonder she came to Skids. She thought only family would be willing to help her.

"What did you do, Tex?" I unsheathed my pistol but held

it down by my thigh. I didn't like where this was headed. He had to have made a deal with the Veins to get the Legion to back off. I was not about to let that fucking weasel touch Maya.

"I saved our lives is what I did. Put the gun away, Hendrix." Tex raised his empty hands slowly.

I glanced back at Skids and Maya. Maya paled. Skids planted himself in front of her, his military background brandished in his posture and fixed, defiant gaze as he remained steadfast. He wasn't about to let anything happen to his niece.

"What does that mean for us, Tex?" I thumbed off the safety.

"It means that if we just bring her back to Slick, her father, not only do we get protection against Iron Legion blowback, but we also get a full patch over. Apparently, he's real interested in gettin' his second daughter back."

"Second daughter?" Maya spoke up. "What did he say about Anna!"

"Slick'll kill her." Skids was too single-minded to keep from interrupting and talking over Maya. Skids didn't raise his voice; he simply made the statement to Tex as matter-of-fact as claiming that the sky was blue or that water was wet. "That's not going to happen."

I could tell that nothing Tex said would make Skids's resolve waver. As long as Skids was with Maya, she wasn't going anywhere near her father. That was admirable.

I imagined how having someone I cared about relying on me like that could make a man even stronger by giving him a sense of purpose. Something larger than just himself to fight for. I wondered if I could ever have something like that. A thought like that would have never trespassed my mind before having met Maya.

"He told me explicitly that nothing would happen to her. He just wants to talk to her. He's her father, for fuck's sake! Let's all calm down for a sec," Tex reassured. "We'll put it to a vote. All in favor of taking the deal? Aye!"

The vote wasn't even close; this time even Miles caved. Only Skids and I were nay votes. I didn't trust a slimy word out of Tex's mouth, and I sure as hell didn't want to be indebted to yet another club. Our record for buddying up with bigger clubs had been pretty shitty so far, and I wasn't eager to try it again.

Behind all that, if I was being honest, my hesitance with the vote was all about Maya. I couldn't deny that I'd grown to actually like the girl. I had to hope that her father didn't know why she was with us. Even among criminals, he had a cruel, ruthless reputation. Could he really kill his own daughter, though? It was hard for me to wrap my head around that. But it didn't matter now because we were outvoted. There was nothing I could do for her, so I had to put my gun away. Maya was going home after all... at least for now.

I headed over to Skids, thinking about convincing him to let Maya go, or else things would get messy quickly. I'd tell him that it was a long ride back to St. Louis and that between the two of us, I was sure we could figure out a way for her to get lost in transit. It was going to be a tough sell, but he'd listen to me, for the most part.

"There was one other condition that was a deal breaker otherwise...." Tex let the words hang. He shook his head, then looked at his guys for support. Without warning, he quickly drew his gun and shot Skids in the chest three times.

Maya screamed. My gun was out and on Tex by the third round with everyone else following suit. Tex immediately dropped his gun and put his hands up as if in surrender.

"Skids! Say something!" I cried out for him to answer, briskly jogging to him while keeping my gun trained on Tex.

"Skids's real last name was Merritt. He was Slick's brother. If we didn't kill Skids and deliver Maya, Slick told me that the Steel Veins would erase us. Our clubhouse, our businesses, our families... everything. It was him or us. I had no choice. I'm sorry."

"Shut your fucking mouth, Tex!" When I got to Skids, his plaid, button-up shirt bloomed in deep crimson. He lay there, eyes wide open, awake and alert but struggling to breathe. Seeing that the other guys had Tex, I dropped my gun and ripped open Skids's shirt.

One of the wounds was bubbling blood, meaning the bullets had pierced his lung, collapsing it. He was dying.

Maya, obviously rattled, shoved passed and immediately applied pressure on his wounds. "Robbie! Uncle Robbie, stay with me! We're going to get you to a hospital!" She then glanced up at me with watery, pleading eyes. "Hendrix, we *have* to get help!"

I grimaced because I knew a hospital wasn't going to happen. Skids couldn't ride, and with the van gone, we had no way of moving him. If we called for an ambulance, there was no way paramedics were showing up to an abandoned train station in response to a gunshot victim without a police escort. With the wake of destruction we left at the Wild Boys' clubhouse and a highway full of coke from the wrecked van, the police were the last thing the rest of the guys would go for. We needed an off-the-books doc.

I ripped long shreds off Skids's shirt and assisted Maya in attempting to stem the blood flow. "Hold on, brother." My crimsoned hands rifled through my phone, urgently scanning for any contacts that might be able to help. The first few numbers I tried were disconnected, the result of five years removed from a culture of people who used primarily disposable phones. Five years might as well have been an eternity. I was probably the only motherfucker that had the same goddamn number!

Skids's breathing went from labored wheezing to ragged gurgling as he was choking on his own blood. Frustrated that we were running out of time to help my friend, I crushed the phone in my hand then whipped the worthless marvel of technology into a steel beam, shattering it. "What the fuck are you all standing around for? Call someone!" I screamed at them.

"This has to happen, Junk. Let him go," Tex calmly explained, as if attempting to comfort a grieving child in a patronizing sort of way.

I was stunned to see the other members had lowered the guns they had been aiming at Tex. What the fuck happened to this club that something like this was allowed to stand?

Tex shot a member in front of everyone! My heart boiled over with betrayal and hate. I couldn't think straight. It all came crashing down—the pact, the brotherhood, everything I had started with this club for. We were supposed to be family! Now my closest friend was bleeding out. I didn't have anyone else outside of the club… or in. "No one gets to kill us! Not the Wild Boys, not the Veins, and not you, Tex." Venomous rage dripped from each of my syllables.

With what must have been the last surge of energy he had, Skids grabbed my arm and stared at me intently, occasionally flicking his gaze over to Maya. There was no fear in his eyes now, just the grim determination of a dying man trying to relay one final message. He could no longer speak, but his features said everything.

*Keep her safe.*

Then Skids pushed us away. Too many bullets in all the wrong places. Too much active hemorrhaging with nothing to stop it. No available ambulance to get here in time. He knew it was the end, and he decided to face it the only way he knew how—on his terms.

"No! Don't do this! We can help, we can!" Maya struggled with him, not allowing him to deny her help.

One eye closed, the other struggling to stay open, Skids gazed back at me. I hung my head and exhaled before I grabbed Maya and pulled her away. She was a fighter, I realized, as she thrashed against me, focusing all her own strength to get back to him, unable to surrender to the inevitable. But there was nothing she could do. Nothing either of us could do.

No one else moved or spoke aside from just lowering their heads as well. When Maya finally stopped protesting, she hugged me and softly sobbed into my shoulder. Skids lay there, motionless, his hacked, last gasps sporadic, each interval between becoming more and more prolonged until there was nothing except the sounds of birds chirping and the wind swaying clusters of branches above in the treetops.

My friend, Skids... my friend Robert was dead.

Maya slipped free of my loosening grip to hold Robbie's hand. I stood as a wave of numbness rolled over me, and my vision tunneled down into the immediate. I was a man inside my own head, watching my body move under its own autopilot. I strode directly to Tex at a slow gait that picked up gradually as I drew closer, my gun abandoned somewhere behind me. My fists trembled.

"Hendrix... I know it's hard, but you have to listen to me. It was the only way. You have got to think about the bigger picture here." Tex probably spoke more than that, but only one in a few sentences pierced my haze.

As Tex spoke, he hurriedly went for his gun. His guys grabbed at me, trying to stop what they knew would come next. So singular was my focus that I barely noticed them at first. People were saying things to me, but I didn't hear them. Everything around me was hazy. Perhaps there was grabbing and then blows landing on my person....

Each man who got in my way crumbled to the ground seconds later. My world was only that of Tex and me. And there was one too many men alive in it.

"Hendrix! Listen! Listen, dammit! I—" The blur of

motion ended with my hand around Tex's throat, choking his words off. A gunshot rang out somewhere close, but it didn't slow me down one bit.

Tex struggled, swinging his gun around to shoot me, but I slapped it away. His hands clawed at me, dragging long lines down my face, searching for my eyes. His thumb slid into my mouth as he desperately lashed at me, but I sank my teeth into and tore a large, fleshy chunk from his hand then spat it in his face.

The veins in my arms raised with the exertion. My hands now shook violently at their approaching muscle fatigue, but I could feel his pulse weaken beneath my grip. I leaned closer, letting the weight of my body add to my strength as I strangled him. The cartilage in his neck clicked rapidly and cracked, his larynx and trachea popped, then collapsed. I watched his eyes bulge, and his face turn purple from undrained blood. His eyes brimmed with tears, disbelief, and terror.

Coldly, I watched the flickering electricity fade from his pupils as they began to dilate and become fixed. I rode his writhing as everything eventually slowed to a stop.

It was done and over now. He'd killed my last friend, and I refused to live in any world where Tex was alive when Robbie wasn't.

Without warning, Tex's bowels loosened, and the front of his pants darkened with urine as it drained down his left leg. Then Tex's head lolled to his left as I squeezed even tighter, dropping to my knees and eventually following the corpse to the ground. Despite the completed kill, my hands needed to tear his fucking head clean off his neck.

"Let him go, Junk! It's done! It's all over!" Miles shouted frantically.

My narrowly focused, merciless glare widened from my singular, murderous task and finally flickered over to see that Miles had his gun drawn, keeping the other guys at bay, but it wasn't really necessary anymore. They had only tried to stop me out of their allegiance to Tex. Had they wanted to, they could have easily overpowered Miles and shot me where I stood, but on some level, they all had to know that it needed to happen.

Death for death.

It didn't matter the justification for it. When a member kills another member without a vote, there would always be retaliation, often immediately. Tex had lost sight of that. He thought that it didn't apply to him because he was The Club. Looking around at the rest of the members made me feel like Tex was right. If I hadn't done what I did, they might have let him walk because of his flawed reasoning. I would never let something like that slide. Robbie wouldn't have either. No, not even the president was above that law. It was the very foundation of the Coffin Eaters.

The old Coffin Eaters, that is....

I rose to my feet as the haze began to lift. My arms hummed and pulsed, vibrating with residual energy. Blood of Tex's maimed hand plastered my mouth, and I was covered in oily sweat. My eye twitched as I matched glances with each man in turn, their discomfort at my brutality written on their faces. Most had their guns out in case I turned on them next.

It was Maya's terrified gaze that woke me fully from my killing fog, bringing me back from the primal brink. I couldn't meet her eyes for long, so I looked away and exhaled what fighting frenzy was still remaining deep within. Goddammit, she had a knack at being there, seeing me at my worst.

I felt exposed and rightfully so, I guess. I'd just killed a man. It wasn't the actual killing that bothered me. Tex completely deserved it. What frightened me was how easy and quickly I had lost control and plunged into the physical, hands-on brutality of the much-needed execution without any warning from my personal, otherwise reasonable, conscience. I could've just shot him and been done with it, but every step toward him made my heart race and sank me deeper into the depths of unyielding rage.

"Everyone, mount up!" Miles quickly stepped up and took control, barking out orders. "We gotta go! Lump, take Maya!"

What did he say? Take Maya? *Where?*

"What the fuck?" I shouted at him. I wasn't just going to let someone else take Maya after what happened to Robbie.

"I didn't know what Tex was going to do. Skids... I'm going to miss him." Miles picked up my gun off the ground near Robbie's dead body. "Tex was a worthless piece of shit, but we're going to finish that deal with the Veins."

"Miles, you can't, man. You know Slick's rep. You do know what he'll do no matter what he might've promised. Maya is Robbie's niece. He's not even cold, and you're talking about delivering her to a monster like Slick?"

"Jesus, brother, look at yourself. You just strangled a man to death with your own bare hands." Miles exhaled deliberately then shook his head. "We're all fucking monsters."

I shot a desperate glance over at Maya. Her inability to meet my gaze stung me worse than any gunshot. So I turned my attention back to Miles. "She's not."

"We don't have a choice!" It was a long time since I'd seen Miles get this riled up. "The Steel Veins weren't bluffing. It's either her or us. It's what's best for the club. I'm sorry, but it's gotta be done." His tone was loaded with deep resignation. Frowning, he aimed his gun and shot the front tire of my bike.

"Don't do this, Miles!" Out of all of us, I couldn't believe Miles would be the one to finish Tex's dirty work. I guess it was a long, five years for everyone.

Miles shook his head again. "By the time you get it towed back to the clubhouse, all this will be over. I'll get you everything that's owed to you. As acting president, I'll make sure you're voted out in good standing with both the Coffin Eaters and the Steel Veins. You get your full freedom, brother. Everything you wanted." He slid out and pocketed the clip, then racked the slide, popping the last chambered round from the gun, completely emptying it. Finally, pocketing my gun's clip, he tossed the harmless weapon back to me. "All you gotta do now is nothing."

"Hendrix! Hendrix, please don't let them do this—Get your fucking hands off me! Hendrix! *Hendrix!*" Maya struggled and pleaded, but I just stood there, paralyzed, and watched them drag her away from me. If I made a move toward them, Miles would've shot one of my legs, if one of the other guys didn't outright kill me.

All I could do was watch.

The bikes started up, and they all sped off as Maya's screams of my name were quickly drowned by the engines and distance. Soon, they were gone from sight.

And just like that, Maya was out of my life.

I sank into the dirt between the bodies of my best friend and worst enemy where all I could do was sit there and think.

In the end, which one of them had I become? Did I get what I wanted? At what cost?

Complete freedom, protection by a much larger club, and enough money to start again in any life that I chose. It was everything I had wanted since getting out of prison, and now it was laid at my feet. I had even got my revenge against the man who killed my friend. What else was left for me to want? Beneath the tremendous amount of grief for my friend, I should have felt at least a little bit of closure and relief at how it was all over now. I could go my own way and never look over my shoulder again. My new life started right now.

And all I had to do was nothing.

Beneath the grief was a profound sense of loss. I felt like I was in prison again, trying to imagine what the stars looked like. Trying to feel connected to something, but instead just floating alone within space. Though I never thought it possible, there was now a pit inside of me that I knew couldn't be filled by pussy, money, or freedom.

The rustling trees swayed indifferently. For hours, I swore I could still hear Maya's pleading voice calling my name on the wind. I saw her face whenever I closed my eyes. I could lie to myself all I wanted, but if the Steel Veins were willing to risk us killing each other by ordering Robbie shot, then there was no way they would allow Maya to live.

I crawled over to Robbie. "She wanted to leave and go home, but I talked her into staying the course. I didn't know it was the Veins she was running from, but, shit, I can't pawn it off on that. This is on me. I'm sorry, brother." It was a worthless apology. The damage was already done.

I studied him once again. Robbie's top half was ringed in a darker brown, dirt drinking up his spilt blood. A little beyond him, I saw a glint of light off something metallic… his ever-present pocket watch. It must have slipped out when he was shot. Picking it up, I wiped it off and opened it.

The clock had stopped and the knob that set the time was broken off, the damage having been done for what appeared to be far more distant than Robbie's death. Why would he have kept a pocket watch that didn't work? Robbie was a problem solver, the kind of guy that filled his downtime with straightening things out and fixing them. There was no way he'd be carrying around something without a function, especially a watch.

Then I saw the picture under the cover on the opposite face—the faded visages of a middle-aged woman holding a baby in her arms. The resemblance of the woman was uncanny.

It had to be Maya's mother, but the baby in the picture wasn't Maya, though. So this must be her sister, Anna.

The one physical possession that Robbie valued was a broken watch with a picture of his estranged brother's family in it? Nothing about that added up. The one possibility I could think of didn't make any sense at all. I closed the watch and pocketed it.

"All I have to do is nothing, man. You heard Miles. When I get back to the club, I'll get everything I wanted." The words rang out hollow. Cowardly. In complete denial.

Could I really let my friend die for nothing?

Robbie's watch weighed heavily in my pocket. Like my cut and colors, it wasn't the leather or metal parts that were the burden. It was the weight of the responsibility that came with it. Symbols and ideals could make a man or crush him.

Tex pulled the trigger, but Slick pulled the strings. I didn't kill the man responsible for my friend's murder. I just destroyed one of that man's weapons. I had to go after Maya. It was easier for me to think that the decision was to honor Robbie and to avenge his death.

I sorted through Tex's pockets and found his cell phone. I didn't know where Miles was taking Maya, but browsing through the recent calls, I could sure as hell could find out.

"Yeah, you're right, Robbie." I was the only person in the world who could help her now. "Besides, I was never very good at doing *nothing*."

# Chapter 8
## MAYA

My resolve wavered as we rode into the gated compound of closed, nondescript warehouses of Batesville Casket Company. It was dusk, and it'd been several hours since Robbie was murdered. It made my heart ache seeing him gunned down so horribly. I didn't know my uncle all that well, but he seemed like a decent man making the best out of some bad situations. I wish I could've had the chance to get to know him better. I still had so many questions that I'd never have answered.

The hard reality sank into my bones. How was I going to get into that safe-deposit box now? I'd spent ten long years endlessly datamining to prove that she wasn't living on some Polynesian isle, sipping tiki cocktails by an infinity pool but never had enough for her to be declared legally dead. Mom left without her phone, passport, or even her purse. It was insultingly obvious for anyone who knew her personally, but the courts didn't care about that. Because of the right of marriage, only my father—*her murderer*—could have her declared legally dead, but he'd never allow that kind of closure. It was his way of diverting attention away from the possibility of foul play being the reason for her disappearance—it was all her fault, not his—while maintaining the air of a heartbroken husband to the authorities and the public at large.

*Fucking bastard.*

As infuriating as it was, I had become numb to Slick's brand of social manipulation. Growing up, I had heard him say countless times that she was a selfish, heartless bitch and had run away, leaving behind two needy children who sorely needed a nurturing mother. The obvious lie used to churn my stomach, but now the memory of his claims only widened the chasm of hate I already had for him in the pit of my soul.

So going through Mom to get into the box wouldn't work.

As for Uncle Robbie, the shortest it would take was a month for a death certificate to become available, but only his heir could get that. Unless I could dig up his last will and testament—*something he probably didn't even have*—saying something else, right now that heir would be Slick again. Long before I could even get any kind of process started, the bank would've closed and none of it would matter.

I only had one option now, and to say it was a long shot was being extremely generous. I'd have to basically throw myself upon the mercy of the bank officers, begging on behalf of my missing mother to recover her property. If they let me use their computer or even one of their phones, I could show them the archives of the *St. Louis Post-Dispatch* for the specific articles documenting her disappearance. Hell, I'd even show them my own research by logging into my personal subscription account.

But all they'd have to do is say no, and I'd be fucked.

All that, of course, assumed I made it out of wherever I was headed to alive, which I wasn't too optimistic about. It would take a miracle, and I was running low on those lately.

Inevitably, Hendrix crept into my mind, and the ache in my heart doubled. I was really beginning to like him, to even *trust* him. Considering they were holding his freedom over his head, I understood why he had to let me go.

Understanding didn't make it hurt any less.

I still felt disappointed and abandoned. I couldn't help it. But then again, what was I to Hendrix? Just a cock tease with a distant connection to his now-dead friend? What allegiances did he owe me? I knew he wouldn't be coming for me, not with his ultimate freedom from the MC life hanging in the balance. I'd never see Hendrix again. I wasn't worth that much to him.

But my brain wasn't allowing me to let it all go. He was handsome, charming, and funny, but he was still an outlaw biker in the vicious MC world. I couldn't hate him for his decision. I was madder that I allowed myself to, I dunno... dream? But in the end, I let myself be hurt by yet another biker.

Anger, heartache, sadness... all of it wilted at the same rate in which one particular warehouse's large, corrugated metal doors opened. Rows of hanging fluorescent fixtures snapped on in consecutive sections with a flash then settled, bathing the assembly line of coffins in a drab, bluish-white light. The shadows lingered sickly and jumped while the bulbs overhead flickered as they heated up to full brightness.

The warehouse was gigantic but was also full to an alarming degree. The near building-length conveyor belt was burgeoned with finished, stretch-wrapped caskets that waited patiently for trucks to pick them up. Seven-foot-long coffins stood on end atop flat, wheeled dollies, ranked and filed like platoons of soldiers to either side of us as we walked toward a silhouette of a man who was exiting a free-standing, brown-doored office in the middle of the assembling plant. He was joined by two other shady-looking bikers as well.

Dread knotted up my insides as a wave of nausea rolled over me. My God... I was going to be killed in a building that actually made coffins. "Please, Miles! Please don't do this!"

"Shut up!" Lump shoved me forward when I slowed to a stop.

"Easy," Miles mildly scolded him then stepped in front before approaching the man who opened the doors for us. There was something off about Miles, the way he succumbed immediately to the Wild Boys' ploy almost like he knew something was going to happen but didn't care to stop it. There was also a regretful look in his eyes when he assumed control of the club after Tex was killed. When he ordered me to be taken, I could tell it wasn't because he wanted to but because he felt that he had to. Miles had the demeanor of a man going through the motions, a man with little left to lose, if anything at all. Robbie had told me that Miles had been ousted from the president's position by Tex after some deal went bad, and that ever since then, he'd been in the club mostly out of habit.

"Take her purse and get her in the office. I'll let Slick know she's here," the tall biker who met Miles ordered. "I'll have my guys watch her."

A chill ran up my spine at the mention of my father. There was something else as well. I couldn't immediately place it, but the man's voice sounded disturbingly familiar. It was on the tip of my brain like a distant childhood memory. But he turned away for more privacy during his phone call before I could get a better look at his face. I immediately recognized the Steel Veins cut and colors. His leather vest said "Rock Springs, WY." I assumed that's where we were, not that I'd ever heard of the town before.

Something about this towering biker made my skin twitch and my stomach turn.

Despite my reluctance, one of the Veins ripped my purse away before I could sneak my phone out. The fat biker roughly spun me around and frisked me so thoroughly, it would have made a TSA agent blush. His hand clamped over my denim-covered pussy and demanded, "What else you got on you, bitch?"

"I'll take her," Miles impatiently interjected, stepping between us then, shoving the man backward. He placed a heavy hand on my shoulder and guided me toward the well-lit office. "C'mon, Maya."

"Please, Miles! I have money. Just let me go!" I pleaded once again. I didn't have nearly enough money to get out of this mess, but the thought of what my father or his goons had in store for me was terrifying enough to promise just about anything.

"It's not about money, not anymore." He opened the door for me.

It was a small, one-desk room with a large window that overlooked the assembly line, an office best suited for a shift foreman.

"Then why do this? You aren't a bad man, Miles. My Uncle Robbie told me you were one of the few good guys left, one of the very few he trusted."

"I didn't want any of this. If Junk hadn't killed Tex for what he did, then I would've. Skids...." He sighed. "Robbie was my friend. He was a good man, and it hurts like hell that he's gone."

"How can you claim that? You're delivering his niece to the man who ordered him killed!"

"This is bigger than us now, Maya. The Steel Veins have threatened our families, and they have the reach and influence to make good on that promise. I had no choice. Slick told me that you wouldn't be hurt. He promised me."

"If a snake could talk, it'd say the same thing to the mouse," I mused sardonically.

"I'm sorry." His shoulders slumped as if in defeat, and he retreated from me, quietly closing the door behind him.

I couldn't be mad at Miles. He wasn't evil. He was just scared and at the end of his rope. When he weighed my life against those of his friends and family... who the hell was I in the great scheme of things? Just another unfortunate girl in a rough world.

I thought about Hendrix again and some of my regrets. Part of me was upset that he talked me into staying, but even now, I realized that he was right. I had to stay, or I wouldn't be able to live with myself otherwise. I just wished I had had a little more time with him because I wanted to see what kind of man he really was. Now I wished I could've gotten over myself and let what was going to happen on that rooftop last night actually happen. My heart fluttered slightly at the thought of that, of him shirtless and nibbling at my thighs....

*No!* I couldn't let myself be distracted, not now. I searched around the office and quietly opened the desk's drawers. Unfortunately, they were empty of anything I could use, and there was no landline. The Veins weren't stupid. They put me in here for a reason. Taking hostages, extortion, blackmail, murder... these were the types of things the Veins excelled at.

*"Argh!"* I ran my hands over my face. *Think, dammit!* No one was coming for me. If I had any hope of surviving, then I had to figure something out myself. I slammed my palms on the desk in frustration and heard the light rattle of a keyboard drawer with a loose, metal slide. I frantically twisted and pried a screw out of the side of one track, but the eagerness of my actions alerted the keen hearing of the Steel Veins who was posted outside. He loudly rapped the glass with his knuckles, which jostled me backward into the

office chair. He didn't know what I was doing, but whatever it was, he wanted me to stop.

I demurely clasped my hands on my lap and sat obediently until he turned his back on me again.

Now my progress was quiet and subtle yet brutally slow. The sharp points of the crosshead screws tore into the free edges of my fingernails to the point that I had to bite the urge to cry out when one of my nails split to the quick on a metal burr. I wiped my hand on my legs every few minutes, but my bloodied fingers kept slipping off the screw heads.

One screw dropped onto the carpeting, which meant that there was only one left, and it was the loose one. I was so close.... It was already halfway out. If I could just get one of the tracks free.

The office door opened stealthily. "Maya Merritt!" the same oily voice from earlier cooed with a touch of perversion. Startled, I shot up and was horror-struck at the biker casually slouching against the doorsill. "You remember me, little girl? You're not so little anymore now."

*"No...!"* I didn't think any words actually escaped my lips, but if they did, they were barely audible. Blood drained from my face, a cold sweat beaded my brow, and my body went as rigid as petrified wood. I was staring at a ghost.... or maybe *my* own personal demon.

"Oh, don't tell me you've forgotten me after we had been so close? I am cut to the heart!" The lips of the St. Louis Steel Veins biker I knew as Ricky-Tick parted into a yellowed shark's grin. His jaundice-eyed gaze was one of famished malice as he regarded me like I was floating chum in bloodied water. His awkwardly long face and intense stare ripped repressed, ages-old scars wide open from the deep recesses of my brain.

I staggered against the back wall like I was hit by a truck. I found myself unconsciously putting as much distance between us as possible, but the entirety of the planet wouldn't have been enough. This man shaped my life almost as much as my own father, but I had been told that he was dead years ago. I was assured that he was very, *very* dead!

"Take off, Boot. Let me know when Slick gets here. I'm going keep his daughter company." He waved off the biker who had been guarding me then locked the door behind him. "Don't want our girl getting lonely, you know."

"It's not possible...." I grabbed the nearest thing within reach—the cheap office chair—and rolled it between us.

"No?" He cocked his head curiously, extending his neck to peer down at me. He stood gauntly at well over six feet, if not more, and the stretching motion made his already too long face appear even more unnerving. His arms and legs were stick-thin, making them look exaggeratedly long and gangly. Before me was a skeleton of a man with a shock of gnarled black hair and bulging, delirious eyes. "What did your dad say he did with me, baby girl?"

I swallowed repeatedly, but the Sahara in my throat refused to ease. "Dead" was the only word I could croak.

"Ow! That's a bit harsh! I was... I *am* his best soldier. No, he couldn't lose me. I caught an ass whoopin' and a relocation, but nothing that dramatic and permanent,"

Ricky-Tick mocked me.

He circled the desk and ripped the chair away from me. The ancient, metal desktop rattled with a series of menacing raps as he casually tapped it with one of his rings while slowly stalking after me. I knew he was toying with me, trying to intimidate me, but I was beginning to think it was working. He only halted to stay out of reach, perhaps sensing the beginnings of a fight-or-flight reaction from which things might not end well for both sides.

"Y'know, part of that night was your fault too. The way you were dressed...." He gazed down and absently drew invisible designs with his fingertip onto the top of the desk. I had no words to protest with, not that it mattered as nothing I had said deterred him that night either.

He lunged and caught my shoulders before dragging me, screaming, over to the desk. I kicked and flailed, but he was deceptively strong despite the myth I was told about tall guys and their awkwardly higher center of gravity that interfered with their leverage. Before I knew it, he had pinned my back onto the desktop and straddled me. I shouted, at least I thought I did, but it was like one of those dreams where you scream and scream but nothing comes out.

"When Slick told me to expect you, I won't lie, I was nervous. Excited but also a little worried." With a free hand, he brushed away the hair plastered to his sweaty brow. "Ten years was a lifetime ago, and I like my lil' darlings to be a little more... inexperienced. I was worried that you might have outgrown me."

He leaned in, the tip of his perspiration-moist nose grazed

my cheek. He breathed me in and shuddered in unrepressed ecstasy. "But here you are, and you haven't aged a day. You are still my good, little girl...."

Then, with the flat of his tongue, he licked the side of my face from jaw to hairline. I gagged, the oppressively rank smell of his saliva on my skin bringing water to my eyes. "You even taste the same. Sweet and delicious. Oh, I have missed you, my little, metal angel."

He sat on my stomach and planted both his knees over my arms, neatly preventing me from clobbering him. His bony hands now free, he rubbed his cock through his pants, his bulge obviously hardening. He let out a repressed moan that sounded like it hurt him as much as excited him then switched to undoing the button on my jeans.

I couldn't relive this again. I just couldn't. I closed my eyes and began to cry. I wished I was dead. Between waves of panic, I thought I imagined the office door reverberating from an aggressive fist pounding, the kind that guaranteed a cop on the opposite side.

*Was Hendrix here to save me?*

The thought was so absurd that something like a sardonic snigger rippled up from the depths of my sorrow. Paralyzed by my terror, I couldn't scream or call for help, but I could still laugh insanely. The body did weird things when under tremendous stress.

There was that pounding again. Then the door exploded inward from a heavy kick.

"What the fuck do you think you're doing?" Ricky-Tick erupted in outrage then was punched right off me.

It wasn't Hendrix. Instead, it was Miles, his face flushed red with anger.

*"Don't you fucking touch her!"* The C.E president's flaming eyes glanced over at me before kicking Ricky-Tick in the abdomen. The gaunt man quickly rolled over then stunned us both by deftly leaping to his feet, only to be cut short when Miles's gun clicked and was shoved into thin flesh that padded his forehead.

"This was sanctioned!" the crazed Steel Vein barked defiantly. "You'd better stop before you do something unforgivable by our MC!"

"Shut your fuckin' mouth, scumbag!" Miles refused to be intimidated by this threat.

"Wait!" Ricky-Tick put one hand up and fished for his phone with the other. He browsed through his text messages then handed the phone to Miles. "Check the number! It's Slick's personal cell. This has been sanctioned!"

The C.E. president stubbornly snatched the phone away from him and read the crystalline screen. I could see in his growing disgust that Ricky-Tick had been right. My father had arranged this *tête-à-tête* and knew exactly what the outcome would be. Miles tossed the phone and slowly lowered his gun. "His very own daughter.... You both make me sick."

"Her father loves her and wants her to know *my* love. This is my reward for following his orders and for being a good soldier."

"He promised me that she wouldn't be hurt. That was the only reason I agreed to this," Miles growled hatefully at the man, and for a moment, I dared to hope.

"Maya betrayed him!" Ricky-Tick retorted, appearing wounded by Miles's words. "She needs to be taught a valuable lesson, one of blood and tears."

Miles still refused to budge.

*Please, Miles, don't leave me with him!*

"Leave us. He'll be here soon enough, and if that lesson isn't delivered by then... well, he said he'll have to teach her another, harder one." Ricky-Tick glared at him, a dark promise glinting in his eyes. "He'll have to teach the Coffin Eaters a similar lesson as well."

Miles started to crack, and with it went what little hope I had left. "Fine," Miles muttered as he put away his gun.

"Good," Ricky-Tick agreed as he reached for his phone on the floor.

Miles's eyes flashed with vengeful malice, and he stomped Ricky-Tick's hand against the cover glass of his cell phone. The tall man yelped like a struck dog, and I heard at least two finger bones gruesomely snap. It wasn't nearly enough.

"Whoops!" Miles ground the heel of his boot into the man's digits, producing another loud crack followed by Ricky-Tick's whimpering, muffled scream. "Must've slipped. Hope you're a lefty."

Miles's bitterness melted into anguish when he beheld me. I could see that he so desperately wanted to help. By allowing this to happen, Miles was pissing on the memory of his friend, Robbie, but the Steel Vein's threat still won out in his mind. As plain as it was that Miles hated doing it, he blinked, his jaw set tightly, and finally abandoned me to my fate.

Ricky-Tick wouldn't be denied. That whimsical cruelty in his eyes and features had been replaced with a grim, sexual determination. I scuttled out of the corner and tried to make a break for it, but he grabbed me. Twisting me around, he headbutted me, knocking me onto my ass.

"Nuh-uh-uh! The fun's just startin'!" he squealed between labored, painful grunts because of his shattered hand.

Dazed from the headbutt, I clumsily crab-walked backward in a general direction away from the psycho biker. I didn't think my nose was broken, but I could feel my warm blood coating my lips.

"Red looks good on you." The sick fuck smiled, wiggling his broken fingers at himself. I didn't know if he was high on PCP, but the pain didn't slow him at all. One moment later, he was sprawled on top of me, yanking my pants down and jerking me toward him.

When he got my jeans and panties down to my ankles, I spiked both knees up and cracked him right beneath the chin. His head snapped back, and his grip loosened enough for me to tear my legs away from him. I grabbed the corner of the desk and the keyboard tray to pull myself to my feet, but I only got about halfway up before Ricky-Tick recovered and tackled me back down. I snagged the keyboard tray with me, the particle board breaking into large chunks, as I hit the filthy carpeting with a dull thud.

"I like this new fire in you, Maya. It's hotter when I have

to work for it." He snorted with carnal excitement, now tightly straddled on top of my thighs.

I squirmed and flailed under the much heavier man until he cocked me right on the chin. My head snapped to the side, and I was immediately knocked out. I woke up a moment later and saw that he had his dark, bent cock out of his pants.

"You were always mine," he hissed into my ear while stroking his erect penis. He then plunged his hand through my pubic hair and fingered around for my pussy. "There's nowhere to run to now."

I groped for whatever I could through the daze of his punch until my fingers touched something long and metallic. The fleeting hope spiked my adrenalin enough to cut through the haze and act upon it. I watched his eyes bulge when I slashed him across the neck with the edge of the twisted, metal drawer track. His erect cock bobbed uselessly as he jerked backward away from me.

I spit out a fleshy wad of clotted blood from his punch, kicked one pant leg completely off to give myself some mobility, and threw myself on top of him in a cowgirl position.

"Who said I was running, you sick, sadistic motherfucker?" As dizzy and disoriented as I was, my words and my nerve returned to me in full force.

This man was the embodiment of all my sexual fears. He was why all the boys I'd ever dated had been weak and submissive. He was what kept me from enjoying a glorious night with Hendrix, a man I'd grown to really like. I couldn't explain the feeling that blossomed inside of me.

It was beyond hate. It was cold, exacting vengeance. Every atom in my body needed to watch this monster suffer for what he'd stolen from me.

The spurting blood from his neck wound spattered across my hand and arm as I rode him like a mechanical bull as he squirmed beneath me this time. I took the metal track in both my hands then repeatedly stabbed him in the crotch and groin, which probably ruptured one of his testicles. Blood pooled beneath him, and I knew right away I'd hit a major artery somewhere.

I was startled that I'd gone that far. It was gross and horrible, but this man.... If ever a man deserved a slow, painful death, it was this vile piece of shit. The urge to continue stabbing him was insistent, but I refrained. His groin was so shredded that nothing would be able to save him.

I stared down at him and reveled in his torment. He stared back at me, his eyes brimming with agonized disbelief as I watched Ricky-Tick bleed out, squirming through his death throes, and allowed all my fear and anguish to die with him.

I stood up and slid my pants back on.

The man with the shotgun in the Wild Boys parking lot came to mind—more specifically, how I felt not being able to kill that man who was trying to kill me. Having watched Ricky-Tick die, I didn't feel upset or scared anymore, but now I was more conflicted.

I'd spent my entire childhood surrounded by one side of the law and my adulthood surrounded by the other. I had been unable to kill, and I had now killed. Part of me felt horrible for having to do what I did, but another part of me realized that it was the only way... and that I could do it again if I needed to.

What kind of person was I now?

*The kind of person that survives,* a spidery voice from a dark corner in my head whispered—a voice I maybe should have listened to earlier… sooner.

Distant gunshots reinforced my resolve. I ducked low, expecting someone to rush in and see what I had done. When no one came, I scrambled for Ricky-Tick and searched for his gun. Where the hell was it? *How could he not have one?* I thought that was standard issue for all outlaw bikers like a hammer was for a carpenter. Dammit! He probably didn't want to risk me stealing it and using it against him.

That anger at who he was remained just below the surface but then boiled over with frustrated suddenness. I kicked Ricky-Tick's corpse again and again as I struggled to get my breathing under control. I was *so* angry! I finally understood crimes of passion and how they could force people beyond what they thought they were capable of. "Fuck you! Fuck you, you fucking bastard! How did that work out for you... you, miserable, asshole *prick!*"

More gunfire. What the hell was going on out there? I decided that whatever it was, I needed to use the distraction to get the hell out of here. I sneaked out onto the assembly line floor, carefully observing a few of the overhead lights that were now shattered and hung awkwardly by one chain, all swinging limply.

Rapid footfalls around a nearby corner forced me to

throw myself behind a raised wall of curved casket panels. I lay down and held my breath. Beneath the barrier, I saw two sets of leather boots run passed me, possibly toward the doors we came in.

I realized that this was the first time since meeting the Coffin Eaters that I was fully alone. No Hendrix to save me. No Robbie to look after me. I was completely on my own. The weight of that burden finally sank into my addled brain.

Rock Springs, Wyoming? Where the fuck was that? The last fifteen minutes of the ride here was virtually barren. I'd need to find a ride to a police station. Jesus, what did I even tell the police? Did I reveal everything? No, I couldn't go there. What if they were on the Steel Veins payroll?

Where then?

I could feel the sick slime of a full-blown panic attack tantalize my psyche.

"Focus!" I angrily whispered to myself. "One step at a time! *Get. Out. First.* Find a back door and worry about all that other stuff later." I sharply exhaled and edged my way along the perimeter of the building, darting passed large, organized piles of materials that were palletized on near ceiling-high shelving units.

"How many shooters?" Pause. "Well, where the fuck is he!" A biker's voice came booming up one of the aisles of standing pine coffins near me, but there was no way I knew which one exactly, so I cut over a few rows, hoping to magically turn invisible via wishful thinking. "No. No! Slick'll be here any minute! I'm going to check Ricky-Tick." Pause. "Slick doesn't care if she's alive *or* dead as long as she's in there when he comes back."

The man on the phone passed by so closely and my heart was beating so loudly that I thought he'd actually be able to hear it and spot me. *Alive or dead?* My whole body trembled. I only barely stifled both my hyperventilation and an audible sigh when he hadn't noticed me.

I forced myself to unfreeze and find a safer means of escape when there was renewed shouting from the biker with the phone, and I knew he had found Ricky-Tick's corpse. I backed away as quickly and quietly as possible, scanning for any illuminated exit signs. I spied motion at the back door, so I disregarded that option, but there had to be a side door or emergency exit around here somewhere. *Where the hell were the building inspectors when this place was built, dammit!*

"Hey!" a man screamed as he caught sight of me scurrying between rows of coffins. I thought I recognized his voice belonging to Lump, one of my father's men. "She's over here!"

*"Oh God, oh God, oh God...,"* I mumbled, dashing blindly in the opposite direction. I cut a diagonal path through the standing pine boxes to get out of eyesight of the man. Too stressed to see where I was heading, I collided face-first into one of the standing coffins, which might as well have been a wall on wheels.

My head swam, but I wasn't feeling any pain, at least not yet. Via the massive concussion, my vision became a series of still images. I watched the wooden casket I hit rock precariously and threaten to crush me. Then, while surprisingly still conscious, my brain cut out all motor control from my waist down, so my legs became a pool of noodles.

Fortunately the casket toppled away from me, instigating a chain reaction as one hit another, toppling at least three or four down the row like gigantic, pine-smelling dominoes. The noise was apocalyptic. My stunned brain registered shouting and more shooting, but the only thing that distinctly pierced my haze was the shattering of wood as the death boxes tumbled.

Semiautomatic rifles spilt out of the destroyed coffins like deadly candy from corpse-sized piñatas. So that's why we were here. This business was owned by the Steel Veins, and it was just a front for moving massive amounts of weapons under the guise of newly constructed caskets.

Suddenly, I felt my body being dragged to my feet by multiple hands, and my escape attempt was now officially over. Thus began the inevitable end.

With two punches from one of the Steel Veins who caught me, I dropped to the ground. My eyes swam with so many tears that I could hardly make out my surroundings, and I could move even less. As my senses slowly returned, so came the pain… so much more pain than I had ever felt at one time in my entire life. The iron taste of blood flooded into my mouth, and for a moment, I thought I was drowning in it. I wiped my mouth with the back of my hand and immediately felt the sharp, stabbing throb in my nose as I brushed against it. It was undeniable.

*He broke my fucking nose!*

Disjointed voices hovering over me finally sank into my foggy brain. I couldn't make out everything, but I got the gist of it. The two men were discussing whether to kill me or to wait for my father.

"...happens now! There's a goddamn shooter in here. Slick said if any complications..."

I recognized the Steel Vein who had initially groped me when I first came in here, but this time he was pointing a gun down at me. Damn, it was so hard to think right then. I just knew that I had to go, had to get away, had to do something because I absolutely refused to just die. I squirmed, attempting to feebly crawl away, but I didn't make it far before a kick to the ribs sent me reeling and rolling. Pain spiderwebbed throughout my midsection, and I collapsed onto my back, gasping for air.

"...a shame. At least Ricky got a taste, eh?" the fat Steel Vein joked as he jabbed the cold, metal muzzle against my head.

I couldn't watch this happen, so I closed my eyes and thought about Anna... and Hendrix....

*Blam!*

I was sprayed with hot wetness. *Wha... huh? I wasn't dead!* My eyes shot open. Something was wrong with the handsy, fat Steel Veins biker. How could his mouth be gaping at me stupidly when the front of his face had been blown out? Suddenly realizing I was staring back at a very dead man, I screamed as I tried to shift out of the way, but I wasn't quick enough to avoid the corpse as it fell right on top of me, his head smashing against the concrete floor to my left. Gray and red lumps oozed out of his shattered, through-and-through hole like a thick Play-Doh soup.

I couldn't stop screaming at the horror pinning me down at an awkward angle with my arms tight against my sides. Even the fright and adrenaline weren't enough to get the fat bastard off me.

"Drop it, Lump. I've just killed three men, and I'd rather not end the night putting down one of my own." *Was that Hendrix?* I must've been delirious from a concussion, but I heard a pistol hit the floor. "Now get that fat fuck off her!"

The familiar rumble of motorcycles faintly grew in the distance.

"You fucked up, bro. That's the rest of the Steel Veins. They're almost here. There's gonna be hell to pay for this!"

I scuttled out from under the lifted heap, dragged myself to my knees, then finally to my feet, nearly fainting for standing up so quickly as the blood rushed from my head downward. God, did I have the worst migraine in the history of migraines.

"Yeah. That's why I'm here." My unreliable ears were still ringing so loudly that I barely heard all the words. I dared not dream at whose voice that might be because all I saw was this fuzzy form slowly coming into focus. "Maya, are you all right?

"Hendrix...?" I smiled and laughed and gasped his name in disbelief all at the same time. I was a ball of exhausted, jumbled-up nerves, but I was also indescribably relieved. I hugged him as tightly as I could, never wanting to let him go. I couldn't believe it was really him. I couldn't believe he actually came back for me.

"Ah, that's broken." Hendrix examined my nose, then my eyes then continued to scan the rest of me, making sure I was in one piece. "I leave you alone for a few hours, and all this happens...." He shook his head yet smiled.

"How? How did you...?" I was beyond elated but was flooded with too many questions.

"Plenty of time for that later. I think we've outworn out our welcome." He was right about that. The motor noise was growing louder. We had to leave before the Veins got here.

"Miles!" exclaimed Lump. "This was all Hendrix, man. Shoot the goddamn motherfucker!"

Hendrix wrenched me with him as he whirled to face the C.E. president who was behind us and already had his gun out, easily beating Hendrix and forcing him to lower his own firearm.

I detached myself and slid out from behind Hendrix. He raised an arm to stop me, but I pushed it away. I wanted to expose myself to Miles, let him see that I wasn't afraid of him. That I had faith in him.

I *had* seen it—that look of defeated resignation in Miles's eyes and the way he kept trying to help me while I had been here. Miles wasn't a bad man; he was just incredibly conflicted. He was doing what he thought was right to protect his family, but I was doing the same. Why the hell was I even here in the first place?

"You don't have to do this," I pleaded with the lone gunman. "Come with us instead. Robbie loved you like a brother."

"You're not seriously listening to this bitch, are you?" Lump protested hotly.

"Don't bother, Maya." Hendrix ignored Lump. "This isn't the same Miles I started the club with. I don't know who the fuck we're even talking to."

"When you were on the inside, Stacy left me," Miles unexpectedly revealed, the only indicator of his personal misery being a slight, defeated slump of his shoulders. "It was while I was on a ride to Omaha with the club. All she took was the kids. She never came after me for money or nothing. She just needed to get our kids away from the lifestyle, away from *me*." Miles may have been addressing Hendrix, but his reflective tone made it apparent that this was some sort of confession to a higher power. "There was always so much fucking damage control I had to do that I lost sight of the things that really mattered. It took me a long time to wrap my head around her leaving me, but she was right. I was a shitty father and an even shittier husband. And now I'm a shitty brother too." Miles lowered his head and exhaled remorsefully.

"Remember the bigger picture, bro! A full patch over, protection, influence, everything we wanted is about to happen! The Veins are here, man!" Lump couldn't contain his exasperation. "Think about the club! This is the only way the Coffin Eaters survive!"

"I'm tired of thinking about the bigger picture!" Miles's previously demoralized eyes raked Lump's visage, the sorrow in his gaze had been rapidly replaced with tempered steel. "The Coffin Eaters are *dead*." With that, Miles shot the startled man twice in the chest, and Lump died instantly.

The demoralized man lowered his gun and tossed his bike's keys to Hendrix. "Police'll be looking for that pickup truck you pulled up in."

"Ah, fuck." Hendrix neatly caught the keys and tried to appeal to his friend. "No, Miles. Not like this, man!"

"What?" My bell was still a little rung from plowing my nose into that coffin that I was a little hazy on what was actually going on here. Was Miles planning on staying behind? With me gone and nothing to offer the Steel Veins, wouldn't that be akin to suicide?

"Go," Miles pleaded quietly.

"There's no fucking way that I'm letting you do this," Hendrix defiantly declared.

The C.E. president cut him off. "It's gotta be me. Getting pushed out as prez, letting the club turn its back on you, and all that we stood for... Robbie getting killed then following through with Tex's plan... all of that is on me. I got a lot to atone for."

Miles always struck me as world worn, tired, and defeated. A good, but beaten man desperately riding the coattails of a greater version of himself. Despite the fact he was around my uncle's age, he appeared to be so much older at that moment.

Hendrix couldn't accept what his MC brother was attempting to do. "That doesn't mean that you—"

"It's not just the club!" Miles angrily interrupted him. "This is for Stacy and my kids. Please! *I need this!*"

"Miles...." Just his name slipped from my lips. I wanted

to convince him to come with us, but I didn't know what else to say. How could dying in this filthy warehouse possibly help his family in any way?

The thunderous rumbling had stopped. From the noise, I could tell that at least a dozen of the Steel Veins had parked just outside the main door and were on their way in.

"Go, goddammit!" Miles hollered impatiently.

He was right. If we had any hope of leaving, it had to be now. Hendrix knew it too, and his face twisted with impotent rage at not being able to help his friend. Without another word, he grabbed my arm, and we raced to the back door.

I rapidly counted fifteen Steel Veins entering the opposite side of the warehouse, and, as I had expected, we were immediately spotted. Several of them scrambled pell-mell toward us. If that wasn't enough, the thick metal door that was to be our escape route was locked. Hendrix threw his shoulder into it, but it must've been dead-bolted as the door rattled but otherwise barely budged. We were stuck. Even worse, we were at an exit, so by law, it had to be well-lit and clear of any obstructions, which meant that we had no cover whatsoever. No place to hide. If we didn't get through this door right then, we were as good as dead.

I shrieked as a bullet smacked into the wall a foot or so to the side of me. I glanced back at the shooter reflexively. Although I couldn't see the short man's face clearly from that range, the familiar hunch of bad posture and the way he moved was unmistakable. It was my father, and he was lining up his next shot. He was quite the marksman and rarely ever missed twice.

I should've been more upset that it was him pulling the trigger, but I really couldn't think of any other way it would have gone. Tex had made the deal with Slick when he found out who I really was.

I thought of Anna and the cryptic words Tex said about Slick getting his second daughter back. *She was safe,* I made sure of that. I needed to worry about myself now.

The risk I posed to my father and his club if I discovered and used any evidence against them was more than enough to justify killing his own disavowed daughter. I had learned the very painful but valuable lesson early on in life that the only bond my father and I shared was strictly a biological one.

Even male polar bears occasionally ate their young.

Hendrix growled at our only exit, the veins popped throughout his corded muscles. He refused to be denied as he struck the door with the enraged percussion of a hostile, coiled snake. The entire locking mechanism wrenched free from the wall with the force of the mighty blow, his boot heel impacting so hard that one of the hinges whined and snapped as the door flung open.

Hendrix was strength incarnate, the embodiment of power. Beneath the charm and devil-may-care attitude was a fierceness and determination that I didn't think was possible in any man. He was perfect.

The last thing I saw before Hendrix's strong arms carried me outside and away from the line of fire was Miles. Gun raised, he alone turned to face the charging bikers. The air exploded with the rapid succession of gunfire inside the building.

Then I heard nothing.

My stomach churned painfully because I knew right then that he was dead.

We quickly found Miles's bike and sped away before the Veins eventually streamed out of the building after us. Hendrix caught sight of them in his rearview mirror and yelled for me to hold on. I squeezed him tightly just below his chest as he leaned forward and gunned the throttle. Bullets whizzed past us, peppering metal signs, empty vehicles, and pavement all around us.

When the gunfire safely faded into the distance, I allowed myself to breathe again. The adrenalin slowly faded, taking with it the intense percussion of blood pumping in my ears. I knew we'd need to stop soon to make sure neither of us had been shot.

When Hendrix pulled us over a few miles away, I convinced him to let me leave an anonymous tip with the Bureau of Alcohol, Tobacco, Firearms, and Explosives. I had briefly worked with them a few times through my law firm, and I knew they would be interested in finding a hidden gun smuggling operation. Being that they were the Feds, they would be much less likely to have been bought off by the Veins. Unfortunately, they would never have enough evidence to incriminate my father, not this time. He was far too wily to remain in the warehouse for long, but the shitstorm the ATF would kick up would certainly inconvenience him. It might even buy us the time we needed to reach California.

After the call, Hendrix examined me once again and decided that my nose needed to be manually reset, which took three adjustments to fix it completely. I squirmed and yelped at the intense pain as he did so in those three tries, the first being the absolute worst. All that grinding and bone-crunching ringing in my ears, deafening me to all other sounds, was worse than fingernails down a chalkboard. Would I be able to breathe through my nose again, as I was an obligate nose breather and couldn't sleep if I had to breathe through my mouth.

"You're all right." Hendrix gently kissed my forehead "You're almost as pretty as me. Oh… I found this inside." He handed me my small wallet. I popped it open and quickly perused through it. It was empty except for my license, a photo of Anna, and a library card that I never used. "Your stuff was all over the place. Sorry I didn't have time to grab more."

It was a selfish and small thing, but I wished he'd found my phone and maybe one credit card too. It didn't matter though. It was wonderful that he had even grabbed what he did as it was more than I could have hoped for. Hendrix didn't have to come to the warehouse at all. Then where would I be?

"This is fine. Thank you." I managed a weak but genuine smile.

"Are you ready?"

I took a deep breath to steady myself and tell him yes, but something else fell out of my mouth instead. "Why did

Miles stay?"

The biker sighed, his strained mirth dissolving, and in a low voice, he answered, "He did it for his ex-wife and kids. If he's dead, there would be no reason for the Veins to hurt his family. That's not a health insurance plan most places tended to offer."

The concept of that level of retaliation was so monstrous to me that my face tingled as I fought back the tears. Never in my life had I hated the Steel Veins more.

"Okay," I mumbled, slipping behind Hendrix on the bike's leather seat. I felt a small piece of my heart flitter away for Miles and another piece for Hendrix. In their places, those terrible holes were filled with something darker, something harder. I'd finally begun to understand what brutality really was and what was truly necessary to survive in this world. "I'm ready."

# Chapter 9
## HENDRIX

Maya spotted the smoke first. While riding it, I'd noticed something was off with Miles's bike, but we didn't have time to check it for damage with the Steel Veins from the casket warehouses on our asses. Fortunately, it was a hot night so I could really stretch the bike's legs without freezing too much from the wind chill. I had been able to lose Slick's gang, and we'd just passed the state line into Utah when the heavy, blackish smoke came pouring out of the bottom of the bike's engine.

It was getting late and there was no one on the highway, so I pushed the bike as far and as fast as it could go as we were only about an hour out from Salt Lake City. If I could get Maya there, then I could get her the rest of the way.

All the dummy lights on the instrument panels flashed urgently then clicked off, taking all the bike's power with them. We coasted down from just over a hundred and ten miles an hour, but it was a struggle just to keep us up on two wheels without being thrown off. We eventually rolled to a stop just off the dark, dusty highway out in the middle of

Fuck-Knows-Where, Utah. I helped Maya off and inspected the bike.

"How bad is it? Is it something we can fix?" Maya asked worriedly.

The bike was completely fucked. The intake valve was cracked, maybe from wear and tear or by a bullet while we fled. Either way, the motor had seized. We were lucky the goddamn engine didn't buckle or explode at the speeds I was pushing it.

"Fuck...," I breathed the word, placing both hands on the leather seat for support. This was probably the worst day of my life, and it wasn't nearly over yet.

"Hendrix?"

I held my hand up for her to wait as I couldn't answer her with words yet. Anything that came out of my mouth right then would've been harsh and strangled with exasperation. Maya didn't deserve that. I just needed a minute to cool off.

Robbie and Miles were dead. My plans for getting out of the club unscathed were fucking ashes in the breeze. We were stranded in a desolate wasteland of rolling hills. No streetlights and a heavily cloud-covered sky robbed us of all but the faintest of light. The stars even refused to shine for us. Even outside of my cell, I was still in prison.

The frustration I felt burning inside me that I was hoping would subside did the exact opposite. It seeped into my bones, causing anger to swell in my muscles and joints as it radiated throughout my entire body and finally boiled over. Soon, I seethed with aggravation at how little I was able to change the outcome.

I was fit to burst, the pressure I was experiencing was overwhelming. The impotent rage I felt screamed toward a breaking point and finally vented as I violently kicked the bike over and stomped the shit out of it. Shattered mirrors. Kicked-in headlight. Bent-around handlebars. Ripped plexiglass windshield, and many more pieces flung as far away as I could. I staggered a few feet back from the remains of the wrecked Harley, away from Maya, away from everything. My energy completely spent, I sagged down to my knees and hung my head, all the fight fleeing from my physical form. Then tears swelled from my closed eyes and dampened my cheeks.

The leather collar of my vest chafed against the skin on my neck. Funny, but I never was all that bothered by the discomfort before because it reminded me that this brotherhood came with a cost, and sometimes that cost was uncomfortable. Today though, that roughness rubbing on my neck was too much to bear. Today, that cost was far too high.

That cost was paid in blood and tears… and probably part of my soul.

Maya's touch was so light that I barely felt it at first. Her soft hand lingered on my shoulder as if asking permission. When I didn't push her away, she sidled around in front of me. I opened my eyes enough to see the outline of her lost-and-found jeans and her worn tennis shoes. I couldn't bear to look up at her. Not yet.

She gently guided my head into her arms and slipped her fingers between my vest collar and the back of my neck. I could feel her warmth all around me… like I was wrapped in a sunbeam. I closed my eyes and embraced that soothing warmth.

"My brother, Hayton, was put into a coma by a drunk driver when I was twelve. Every day on my way home from school, I'd walk to the hospital to visit him. On the way there, I'd steal the funny pages out of a newspaper on someone's porch. Once I was in his hospital room, I'd describe the visuals in the comic to him as best I could and then read him the captions," I reminisced slowly and deliberately. The memory was so hard to put into words.

"Did your brother have a favorite comic?" she asked patiently.

"No," I replied, coughing at the innocent question, which then turned into a dark chuckle. "Hayton was a few years older than me and hated those comics, especially *Family Circus*. When I got there, I would always begin by telling him, 'All you gotta do is wake up and tell me to stop, and I promise I will.' My parents would beg and plead for him to wake up, but that, of course, would never work, so I figured if I could piss him off enough, he'd have to wake up and yell at me to quit it. I did that for six months… but he never did. The night of December 22, 1990, around 7:00 p.m., his heart stopped and... Hayton died. That was my first meaningful experience with death, and it feels like death's been chasing me around ever since… 'Just tell me to stop.'" Those words I told Hayton floated from my lips like the whisper of a ghost.

That night of my brother's death was the last time I was physically consoled by anyone.

Mercifully, Maya was silent, but she just pulled me in tighter. Her arms wrapped around me were enough to soothe the sharpest burrs of my long-suppressed sorrow, enough to part the storm clouds of a heavy rain.

I never told anyone that story, and I'd probably never tell it ever again. I wasn't really sure why I did this time as it left me feeling exposed and vulnerable, but maybe it was necessary. There was a small degree of relief in letting something like that off my chest. It must be that absolution Catholics feel when they are truly repentant of their sins and are forgiven of them.

But maybe it was just budding trust. Maya outpaced everyone in the circuits she ran in my mind. I already liked the girl. Originally, she was just a breath of fresh air and a symbol of what life could be outside of my MC. After that, she was an obligation to a friend and now... she was something else entirely to me.

I didn't know fully what yet, but I was starting to actually care for her.

Beneath all my bullshit, I didn't think I would've gone after her when Robbie died if she didn't mean something important to me. I'd like to think that I did it for my friend, but I was too selfish for that. I needed to rescue Maya because *I* needed her to be safe.

I sat there in silence with her along the side of that endless, dark highway for a long time. It took a while, but in her arms, I found the strength to stand up and fulfill one last obligation to the club.

"Where are you going?"

"Stay here." I touched her cheek to ward off her worry then wandered off into the flat, starless landscape. It was hard to see, but I found my way. I wasn't sure what I was looking for, but I knew I'd find it.

Before long, I came across a patch of semi-loose earth and went to work. A shovel would have made everything much easier, but all I had with me was my knife, and it would have to do. I stabbed the packed soil to loosen it up then dug the hole with my bare hands. It would take a little while and the going would be tough, but fortunately for me, this grave I had to dig would be a shallow one.

All this time I was trying to get out, to leave the club. I thought about Robbie, Tex, Miles, all the guys we lost to the Wild Boys, and all the portraits of fallen members that hung on the gray wall back in the war room at our clubhouse... I was all that was left, a lost rider that just wanted to hang it all up but instead was dragged into a desperate plan and a losing fight.

In the end, it was the Coffin Eaters that left me.

"You boys remember why we started this drinking club on wheels?" I let my mind drift back to the four of us around the table in the clubhouse when both it and we were still shiny and new. "We were drunk and directionless, looking for new ways to stir up a little trouble on Saturday nights. Turns out others were like-minded, and before we knew it, the Coffin Eaters was born."

I stripped off my cut, folded the vest neatly, then held it in my arms, just feeling the weight. I dragged my hand across the leather one last time. There was so much history in each scratch and hole of that vest. Finally, I laid it in the hole and buried it.

Standing back up, I clapped my hands free of most of the dirt and spoke a few words *in memoriam*. "To every man worth his salt, to each brother come and gone, to the reaper that rides for us all. May each man eat the coffin of the last so that the club may live on. Rest easy, you ugly bastards, and save me a beer in hell."

It wasn't much of a eulogy, but it would have to do.

Gravel shifted on the ridge above me, startling me into reaching for my gun. I quickly relaxed my hand when I registered that it was Maya.

"That was really nice," she ventured.

"I thought I told you to wait for me."

"I did, but you were gone so long, I was worried you had been eaten by wolves. I'm a city girl. There's a shelf life on how long I can be left by the side of a highway in the middle of nowhere before I start to freak. You're lucky I let you out of my sight for as long as I did," she berated with feigned indignation.

It was damn near impossible to be mad at her. The little biker-hating princess was genuinely concerned about me. It was a hell of a feeling.

Compassion settled into her voice as she asked, "Are you all right?"

I gazed at her slender outline on the hill above me, her presence alone already making me feel better. *Robbie, where the hell did you find this girl?* "Starting to be."

"You did a number on that bike, but I managed to find a

blanket in one of his side boxes." She held it up triumphantly.

"Now we just need a basket and some ants, and we can have ourselves a proper picnic."

"I was thinking more of a campout, especially being that I haven't seen so much as a headlight in the past hour."

"Yeah, we're really out there. C'mon down. Let's set that up." I climbed toward her as she carefully navigated the hill in almost complete blackness.

The gravel beneath her shifted, and Maya lost her footing. She let out a surprised squeak as her foot abruptly skidded forward and threatened to betray her. It wasn't too steep of a grade, and the soil was soft enough that she wouldn't have been hurt much if she fell, but I launched myself to grab her anyway. It was now an automatic reflex for me. An impulse. It would have taken longer for me to realize that she'd be fine than it would have been to actually catch her. So I snatched her out of the air right as she pitched forward and really started to panic.

Unfortunately, the momentum shift of her in my arms toppled me over too, so we tumbled the last few feet together, rolling out at the bottom in a jumbled mess. I managed to take the brunt of the fall, positioning myself to have her land on top of me rather than me crushing her. Strange how the blanket she brought managed to have woven itself around us like a tight cocoon.

There I lay for a second, slowly easing into a smile. My life was a maelstrom. It was a roller coaster of horror, sex, violence, and drugs. This... whatever this was... was completely alien to me. Never had I been wrapped in a blanket at the bottom of a hill with a beautiful lawyer after our only ride out of nowhere had been destroyed. This was a first for me, and firsts were hard to come by nowadays.

"I take it there aren't many sandy hills in downtown St. Louis?"

"I think we paved over most of them." Maya wriggled and eventually poked her head out from the swaths of fabric.

I didn't know if she was just a welcome distraction from the pain, or if she was the staples and duct tape that my heart needed in order to mend. It was hard to let that grief go, at least enough to enjoy anything good, especially when that hurt was so raw, so fresh in my mind. My vest—the bleeding, open wound of my recently buried past—was only a few feet away.

How was I supposed to set something like that aside and look beyond it? My club and my closest friends were dead. I liked Maya a lot, but how the hell could I justify enjoying myself with her?

I had asked Robbie that once after a friend of ours was killed. He'd lost a lot of friends in the service and a few more after that. He had a girl in each arm when he replied to my question, saying that we feel an obligation to the dead. We grieve because we feel that they deserve our full attention, that they'd somehow want us to keep them on our minds. But really they're just gone. They don't want anything from us. And if they did and were worth grieving over in the first place, then they'd want us to not be in pain when we thought of them. Let the memory of the dead enrich our lives, not make them shittier than we already make them ourselves.

*That's how*, I thought. I wasn't trying to find a way to distract myself with Maya and forget about my pain. No, I would honor those I'd lost by not letting that loss destroy me by embracing the good things in life rather than pushing them away.

Maya, in this moment, was the best thing in my life. Despite everything—no, *because* of everything, I couldn't push her away. Not tonight.

Maya approached with a hint of shyness, her hot breath brushing against my lips, her face being only a few inches away. I let the rest of the world melt away. We might as well have been floating in space where there was only her and me.

Her slender body draped over me, robbing me of my grief and pain. I was tangled in her and she in me. Either of us could have easily escaped if we wanted to, and although she stirred, she eventually sank back down and pressed herself all the more tightly against me. She matched her breathing with mine. I could faintly make out the whites of her dark, almond eyes. We were one form.

I shifted enough to get an arm free and swept her silky hair over an ear. Maybe I imagined it, but even now I could just barely pick up the faintest notes of lilacs on her skin, which was quickly becoming my favorite scent. I wanted to live in that moment with her forever. I wanted to steal it and tattoo it across my flesh so I could never forget her.

"I think I need to tell you something I overheard," Maya started, appearing a bit embarrassed. "I meant to tell it to you earlier, but with all the deadly excitement, I just kinda forgot."

"What's up?" I asked, pulling my head back a little further to read as much of her expression as the dark night would allow.

"It's about my fath—" She cleared her throat, not able to get the word out. "It's about Slick and his chapter. I think they're going rogue from the Steel Veins now that the new guy's in charge. They're apparently really pissed about how all that went down."

"Forming their own MC?" I asked, the old adage *the enemy of my enemy is my friend* stirring in my head. It also reminded me of just how over his head Tex had really been. He had no idea what was going on, the selfish prick.

"I think so. He told his guys to reach out to support clubs and bikers that were pissed off about the new policy changes. He wants to build an army." Maya's face went deadly serious. "And if there's anyone that can do it, it's him."

"He seems like quite the cult of personality type," I replied cynically, remembering the way he mercilessly tried to kill his own daughter. Then something clicked in me. "Why are you telling me this?"

"I, uh, I just didn't want there to be any more secrets between us." Her face screwed up to one side as her beautiful eyes appealed to me.

She was beginning to actually trust me.

"No more secrets," I agreed.

My filthy hand grazed her cheek as I cupped the side of her face and pulled her into me. Her wide, full lips crushed mine, the last barriers of my resistance shattering. Tomorrow, I'd see to it that Maya was safely on her way to San Francisco and out of my life, but tonight…

Tonight, Maya, the fallen Steel Vein angel, would be mine.

# Chapter 10
## MAYA

I didn't know what to think when I crested that hill. I figured it had to be something to do with mourning. Then he caught me when I slipped and... I hadn't planned on any of that. Hendrix was in so much pain when he left me. Who wouldn't be with the losses he had suffered today? That's why I went after him. I just wanted to console him, to let him know that I was willing to help him. It was the least I could do.

I was also a little scared as well. I wasn't joking about that whole being left alone out in the middle of nowhere thing. I was raised in a city. The wilderness, although incredibly lovely, was also very intimidating. The sheer size of it all….

Hendrix had saved my life several times over now, but it still struck me as funny that I'd somehow come to associate him, a murderous biker, with safety. He yanked me out of the fire that was his normal lifestyle. By virtue of being near him, I'd given up my sense of security. Intellectually, I understood all of that, but I couldn't change the way I felt. I really did feel safe around him.

Safe enough to open up about everything. It felt good to tell him what I'd overheard from Slick about splintering off from the Steel Veins. I didn't think telling Hendrix was going to fix anything, but it was nice just to share that burden.

"Is this a good spot for a blanket?" It was a silly question to ask a man wrapped up in a blanket with me. I guess I was trying to diffuse whatever *this* was because I didn't know if the whole situation was a good idea, considering what he was probably going through and what I had just been through with that psycho Ricky-Tick.

Still, pushing myself away was so difficult. I wanted him almost beyond words and especially after every time I thought about him coming back to rescue me. Wrapping my head around just how much he had to give up for me made my heart swell to bursting. No one had ever done anything like that for me before, and ever since then, thoughts of him invaded my mind with the destructiveness and unpredictable nature of gale-force winds in a wild ocean storm.

I needed to stop myself before it went too far like last time.

I prayed that it would happen with Hendrix eventually but on some other day, not now. On a day that wasn't so full of death or near-death or almost-rape or so much loss or….

*When the hell would that* normal *day be?*

I was almost killed a few hours ago, and there were still so many miles to go. We were dirty, beaten up, and stranded in a near-hopeless situation that we barely escaped from. There may never be an ideal time for Hendrix and me. We may never have our perfect moment, if there even was such a thing. This might be all we got—right here, right now.

How could I possibly give that up?

So I let my arms give way and allowed his darkness and warmth to take me. I drew a long, deep breath and released all my doubts, sending them to float away. I gave myself to him completely. Now it was his turn to decide what came next.

Under the blanket, it was impossibly black. I couldn't see where I ended and he began. My heart beat only for him. My chest rose and fell on his whim. His fingertips dragged through my scalp, leaving trails of tingling heat in their wake. Tonight, I was his. He was in mourning, and I was recovering from shock and PTSD. Maybe this was the best we could ever hope for?

He cradled my neck and cheek, and I let him guide me to where I really belonged. He aligned my curves against his rock-hard form and kissed me. Unions like ours were colliding comets, our trajectory hurtling straight toward the sun to be irrevocably consumed. Fast, unpredictable, and absolutely ruinous for us and anything in our way. It was amazingly rare and incredibly brilliant. We were doomed but gloriously so.

He stretched, pulling the blanket apart far enough to free his other arm then wrapped it around me, mashing my small tits into his hard pecs. Quick, hard, wet, and searching—we kissed like desperate strangers with only a few hours left to live. I lost myself in it all. I lost myself in *him*.

"Ow!" I grunted, immediately wrenched back to reality

once again, or at least the reality of my still very broken nose. His own pressed against mine, sending shooting pain up into my face.

"Yeah, that's still broken," he mused wryly.

"I'm okay." I didn't want him to stop, but it hurt so much.

"I have no doubt, but why don't I find new places to kiss... just to be safe." I could feel his highly skilled lips smile against the skin of my oh-so-sensitive neck before he proceeded to kiss downward. The pain in my face subsided even more in response to his intimate expertise.

He rolled me over onto my back then tugged me up into a sitting position before yanking my shirt off. I fumbled to unclasp my bra, hoping to save it from being destroyed this time, but Hendrix caught my arms. "Nuh-uh-uh…. Trying to steal all my fun?" he accused devilishly.

I released a resigned giggle. "If you can handle—" Before I could finish, he had pinched, released, and popped the wings of my bra away. "Uh, okay, apparently you can." I felt my face redden.

"That's not all I can do," he purred in my ear, slipping a finger between my breasts and ripping my bra off my chest. The chilled air tickled my hardening nipples, and an excited shiver rippled through me. This all was a promise of what was to come, and it transformed my spine into jelly.

He lifted my chin and kissed along my hairline until he reached my ear. Suddenly, he was all teeth and tongue. A quick jerk forced me back down as he clamped a mighty hand over both my wrists, restraining them over my head. The thrill of exciting kink danced in my mind as he worked my panties off with his other hand. God, I still felt a little self-conscious that I hadn't shaved, but if he minded, he never let on about it.

I'd never done anything like this, and now I wasn't certain if I could handle it.

With two, exploring fingers, he located my clit and slowly began to rub. His tight, little circles had me breathing heavily almost immediately. I swallowed hard. Those old anxieties began to whine in the back of my head, warning me of whom Hendrix was and what I had already lived through at the hands of my father's club—

*No!* I refused to allow parasites like Ricky-Tick and Slick to ruin my life any further. *I wanted Hendrix.* Every filthy, flexing, fleshy inch of him. Besides, without a motorcycle or a patch, Hendrix wasn't officially a biker anymore—

Dammit! I couldn't fool myself. Hendrix *was* still a biker. It would always be a part of a man like him, but right now, with *me*, he was just a man. That was all that mattered. A real man who wanted *me*. So I finally disconnected my nagging superego and decided to relax and enjoy him fully. I wasn't sure if I would survive it, but I now was frantic to find out.

He withdrew his adept fingers, licked them, then ground harder on my clit, matching the rhythm with my body's natural tempo. Not too fast. Not too hard. God, did he make my pelvis buck uncontrollably as he coaxed my first squeak and moan from my lips, which then never stopped.

How was he so good at this? I didn't think it was possible to be touched like this, to eke out such a response from me like I've never experienced before. Because it was too dark to see, I could never prepare myself for his touch. My skin was awash with goose bumps in dripping anticipation, so when I felt his wet teeth abruptly sink into my neglected nipple, my skin caught fire and I exhaled crackling electricity.

"Fuck," I whispered, my whole body contracting. I was a steel board. Guttural moans flowed from me like water. I was so close to coming that I could feel it in my clenched teeth. My God, he was amazing.

"Say it again." His voice was smoky and thick.

"Fuck me...."

"Louder," he demanded, flicking over my bean, my body jerking at his every movement. I was a marionette, and he was tugging my strings to his will.

"*Unh*... fuck me...."

"Again," he growled fiercely in my ear, the edge in his voice slicing through me.

I couldn't stand it. My whole body vibrated, yearning for his touch. I wanted to feel him inside of me more than I had ever wanted anything else. "*Please!*"

He knew what I wanted but refused, decelerating his fingers to an agonizingly slow speed, which drove me crazy.

"*F-f-f...,*" I stammered, teetering on the cusp of divine ecstasy. He was so heartless, demonic even, to torment me so badly.

"Scream for me. I want to hear that you really want it this time." He slid two fingers into my pussy, and I immediately came. He felt it, too, and didn't stop. Instead, he sped up in rhythm with my pussy's spasms, making a beckoning motion with his fingers inside of me. He oscillated them, one after the other, in short bursts of movement, stroking them against my ribbed walls. I was sopping. My whole body went rigid. My pussy, thighs, and lower stomach rocked involuntarily.

The growing bulge in his pants became a hardening rod. Hot and thick. Grinding down my thigh. I strained against his iron grip, desperately wanting to grab his cock, to feel it every way possible.

"Fuck!" I screamed it. I'd never been more ravenous. *"Fuck me! Fuck me! Fuck me! Fuck me!"* I shouted at the top of my lungs until my throat was rough. I had let the whole world know what I wanted, but I didn't care.

He released me to pull his pants off. My hands rocketed down to my pussy; he had me so close to coming again! I was right on the verge when he grabbed my hand and flattened it onto my pussy. The pressure was pleasurable, but it wouldn't be enough. He refused to let me consummate that ever-evasive orgasm, *the bastard!*

"No! No! I'm so close! Don't be so mean!" I rubbed my pussy against his hand. I was almost there again. All I needed was a little more....

"All I am *is* mean." He jerked our hands away and laid his massive cock on my pulsating pussy. I was losing my goddamn mind now. How could he be so much in control?

The cool air licked at my soaked pussy and thighs but didn't chill me one bit. The heat I had that burned for him could set the chilling wind on fire. I felt like I was going to have a fucking heart attack if he kept teasing me. If I exploded, they would be finding pieces of me across these hills for weeks.

"Give it to me!"

And then he finally did.

His cock split me open wider than Tyrone, my favorite vibrator at home did, but his incredible girth continued to invade my very core until I feared that I might feel him in my throat; it was so fucking amazing. My quick, shallow breaths were a mockery of breathing. God, the things Hendrix made me feel….

He threw one of my legs over and rolled me on my side. The new position allowed him to somehow get impossibly deeper, sending pangs of pleasure all the way up to my rib cage.

The blanket was a distant memory as we copulated in the dirt.

"I've needed to fuck you since the second I laid eyes on you." His voice was raunchy and betrayed cracks in his stoicism as he pumped harder and faster. Asphalt-darkened earth packed underneath my nails as I dug my fingers into the ground as it was all I could do to just hold on.

*"I'm coming! I'm coming! Don't stop!"* I seized, momentarily arresting my writhing. The orgasm ripped throughout my entire body like I was made of paper. My eyes rolled back in response to the deepest ecstasy I'd ever felt.

"You won't scream for me?" I croaked between gasping, ragged breaths.

Hendrix squeezed my leg and ass tight enough that

I would bruise. Good! I wanted to remember this for as long as I could. The thought of me being the girl to make a man like Hendrix lose control, if only for a second, was intoxicating. The most dangerous of all drugs.

I ran my dirty fingers down the ridges of his sweaty, sculpted chest and abs. He yelled both loud and guttural, both frightening and thrilling. Then he snapped my hand up and bit my fingers, dirt and all. My swollen pussy clamped down on his corpulent, throbbing cock as he filled every part of me. His cock swelled even larger and pulsed, and I felt him explode.

I curled my fingers in his mouth and jerked him toward me. He lay on top of me and pulled my lips into his, kissing me with fervor. So personal and so very intimate. He even remembered to be careful of my nose, which reflected the kind of man that was hidden within that rough exterior.

How could I possibly have been able to write him off?

Eventually, he slid back in what was the longest pulling out of my life, then found and straightened the blanket. With a quick jerk and without any hesitation, being that we were both filthy, he trapped me against him. Our bodies, a sweaty, dirty mass of flesh, collided. I relaxed on his chest and listened as his racing heart eventually decelerated back down to normal. Everything about what had just happened was wet, sloppy, and strangely wonderful.

Hendrix was a man who made no apologies for what he was and what he wanted. If there was something worth taking, he took it. Tonight, that was me. I hadn't felt this good, this accepted, in... God... I couldn't even remember when. Worse,

I thought I was actually beginning to fall for him.

"Oh shit! Did we just do that without a condom?" The harsh realization dawned on me with the subtlety of a sledgehammer.

"It was good for me too. Thanks for asking."

"And you came inside me!" I ignored him and climbed against him into a sitting position, the consequences of what we had just done piling up in my head. And I was worried about what that might mean for me. Jesus, what if I got pregnant? I wasn't ready for that. What about him? Was he clean?

"You get wound up pretty easily, don't you?" He tried to drag me back down, but I thoroughly resisted.

"I'm not on birth control, and you came in me without asking!" I ranted in his face.

He sighed and released me yet made no other move to comfort or reassure me. Why wasn't he taking this seriously?

"I had a vasectomy years ago, and they tested me in prison. So as long as you're clean, we're good," he finally revealed, and my panic gradually melted. Only then did I allow him to pull me back into his embrace. "You *are* clean, right?" he inquired discreetly.

"Of course! What kind of woman do you think I am?" I choked on the absurdity of the question. I hadn't had many partners, and up until now, I was always extremely careful.

Hendrix rolled me onto my back, and his big cock slapped against my thigh then slid over my pussy, eliciting a sharp thrill that ran up between my legs. "The kind of woman who likes to be held down and fucked in the dirt."

"Oh, you smug son of a bitch...." My cheeks reddened profusely while my smile beamed. He was right though. I loved every filthy second of it. "What about the girl you were with at the clubhouse before we left?"

"Jackie Blow? I had a condom, not that it came to that. Guess what her specialty was?"

"You are such a pig," I scoffed, mostly jokingly. A small part of me was jealous of that girl. But why? It was only a few days ago, but it might as well have been a lifetime.

I didn't know what this was that we had—if it was anything at all. The sex was incredible, and I hoped I would get that chance again. Though, feelings for him aside, I didn't know what was in store for me in the next few days, let alone us. This was no time to go foolishly falling in love.

"What is your last name?" I asked as it suddenly dawned on me that I had no idea. He knew mine, of course. That was one of the reasons that we were in this mess.

"Are we already at that stage of the relationship? You're moving a bit fast for me, Maya." He chuckled then added, "It's Cedro. Hendrix Cedro." I could feel the smile in his kiss. "It's a pleasure to meet you, Miss Merritt."

I liked the way he said my name. It was a silly little thing, but I liked how he could swing between vulgarity and propriety. He had me, and even worse, he knew he had me. Keeping him emotionally at arm's length might be more difficult than I thought.

It was a nice thought to fade into sleep with. I was a little cold, but Hendrix was a two-hundred-pounds-plus heater who held me close all night. I had never felt safer or slept more soundly than I did with him.

***

"Um, hello? Hul-lo?" The old, gruff voice groggily awoke me to an early rising sun.

It took me a few seconds to figure out where I was and what was going on. Hendrix stirred beneath me but continued sleeping.

"Oh my God!" I blurted out sharply, jerking the corner of the blanket over me. We were laying on too much of it to cover myself in any meaningful way, so I rolled onto my stomach and prayed that I would melt into the ground and disappear forever. "Hendrix! There's someone here!"

Hendrix startled awake and was up into a sitting position at a hundred miles per hour in a few seconds. Dazed, he groped around for his gun before relaxing when he saw the old man and deemed him not a threat. Hendrix was utterly unconcerned about his lack of clothes and took the opportunity to stretch and scratch himself before standing up.

"Are you youngsters all right?" The old man, bent over by age and using a cane, stood on the opposite side of the hill that we came down hours before. "I heard noises last night but didn't want to come out till daytime."

Noises? Jesus... I didn't think it was possible to be more embarrassed. There was no way to explain what we were doing out here that left out the fact that we were fucking in the dirt like animals. I was mortified.

Hendrix cleared his throat, shaded his eyes, and asked,

"You call the cops?"

"Couldn't. They're closed for another hour."

"The police station is closed? Where the hell are we?" It seemed so surreal to me that what he said was even possible.

"Technically you're between two towns, miss. Right on the line, really," the old man replied to my mostly rhetorical question in earnest. "I saw the wrecked motorbike. Are you hurt? Do you need help? You look a little banged up, miss." He twirled a circle around his nose with his index finger.

"No, no, that was, uh...." An impossible story to tell right now. "I'm all right. I just, um... Broke. It." Fuck. I was no good in the morning. I was a morning-coffee-before-I-could-function kind of girl, not a wake-up-nude-covered-in-my-own-filth-in-front-of-strangers kind of girl.

"How far are we from Salt Lake?" Hendrix casually asked.

"Oh, not far. I've been meaning to head there for a little while. I can take you if you'd like."

"Yes, please! That would be wonderful!" I wrapped myself tightly in the blanket.

"C'mon to the house. We'll get you cleaned up and with some food in you before we go."

Both suggestions sounded wonderful. I was covered in dirt and dried... bodily fluids. I needed a shower so badly. I reached up, and Hendrix easily hoisted me off the ground. I didn't realize how sore I was until I stood up. I had a lingering headache from my concussion and broken nose, not to mention how tender the rest of my face was. But it was the soreness in my thighs and my pussy that surprised me.

I hadn't been fucked in a while and never like that. His big cock certainly did a number on me.

"Thanks." Not bothering with his underwear, Hendrix carefully tucked his cock into his pants as he slid them up. Getting a good look at it up close, no wonder I was sore! Jesus, his member should come with a warning label. He grabbed the rest of our clothes. "You got a name, old man?"

"Benny. My wife's Agatha, and we're just over the next hill." The old man turned and started hobbling toward his house. "Agatha! It was just two young folk. You was right. They was having sex. Turn the heat on. They're needin' to bathe."

"Oh for fuck sake...," I muttered, burying my head into Hendrix's shoulder. He just laughed, thoroughly enjoying my discomfort. "Kill me. Just kill me now."

"No way I'm letting you leave me alone with Ma and Pa Kent." Hendrix smirked.

"Who?" It was a reference to something, but I couldn't place it.

"Never mind." He frowned in mock disappointment then wrapped an arm around me as he escorted me up the hill after Benny. Walking was slow and deliberate at first, and climbing was hell. "You all right?"

"I'm just... a little sore." It felt like I hadn't stopped blushing since I woke up. It was awful.

"Yeah." He licked my neck from my collarbone to behind my ear. It made me quiver with wanting. Goddamn him. "Next time I'll have to carry you around because you won't be able to walk comfortably for a week."

"Is that a threat or a promise?" I moaned, enjoying his nuzzling my ear.

He let the words hang and bit my ear instead. He lifted me up and carried me to the top of the hill.

Benny's house, which was a few hills off the highway via a nearby, invisible dirt road, was tiny and appeared to have been in the family for a few generations. Strangely, the place seemed even smaller on the inside, consisting of a modest living room with a fireplace and a kitchen in the corner, two bedrooms, and a bath. That was it. There were virtually no electronics that I could see aside from a modest microwave.

His wife, Agatha, who just as elderly, eagerly welcomed us in. "Can I get you some coffee?" she offered while already in the process of making it without depending on our response.

"God, yes!" I nearly shouted and then bit my lip at the abruptness of my reply.

Agatha didn't mind at all. She seemed like the unflappable type. Once the coffee was set to brew, she dusted her hands and surveyed me carefully. "Is that from the sex?" She pointed to the bruising and swelling on my face.

"No! No!" Horrified by the question, I told her the first thing that came into my head. "I fell when we crashed the bike."

Apparently she had her own agenda, and without skipping a beat, she told us that she understood the exciting vigor of a little rough love. Then she went on to regale us with stories of their sex life. She related in extremely uncomfortable detail how she and Benny were still physically intimate, and despite the various challenges of their bodies over the years, sex was what had kept them feeling young. There was no polite way to change the subject, either, and Agatha was quite the rambler. I glanced over at Hendrix, who appeared equally bemused. After an insightful conversation on vaginal changes with age and the ever-present threat of incontinence during sex, she finally asked who wanted to bathe first. I nearly leapt at the opportunity, mouthing an apology at abandoning an ill-at-ease Hendrix to his fate.

Much to my surprise, they only had a bathtub. No shower. I had just assumed they were speaking in colloquialism when they said "bathe." Obviously, they were not. I hadn't taken a bath since I was a child. It just wasn't a thing I did anymore and was never even a consideration when at another person's house. Showers were more efficient. I had never been into relaxing baths, either. It always seemed like too much work or something you did on a romantic evening, and I didn't have many of those, even if it was only with myself.

There was no escaping Agatha, even while bathing. She unexpectedly barged in where I gently turned down her offer to wash my back, not that it did any good. "Nonsense," she exclaimed and did it anyway. I would have been far more freaked out at their obscene lack of privacy and personal space if they weren't so genuinely good-natured about everything. Their intent was innocent and clear. They only wanted to help.

Apparently, she did the same thing with Hendrix when

it was his turn. I stole glances at him when she abruptly pushed open the door, displaying to all his worsening predicament. The tub was way too small for him with most of his bent legs sticking out and the water barely covering his abdomen. I had to suppress a giggle at the image of this tiny, old lady pleasantly chatting while scrubbing the back of a giant like Hendrix. He sat quietly, utterly miserable.

When Agatha finished, she dutifully left him to finish up, then came back into the kitchen to start breakfast. "Oh! The trunk on him!" She winked as she swung her arm between her legs when she walked passed me. "It's a miracle you survived."

I chortled, covering my face with my hand while trying to hide the renewed flushness. It was incredibly hard to be mad at her unfiltered honesty without the Puritanical taboos. She had obviously lived far too long to care about upsetting others with her opinions. If I survived to be her age, I hoped I would have a fraction of her uninhibited personality. I liked the dynamics of their relationship as well. Benny and Agatha existed seamlessly in their own spaces. Without having to discuss anything, they just knew what they needed to do to further their mutual goals such as when Benny kissed Agatha on the cheek as he passed her to switch over our laundry. They lived perfectly symbiotically.

Hendrix emerged a short time later, having been more comfortable dodging bullets than he did with the elderly couple's brand of hospitality. I was able to wear Agatha's bathrobe, but they didn't have any clothes large enough for him. Instead, they gave him a sheet to wear as a toga while our clothes were placed in the dryer in the other room. Despite his obvious embarrassment, Hendrix was resplendent, tattoos and all, like a noble Viking emissary to Rome.

Hendrix asked to use their landline while Agatha finished up with breakfast. Instead of his Viking composure, he now appeared as if he was posing for a sculptor as he uncomfortably sat on a small stool with short legs, his body all hunched forward. When I asked him what he was doing, he smiled and reported that he was making friends with our enemy's enemy.

Nearly a dozen phone calls later, we ate a gigantic breakfast, and before long, the dryer dinged loudly, announcing our clothes were now ready. We quickly changed, thanked them for their generous hospitality, and headed out to Benny's truck. On our way out, Agatha gave us both a big bear hug and wished us well. "You two are a cute couple. You take care."

When we finally situated ourselves in the vehicle, I turned around to wave to Agatha one last time. My eyes went wide when she brazenly swung her arm between her legs again before pointing at Hendrix and giving me a thumbs-up. What a dirty old lady! Hendrix caught a glimpse of the spectacle and chuckled deeply. Agatha winked at me and finally waved back as we pulled away. I wasn't sad to leave, but I would definitely miss the plucky woman. I admired her fearlessness.

We didn't have much to offer Benny for the hospitality or the ride, so Hendrix told him he could scrap Miles's bike for a few hundred bucks. Benny agreed and reassured us that the whole incident would stay between the four of us. He wasn't a foolish man. He knew that, for whatever reason, we didn't want the cops involved. He probably talked it over with his wife, and they had gone with their gut that we needed help, not trouble. They both were just good, salt-of-the-Earth people who wanted nothing more than to be as helpful as possible.

We all had to share the one bench seat up front, which was the style of the old pickup trucks. Hendrix placed an arm around me and made it too comfortable to stay awake for long. I was running on fumes, still exhausted from the previous day's events. Between that, the sex, and being woken up at the crack of dawn this morning, sleep took me pretty easily.

"Maya, time to wake up," Hendrix's voice was so distant at first that when I opened my eyes and saw the airport, I thought it was a dream. Then some asshole behind us laid on the horn, and I knew it wasn't. "Salt Lake City International Airport" read a giant mural in the drop-off area. Why were we here?

There were people yelling and crying, taxi drivers arguing, and the general hustle and bustle of over-encumbered, stressed-out travelers rolling their small worlds behind them. Everything was extremely loud.

I had finally become comfortable with the silence of being out of the city. Last night by the side of the road, the motel in Laramie… before that… it was all very peaceful. Growing up in a city, it was easy to forget about what you didn't have—the rich beauty of silence.

Hendrix had disappeared by the time I'd rubbed the sleep from my eyes and acclimated to the din. He hadn't gone far, though. A loud crunching alerted me to his presence behind the truck as he was having a spirited discussion with the guy laying on the horn behind us, or rather, Hendrix was talking and the man behind the steering wheel was listening while in a state of terror.

"Benny, why are we here?"

"You'll have to ask your boyfriend. I just do what I'm told, a skill I picked up from Agatha." Benny winked at me just like his wife had. Those two were perfect for one another.

Hendrix, my boyfriend? I thought about correcting Benny, but I didn't. Part of it was because I'd never see the old man again, so why bother? It was a nice feeling knowing that there were at least two people out there somewhere that thought Hendrix and I were a couple. Even if it wasn't true, it still brought a slight smile to my heart.

Something metallic dropped from Hendrix's hand and shattered on the ground as he opened the passenger door to let me out. I saw the car that had been making all the commotion behind us quickly drive around Benny's truck and speed away—now missing its driver's side mirror.

Hendrix shook Benny's hand, and I thanked him for all his help. Then Benny's truck sputtered a few times as it navigated the drop-off platform before it disappeared from sight.

"So the airport, huh?" I gazed up at the big man. A plane

made sense.

"Fastest way to San Fran." Hendrix peered down at me and smiled weakly. His usual confident, troublemaking smile was replaced with one that was just going through the motions. It put me off right away. Something was wrong, and that made me uneasy.

He read the skepticism in my face and smiled deeper, trying to cover up something that weighed heavily on his mind. He held my hand. What could he be thinking that had him looking so dour?

I stared at the wad of cash he pressed into my hand. "What is this?"

"Airports charge money for their plane tickets." Even his snark was forced.

The realization that I didn't have my purse flashed across my face. I couldn't believe I hadn't remembered that until now. Everything had been so crazy that I hadn't had time to even think that I hadn't had it since the warehouse.

"I had Benny stop and withdraw money from one of my accounts on our way here."

"Are you...?" The words were surprisingly difficult to say out loud. An anxious feeling broiled from within my belly. "Hendrix, are you not coming with me?"

"I'm still on parole. I can't step foot in a place with that many cameras. If I gave them my info to buy a ticket, it would prove that I'm not in Kansas anymore, Dorothy."

"But...." I couldn't name it but something—maybe confidence or a sense of direction—whatever it was, it was slipping through my fingers like sand.

"My usefulness to you is about up, Maya." Hendrix's faded smile renewed but only in size and was more of a mockery of happiness. "One way or another, cops'll be able to place me at one of the crime scenes. If they're not already looking for me, they will be soon. If I stay with you now, I'll only slow you down."

"Hendrix, no...." I needed to find the words that would make him stay. "Together, I know we can find a way to figure this out."

"It's all right." This time his smile was genuine. "You don't need me anymore. We had some fun though, didn't we?" He kissed my forehead as tears flooded my eyes.

Was this really happening? How could it already be over? I knew it had to end sometime but not already. I wasn't ready... not yet.

"Where are you headed?" My voice started to crack.

Hendrix shrugged. He looked off over my shoulder and nodded to some vague direction. "That way, I guess."

He thumbed away the tears that streamed over my cheeks and put something else in my hand. "This was Robbie's. I think he'd want you to have it."

It was my uncle's pocket watch. I opened it and found an old picture of my mom and Anna.

"Robbie always had that on him. I don't know why he never had it fixed, but it looks like he really cared about your mom."

"They were lovers?" I wondered aloud, letting the words tumble out of my mouth to answer the hunches I'd been forming in the back of my mind during this whole trip.

My heart sank, and my stomach contracted tightly. It felt like the air was crushed from my lungs when the realization came as to what happened next. "And Slick found out...."

I had a sneaking suspicion that Mom and Robbie were in love, but this locket actually confirmed it.

Frustration rolled over me like the exhaust of a backfiring car. Why couldn't we have more time together? I didn't know if he didn't trust me enough yet or if he was just trying to protect me, but Robbie had been so damned guarded about his past with my mom every time we talked. He'd only really started opening up to me back at the Lost Boys' clubhouse when Hendrix came yelling that we were being attacked.

Then Tex killed him on Slick's orders.

"Is that why your mom disappeared?" Hendrix asked.

"That's what I'm hoping to find out when I get that safe-deposit box," I replied distantly, lost in thought.

"You'd best get to it then." He lifted my chin, breaking my bleary-eyed gaze at the ancient picture of the two people I loved most in the world. I met his sad eyes only briefly before he kissed me. It was the last, desperate kiss of a goodbye without compromise. Just as we broke away, he leaned in and whispered, "Take care, Maya. I'll miss you."

Hendrix pulled away, leaving me grasping at air. I didn't want the moment to end. I didn't know how this was supposed to end, but I knew it wasn't supposed to be like this.

Without another word, he turned and walked away.

I stood on the sidewalk and watched Hendrix vanish into

the crowd. I would never see him again. I was devastated. A hard but wonderful chapter in my life had now ended.

I was surrounded by tearful, hugging families and friends that were forced apart by their plane tickets and departure times. There were teens flying off to colleges, relatives returning home after vacations, bridesmaids flying out for their friends' weddings. All of their parting dramas seemed so petty to me… so temporary. What could they possibly know of the sadness that I felt at that moment?

I stumbled into the airport in a daze and was a teary, swollen-faced mess when I reached one of the counters that offered flights to San Francisco. I took some solace in the fact the airline employees must be used to dealing with distraught people. Heartbroken as I was, the last thing I wanted was unnecessary attention.

"Ma'am… uh, are you okay?" The lady behind the counter beheld me with worry, and that's when I caught my reflection in the mirror behind her.

Sad people were one thing, but I looked like I was hit with a shovel. Two black eyes, bruising and disfigurement of my nose, swelling and discoloration of most of my face, and facial scratches from Ricky-Tick's jagged nails. I was a walking horror show. I didn't realize I appeared so bad. For whatever reason, the elderly couple didn't have a mirror in their bathroom, and their place was so rustic that there weren't many reflective surfaces at all, none that I could've even subtly used as a mirror.

"I need a ticket to San Francisco. The sooner the better." I groaned, extracting the wad of cash and my license from my pocket. I had no intention of explaining myself or what happened to anyone as I was simply out of fucks to give.

The lady saw my disposition and decided against any other questions about my well-being. She pursed her lips and accessed her computer terminal. "I'm sorry, but we don't have any available seats until... Flight Four-Thirty-Nine tomorrow at…."

Her voice nervously trailed off as she saw the hardening look on my face. It was an expression that said tomorrow would *not* work. She cleared her throat and began again. "Would you like me to check the other airlines? Maybe they have something available that is leaving sooner."

I stood there for at least a minute, my mind drifting over the events of the past few days. I tried to focus on the task at hand, but my brain and my heart kept returning to Hendrix. I thought about just how much I had misjudged him initially. How I wouldn't be here without him. I probably wouldn't even be alive right now if it hadn't been for him.

Sometime later, when I came back to the present, I saw the service agent behind the counter start and stop like she wasn't sure if she should repeat herself or call her supervisor over. Her discomfort almost made me laugh. It wouldn't have been a laugh at her but at the fact that I had become an entirely different person than when I first met the Coffin Eaters. I used to be overly accommodating and empathetic. The hardness that I wore for work was a façade, an ill-fitting, uncomfortable mask. I was so much tougher now. Tempered in the fire of pain and tragedy, I now found it difficult to care about the discomfort of others. Social niceties were beyond my capacity at the moment.

She coughed, finally mustering up the courage to repeat herself. I ignored her again and let my gaze wander. The loss that settled throughout me was so palpable that I felt physically heavier and awash in numbness.

The current date and time digitally hung above the various airline kiosks and booths. I still had two days before the cut-off date with the bank. The flight from here to there was only around two hours. That wasn't that long when I thought about it. My brow furrowed. These two locations couldn't have been all that far apart, right? "How long of a drive is it to San Francisco?"

"I'm not—"

I left before she finished her sentence and went straight for the car rental kiosk. There was the faintest kindling of hope smoldering inside me, and I didn't have time to waste it on people who didn't have answers for me.

"A little over half a day if you're quick about it," the car rental agent answered when I asked him the same question.

Embers of that fleeting hope suddenly flared to life. My sorrowful haze dissipated like burnt flash paper. I dared to dream the impossible once again. He told me where they kept the rental cars and called ahead for me. Unapologetically, I pushed my way through the crowded airport, running my heart out to get that rental car, praying that it wasn't too late.

I couldn't fill out the forms and throw money at him fast enough as I rushed the on-site representative through the mandatory paper signings and visual checks on the car. I threw another twenty-dollar bill at the man just to get him the hell out of the way. I didn't give a fuck about any of it. I needed to leave immediately, and he wasn't getting it. He tossed me the keys and shouted policy reminders at me as I peeled out of the parking lot. *God, please let it not be too late!*

The roadways in the airport complex were designed to be a giant traffic circle so that if you missed your drop-off or pick-up point, you could loop back around again. I frantically drove through the entire circuit twice before finally spying what I was searching for.

Hendrix's unmistakably broad figure boarded a shuttle that would take him somewhere off-site, somewhere out of my life completely. What I did next would have been unthinkable to the old me of a week ago. I sped up and passed the shuttle right as it began to pull away from embarkation. Then I jacked on the brakes in front of it. The bus screeched and skidded to a halt. I had no idea if it would be able to stop in time, but it did with under a foot to spare. I hadn't been listening to the car rental agent, but only now did I realize that I probably hadn't bought additional insurance that covered "idiot drivers." I jammed the vehicle into park before jumping out of the car. The only thing I cared about was getting to Hendrix.

The shuttle doors opened, and the driver commenced the scream-a-thon. "What the fuck, lady? I'm calling the cops!" I ignored him and forced my way on the bus. Right as I passed him, the driver grabbed my arm and violently jerked me backward. "Are you out of your ever-fucking mind, bitch? Do you know how much trouble you're in?"

"Not nearly the trouble that you'll be in if you don't take your greasy hand off her," boomed a deep voice from the back of the bus.

Hendrix's hulking form rose to his feet, towering over the seated passengers like an angry, marble sculpture of a wrathful Norse god. When the sculpture moved, the passengers quieted and the driver released me.

I ran to Hendrix. His disposition shifted from anger to confusion, but he caught me as I barreled into him. "Maya...."

The words spilt out of my mouth. I couldn't handle hearing him reject me without explaining myself first. "There were no flights available, so I rented a car. Come with me." I buried my face in Hendrix's chest. "Please come with me!"

"Just go before I—" The bus driver stammered through the pathetic threat before he was interrupted by my Norse god.

"We'll take as much time as we damn well please," he growled at the man with a fierceness that was unquestionable.

The rest of the passengers were becoming restless. This wasn't a scene from a movie from which they would get screen credit. They didn't rally behind the notion that love conquers all. We were the equivalent of a car wreck, a delay that came with a spectacle during the morning commute. Everyone who wasn't frightened was becoming impatient, and some already had taken out their phones.

Hendrix saw that too. His eyebrows tipped up in a look of concern as he regarded me. "The cops'll be here soon."

If the police caught Hendrix, they'd quickly discover that he had broken parole, and they would arrest him. I risked too much to let that happen to him, especially after all he had done for me. I released him from my hug, feeling the onset of a crushing emotional defeat creeping in. I had to leave him again before I was destroyed by it.

I didn't know what I was thinking about trying something like this. Of course, it wasn't just because he couldn't get on a plane with me. He'd fulfilled his promise. He got me safely to where I could finish the journey. There was no reason for him to help me further. I felt like such a fool.

"Yeah. Okay." I turned away from him this time. I didn't want him to see how badly this hurt me.

"Aw... hell, I've been meaning to work on my tan anyway...."

Those words turned my legs into lead and stopped me dead in my tracks. Could that have possibly meant what I desperately hoped it would mean? Turning, I saw him smile. It did! It fucking did! He was coming with me. My heart cartwheeled.

Hendrix kissed me, and we exited the bus together. He grabbed my hand and halted me as I opened the driver's side door. "No way," he retorted, shaking his head. "*I'm driving.*"

I guess that was fair. I had the car for fifteen minutes, and I'd almost crashed it into a shuttle bus. I circled around to the passenger side, let myself in, and buckled up. The bus driver scowled at us through the windshield but drove around us without any more complaints. One girl in a window toward the back of the bus grinned impishly and gave me a thumbs-up as they passed. I smiled back before facing Hendrix. I was still stunned that such an unlikely gamble actually paid off.

"Is this a microcompact? It's smaller than my bed in prison! No Harleys were available?" Hendrix struggled to adjust the seat just to get in as he was much too large to be driving such a small car. It was kind of adorable.

"Sorry, the rental place only had Japanese motorcycles," I smirked.

Hendrix's face screwed up in disgust. "Compact it is, then."

I laughed. Having him with me felt night and day better than being on my own. It was horrible thinking I had lost him forever. For now, the path before us was paved with uncertainty, but at least I didn't have to lose him just yet. That's all I wanted... just a little more time with him.

We drove out of the airport and cruised back onto the highway. We had a long drive ahead of us, but it would just be him and me with hopefully no one else trying to kill us. I really liked the idea of being trapped in a car with Hendrix as it would give me the chance to really get to know him.

The windows were down, and the radio was on, but faintly. The sun peeked out behind a cloud-dotted, light blue sky. I leaned the seat back and put my bare feet on the dashboard. Riding with him without being chased felt delightfully normal... relaxing even. I could breathe easy.

With the scenery blurring by, I glanced over at Hendrix with a warm, contented smile. His long hair was brushed back by the warm summer wind as he thumbed his way across the tuner controls on the steering wheel, trying to find some decent music.

Was this happiness? Actually happiness? It was impossible not to feel hopeful. Hendrix had a way of instilling that in me. Maybe, just maybe, everything would be all right after all.

It was such a beautiful lie, I could almost believe it.

"Wait! Go back! Turn that up!" I exclaimed reflexively but reached for the volume knob without giving him a chance to do as I asked.

"Underground victim-sheltering network—" the radio scratched out through static. I quickly found the frequency for the clearest sound and listened with rising dread. "Kansas attacked. Dozens dead in 'safe house' slaughter."

"No...." The word escaped me as if it was squeezed from my chest by a vice. I froze, immediately thinking of Anna. It couldn't be her safe house. That was impossible! The organization I dropped her off at moved victims several times before they finally found a place for them. There was no way Slick could've found her.

They couldn't even tell *me* where Anna was.

# Chapter 11
## HENDRIX

The drive itself was rough with Maya needing to stop every hour to make calls, hoping to find out more about her sister. After the fifth, frustratingly futile hour of uncertainty, I was finally able to convince her that her best bet was to make it to her aunt's place and the safe-deposit box as quickly as possible. It took some time to convince her, but after a while, she relaxed enough not to be utterly wrecked with concern over her sister, and we talked about some lighter and more irrelevant topics.

Despite the desperate air of worry that hung over us like pregnant storm clouds, I loved stealing some time with Maya. It was the only thing that made those endless fucking desert roads, consisting of a vanishing point in front and behind and nothing else in between, bearable. There were some mountains on the horizon, but they were so far ahead they might as well have been on another planet.

I drove until I damned near passed out.

Maya offered to drive, but even she didn't have much stamina. She did her best to stay awake and keep me company, though.

A collision in Utah delayed us to the degree that we had to spend the night in the car somewhere along the highway in Nevada.

The following day was much easier. Once I got her rolling, it was hard to keep up with the conversation at certain parts. Maya was such a smart girl, a hell of a lot smarter than I ever was.

I had hung out with rough-and-tumble thugs most of my life, so stimulating conversation was hard to come by. Hearing words with more than one or two syllables pour over me... she was like a cool glass of water, and goddamn if I wasn't thirsty.

We talked about anything and everything—hobbies, interests, past experiences, even favorite positions. The more she talked, the more there was to like about her. The chord that struck me the loudest was what she said about her family. All the shit about her scumbag father made me really understand her mistrust of the MC lifestyle.

We had to stop for gas about an hour away from Maya's aunt's house in San Fran. Before pumping gas, I took the opportunity to buy and activate a pay-by-the-minute burner phone then followed up with the contact I had found while calling around at Benny and Agatha's place. With my club dead, there was only one group I could turn to that might actually be of any help—the Steel Veins MC proper.

It took some time, but I finally obtained the number to the new national chapter that had relocated to Leslie, Ohio. I was hoping to get ahold of the big man in charge and explain what was going on, but all roads led to Remy's ol' lady, a woman by the name of Star.

My first impressions? Star was sharp, fiery as hell, and quick to put me in my place when I told her I'd only talk to Remy.

"I want to make it perfectly clear," Star harangued like an unapproachable mother hen. "You've reached the top of the food chain, Hendrix. Remy and I work as a team. The only place left to go is down if you don't mind your words very carefully."

"Well, hell…." I rested the back of my head against the outside convenience store wall I had been leaning against. "All right, then. Let me catch you up to speed."

Star was guarded and skeptical when I started telling her everything that went down between the Coffin Eaters, the Lost Wild Boys, the Legion, and the Hangers but only really perked up when I mentioned Slick and his splinter faction of the Steel Veins. When I told her how Slick—and by extension, the Steel Veins—had probably been the one who had massacred that underground safe house, Star became extremely quiet.

"Those motherfuckers…." Star couldn't keep the disgust from her voice. "I was wondering why we hadn't heard back from St. Louis. There's been some trouble getting a few chapters on board with the changing of the corrupt old guard."

"I don't know if you can do anything, but there's a scared teenager being held hostage in Slick's new club somewhere. We can't go to the police—"

"You won't have to," Star was quick to reply. "It's our mess now. We'll handle it. If what you're saying is true, Remy will want to go pay Slick a *personal* visit."

"Handle it how?" I asked cautiously. The last thing I wanted was to put Maya's kid sister in someone else's crosshairs. "Anna had nothing to do with this."

"We're not that kind of club, not anymore. Remy saw to that personally." There was a pause as if she was caught off guard by my genuine concern about them killing to clean up any loose ends. "Keep our number, Hendrix. If you're looking for a place to land when this is all over, let us know. We might have an opening for a guy like you."

"Appreciate the offer." I chuckled, which then ended like a sigh. "But I've spent every waking moment since I've been out of prison trying to get out of the MC life. All I'm interested in now is freedom."

"That's fair." There was a knowing tease in her voice as if she'd tasted the freedom I was after and found it wasn't all that it was cracked up to be. "Well, if freedom gets too lonely for you, let us know."

"I guess we'll see. One train wreck at a time," I replied with a short air snort. That was whether we even made it through this adventure without getting killed or arrested. I thought about asking Star to send us some backup, but adding more bikers to this party was just going to get the cops called on us that much quicker. It was better to keep a low profile, especially if we were going to be heading to some banks.

"Oh, hey! One last thing!" I couldn't help myself. I just

had to know. "All the rumors of Remy coming back from the dead, fending off a kill team, and tearing apart the Lobos, that's all bullshit, right?"

"You'll have to ask him yourself." Star just laughed, again with that tantalizing allure in her voice.

This now made me wonder what the hell Remy and Star's story was. Who knew? If I stayed out of jail and the grave long enough, maybe I could ask them in person.

Feeling a little better about Anna's situation, if nothing else, I filled the car with gas from the pump, then laid my arm and head on the roof of the vehicle. It had been a long haul, but for better or worse, the end of all this was just around the corner.

The pump dinged and slowed to a crawl before stopping at the prepaid amount. I picked my head up, and I was back in the present. I could see Maya browsing the aisles inside through the convenient store's large windows and open floor plan. Man, I could watch her forever.

Maya was much stronger than she originally thought, although I thought she was finally starting to see that now. All the shit that girl had been through, and I thought I had it rough. I'd known a lot of men who weren't half as durable as that sweet thing. And here I was, completely incapable of taking my eyes off her. I tried to think of the rest of my life without this woman, but it was like dreaming in black and white and trying to imagine color.

I knew she cared about me or else she wouldn't have nearly crashed into a bus to get me. That made this ending that much more bittersweet. She'd been trying to escape the conclusion of this trip, pushing it from her mind and focusing on the tiny moments of time we actually had left.

I was envious. All I could think of was the end and how impossible it would be to have to let her go. I didn't know how I would find it in me to do it. I walked away from her once, and that took everything I had in terms of physical and emotional strength. This time, it just might kill me.

Seeing her face light up when she saw me watching her leave the building was the twist of a beautiful knife. It made all the thoughts of joining the Steel Veins dissipate like cigarette smoke.

*If we're looking for a place to land....* Who was I kidding? We were heading into a major metropolitan city with cameras and eyewitnesses and live streaming on every corner. One way or another, landing anywhere didn't seem likely.

I doubted I'd ever see the ground again.

It was selfish of me to come with her. I should have forced her to leave Utah without me. All I was doing was stealing time and making it harder to eventually part ways. Whether she found what she was looking for or not, the cops would have to be involved at some point, and that was the point at which I would have to leave her.

I was willing to die for Maya, but I didn't have it in me to be locked in a cage again. I just couldn't.... I could either leave her of my own accord or leave her in a body bag. Either way, we both knew there was no future for the likes of us. It had been a few days since I checked in with my parole officer, so the cops would've found out that I had jumped bail by now. With all the bodies that I'd dropped on the way here, I must have at least one murder charge going, God knew what else.

There was no saving me now.

"I grabbed us some snacks. They even had caramel Cadbury eggs!" Maya exclaimed proudly.

I pushed the cloud of hurt away. It wouldn't do Maya any good to worry her. "You're braver than I am. Easter was a long time ago, and I doubt those are preorders," I joked. Humor had always eased the pain. I glanced away and hung up the nozzle. I couldn't look at her yet if I wanted to sell it as just a joke. She'd probably see through it if she saw my face. "You grab anything that wouldn't survive a nuclear holocaust?"

"I don't care. I love these things. If this is what kills me, I'll at least have died happy." Maya saw my souring expression and laughed before continuing on. "Don't worry. I called my aunt this morning, and she said she'd make us lunch. I also told her what happened to Robbie, and that apparently reminded her that my mother sent her a document before she disappeared. Aunt Gina looked at it once, but that was a long time ago and she couldn't remember what it said, but maybe it might help us get access to the safe-deposit box."

"That's good," I replied, weathering the sting that came with the mention of my dead friend. His loss was hitting me in waves once again. Sometimes I felt completely fine, and other times, I wanted to break down and bawl my eyes out.

"Are we almost ready?" Maya cleared her throat and

smiled with sad, concerned eyes, trying to pull me out of my sudden depression. "I didn't mean to—"

"It's cool. Gotta deal with it one way or another." I returned her smile. Seeing her soft, warm face helped me get my weakness under control. It was funny how she could be my weakness and my strength at the same time. "I gotta go stretch my legs first. Come with me."

The rest stop was built along the top of a range of rolling hills and had a fantastic view, overlooking yet another clash of urban/suburban sprawl. Maya told me it was the southern part of the city of Berkeley, but that didn't mean a damn thing to me. The parking lot had a five-foot-tall foundation cinder block wall surrounding it, but when I had peered over it earlier, I discovered that it was really a ten-foot-tall retaining wall from the viewpoint of the other side. Live oak and knobby-coned pine trees dotted both sides along the barrier with intermittent, flowering bushes demonstrating a riot of purples, blues, and reds. I found an easy spot to climb over and drop down between the vegetation on the retaining side of the wall for some privacy and a better look at the scenic vista.

"It's so pretty. I think I'm beginning to like cities better from afar," she murmured in awe.

"The forest for the trees...." I didn't give a shit about the view. Maya was the only thing I wanted to see. The sun filtered through her lashes and played off her russet-colored eyes that shone so brilliantly.

"Hey, I just talked to a new friend in the Steel Veins' new national chapter, a woman by the name of Star. I think you'd like her." I went on to tell Maya everything about the conversation. No more secrets.

"Oh, thank God!" Maya sighed with relief. We didn't know what, if anything, actually happened to Anna, but it was a good feeling knowing that there was someone out there looking for her. "Do you think we can trust them?"

"I think so. Everyone I've talked to recently said that Remy and Star are the real deal." I couldn't speak in absolutes, but I did have a good feeling about them now that I had talked to Star. If even half the rumors were true, then I was right about Remy being a real devil. It was the side that devil was fighting for that I had all wrong.

Maybe the Steel Veins really had changed?

She soured a bit, darkness spreading across her thoughts. With the end in sight just beyond the foothills of the range, I knew she was finding it hard to ignore the fact that the trip was almost at its end.

"What happens when this is all o—" She couldn't stop herself from asking the inevitable questions, so I stopped her by filling her lips with mine.

I didn't want to hear the words out loud despite us both feeling the acrid rush of finality breathing down the backs of our necks. The kiss was supposed to allow us one last escape from reality, but it turned into the bursting of an already buckling dam. Neither of us could pass up this last embrace. If this truly was the end, then I needed one last taste of her, something to warm my heart on those cold nights to come.

When she wrapped her arms around my neck and kissed me back furiously, the constant din of the rest stop's traffic and commotion melted away. All that was left in the world was Maya and me.

I picked her up and pinned her against the cinder block wall. Our lips broke apart but only for short, staggered intervals, just long enough to start ripping each other's clothes off. I pulled her shirt and bra over her head in one swift motion before lightly pressing her bare back against the concrete again. I ran my hands over her shoulders, tits, and stomach, feeling her core heat up. She clawed at the zipper of my hoodie, stripping me out of it, then the shirt, too, with a relentless urgency to it all. This wasn't simmering foreplay to explore our limits and reach the depths of pleasure. This was desperate. We tore at each other like animals.

This was the flash boil of passion before a fall.

So singularly focused on who could divest each other of one's clothing first, we barely looked at one another. I kissed her lips then her neck, letting my searching hands do the rest of the work. Her stomach tightened and arched backward as I grabbed her side tightly and pulled her into me.

Maya gyrated and seized my back and chest like a madwoman. She was completely into this moment without any more hesitations as her inhibitions had since withered and died off completely. I could wreck her, and she'd let me.

I stole a glimpse at her small, light olive-skinned hand clawing across my tattoos and scars just to grab a matted fistful of my chest hair. The innocence of her features and the sting of pulled hair made my cock swell. Maya was perfect.

Her fingertips rounded the hardening length of my cock.

She popped and parted the metal teeth of my jean's zipper then tucked her cool fingers into the elastic band of my briefs. I felt the released heat of my crotch roll up between her fingers.

"Me first," I teased as I slid both hands into the back of her pants and wrenched everything down. Maya's eyes flashed at the quick motion, and she was jerked forward when I got her pants and panties over her ass. Smiling, she suppressed her provoked squeak. I paused for a moment, drinking in the sight of her tiny slit. I let my eyes creep up along her smooth, eager body. Voraciousness consumed my gaze when I finally found her eyes. This would be the only reprieve she'd get from my appetite.

I slipped off one of her tennis shoes and yanked the pants off one leg, allowing her jeans to dangle from the other. Then I threw both her legs over me to straddle my neck, the bent of her knees resting on each shoulder. She bit the corner of her lip, her eyes flaring again as if to say *Oh my God! Is he really going to….*

I smiled. Yes, I was. I lifted her off the ground and gently rested her back on the gray, retaining wall. I needed to stand up for this, using my whole body to eat her delectable pussy. I closed my teeth on her thigh, causing her pelvis to quiver. I could tell she was a little embarrassed about not being shaved, but it was fine with me. I didn't mind it a little wild.

Then it occurred to me. A sweet girl like Maya... "Have you ever had a man go down on you before?" She bit more of her lip and shook her head. If I didn't have my head buried between her legs, she would have noted the triumphant grin plastered on my face. "You are in for a treat. Just try to hang on."

My tongue drew lines everywhere but her pussy. I could see her lower lips glisten in the sun. She was wet and ready for me. She dragged her fingers through my scalp, grabbing tufts of hair in her needy fists. Before long, she was pulling me toward her rather than pushing me away. Not that it mattered. I went at my own pace, but I could tell it was driving her crazy.

My tongue slithered over her slit before finding and spreading each and every one of her folds and ridges. She gasped, her legs taut cords, her heels digging into my back. I abruptly stopped at random intervals and waited for her hips to buck. When her body screamed for more, I gave it to her.

I did circuits with my tongue around her engorged clit, tickling her nub then plunging it into her pussy. She pulsed, already so close to coming. I nibbled and pulled, my teeth lightly catching her hood before wrapping my mouth around it and sucking. She sank her nails into me and moaned, stifling back each building scream with a gasp instead.

She almost swooned when I touched her soaked pussy lips with the tips of my fingers. I slowly pushed them inside of her, just clearing my first knuckle when I found her G-spot. She came at its slightest touch, her legs extending out like TV antennae. Thighs squeezed around my head and neck as the orgasm erupted from her like an exorcism.

Maya groaned loudly. Oblivious motorists came and went, children whined, parents shouted. Who knew what they heard from this side of the wall? Neither of us cared.

To us, they didn't exist. It might as well have been the Great Wall of China that separated us from them.

Maya's whole body rocked, her limbs shattered from the ongoing aftershocks. I carefully eased her back down as she slumped against the wall and rode it to her knees. "That was.... I… I.... Wow. I just…."

I wiped her juices from my chin and beard and smiled at her, letting her regain her composure. "You gonna make it… this time?"

"Asshole." Maya's eyes flared with disbelief that I would bring up the motel rooftop again. I was trying to rile her up, and from the crack in the defiant smirk on her face, it looked like I had succeeded. She roughly grabbed my cock through my briefs. "I'll survive."

It took both of her small hands to get a handle on my hard-on. Her indignation and confidence got me stiff enough that she could swing from it. Yet she didn't have any of my restraint. My pants and briefs didn't make it down to my knees before she was licking and stroking my cock. She foolishly attempted to take too much of me in right away and choked. I didn't want her to feel embarrassed at her amateur technique, so I grabbed her hand and worked it rhythmically over my tip. When I let go, she kept going. "Squeeze," I urged.

She did.

"Harder. With both hands. Strangle me."

So she did just that. The pressure felt great. I knew what I wanted and wasn't afraid to make demands.

"I want you to suck me and jerk me off. Stay near the head."

She followed my orders as I plunged my hard cock as deeply as I could into her mouth. She sucked and squeezed, now with greater confidence.

"Faster!"

She squeezed even tighter, picking up the tempo. My dick swelled within her mouth. I was close. She felt it, too, and jerked me faster, her lips smacking as she whipped her head back and forth. I was right on the cusp.

I rolled my head back and groaned as I exploded into the back of her throat, my cock pulsing like shotgun blasts. She slowed her motion as she tried to swallow all my cum. I didn't think she could handle it, but before I knew it, she was milking me, sucking me clean.

I exhaled, dragging a hand through her scalp. I pulled out and leaned back into the retaining wall behind me. Goddamn, that was good.

"Come here." I motioned for her to join me. When she got within arm's reach, I pulled her into me. Our sweaty bodies slapped together, and I hugged her. I'd never been much into cuddling, but I felt like if I let her go, I would never get her back.

"I don't want this to be over, Hendrix. Can we stay on this hillside forever?"

"I don't see why not."

*  *  *  *  *

"I think this is it." There was hesitance in her voice. She hadn't been there since she was a kid, well before her sister was born. "Two twenty-six. Yeah, this is it. Just park along the street. If we need to move it, she'll tell us."

Maya jumped out of the car. She was so excited but also a little nervous because she had only met her Aunt Gina twice in person, although they talked occasionally on the phone and through Facebook. The neighborhood was nice enough—a lot of brightly colored, single-family homes. Being that it was the middle of a weekday, there weren't many people around.

I didn't know if it was the distrustful glances by the few passersby that were around or if it was just me looking for something that wasn't there, but I had a bad feeling about this place. My gut told me something was off, but I could be just looking for trouble because it was what I was most comfortable with. Yet actually being here meant that it was real, that I'd have to give up Maya sooner than I wanted to. I couldn't outrun or outgun the inevitability of the feeling. One way or another, it was all coming to a close.

Maya frowned at me. "You promised you'd at least come in with me. Don't tell me you're—"

"No." I smiled, recovering myself. "I'm coming."

Maya saw me tuck the gun in the back waistband of my jeans. "Would you mind leaving that in the car?" she quietly requested. "Aunt Gina said she always hated guns. She... ever since Mom disappeared, she...." Maya smiled, took a quick breath, and started all over again. "She blames my dad for what happened to my mom. Aunt Gina hates bikers as much as I... did."

"You sure you don't want me to stay in the car until we go to the bank?" I sat back down in the driver's seat and discreetly slid the gun under it.

"No, it would be too weird to bring lunch out to my bad-ass chauffeur. Besides, I'm a little nervous, and I'm braver when I'm with you." She gave me a look that could melt iron.

"Chauffeur, huh?" I mulled it over, thinking about Benny and Agatha. There was only so much hospitality I could endure. But Maya gazed at me with those big, rusty-brown eyes of hers. I hated how quickly those were becoming my weakness. So I shrugged, giving in. "Lead the way, Miss Daisy."

Maya grabbed my hand and led me briskly to the front door before letting go to knock. No answer. We could hear the TV on, so Aunt Gina was probably home. Maya knocked again. Still nothing. Aunt Gina was expecting us, so it was odd that she didn't answer. That uneasy feeling returned in spades. There were dozens of explanations that could explain her not answering, so I forcibly convinced myself I was just being paranoid.

Maya tried the doorknob and found it unlocked. She opened it slowly, revealing that the living room and first-floor bathroom were visible and empty. "Hello? Aunt Gina? It's Maya. Are you home?"

The TV must have been blasting in a room down the hall. Maya shrugged and walked in. "Maybe she's exercising?"

I remained quiet and scanned for any signs of a break-in or foul play. There were some boot marks and tracked-in dirt in an otherwise immaculate house, but nothing else appeared out of place. The lack of a presence was odd, but maybe Maya's Aunt Gina was a fitness nut and wanted to squeeze in a session before we got here. A little weird, but this was San Francisco, after all. Appearances and trends were king out here.

I felt the vibration of a scuffle through the floorboards from a room beyond my view. Something heavy or someone hit the floor, and that's when I knew something was definitely wrong. I was wary before, but now I was certain. I grabbed Maya's arm just before she reached the closed door down the hall. When she tried to jerk away from me, I shook my head and started to bodily drag her back toward the front door.

This house wasn't safe. I needed to get her out of there immediately. My plan was to stash Maya in the car, grab my gun, and head back in. I'd have her drive a few blocks away if she didn't see me leave the house in ten minutes. Then she would find the burner phone in the glove compartment and call the cops. By that time, I'd either be gone or dead.

We hadn't made it to the door before my plans went up like kindling.

"Stop."

I didn't recognize the voice, but I knew exactly who it was by the way Maya tensed up like she was flash-frozen.

It was her father.

Three armed men rounded the corner, one of them dragging a woman who was tied to a chair. This had to be Maya's Aunt Gina.

Slick's splinter MC organization was probably too new for them to have official symbols yet, but that didn't stop them from a uniform improvisation. They all wore the traditional leather Steel Veins vests, but the Steel part of all the patches was removed. In its place in bold white marker was the work "BROKEN" and a white skull over a large X had been drawn over the existing back patch.

The message they wanted to get across was pretty clear: *The Steel Veins are dead, and we're what killed them.*

Maya had overheard correctly. Slick and his crew had completely broken away from their host club. If he really was putting together an army of bitter, pissed-off, and morally destitute bikers, Remy, Star, and the rest of the Steel Veins had a much bigger threat on their hands than they may know.

"Lock the door," Slick ordered one of his guys.

I pushed thoughts of the Steel Veins from my attention. I didn't have the luxury of thinking beyond this room. Small number of guys, no bikes out front, and everyone wore black riding gloves to protect their fingerprints. It was clear what these Broken Veins were here to do.

This wasn't going to end well for us.

One of Slick's enforcers brushed past us, locked the door, then patted us down. "They're clean."

"Set them up in the kitchen," Slick snarled. "And tie his fucking hands up. No surprises."

There was no greeting to his daughter in any way. He was so detached from her that if I didn't know better, I'd think he had never seen her before. It was a sad thing to see a father write off his own daughter so completely, which only meant that he wouldn't think twice about killing Maya when it came down to it.

The shades in the kitchen that adorned the sliding patio door had already been drawn, preventing anyone from seeing inside. Aunt Gina and her chair were placed near the kitchen counter. She appeared frightened, as would anyone, but she mostly just glared at Slick angrily. Given what Maya told me about Aunt Gina's outlook on bikers and specifically about her views of Slick, I could tell that hers was a rage that had smoldered for quite a long while.

Slick grabbed an apple and a knife off the linoleum countertop then leaned against the counter where he began peeling the fruit. "Your sister says 'Hi'."

"If you've hurt Anna...." Maya's voice was shaky, but there was an unmistakable edge to her tone. She'd become a person not to take lightly.

"You'll what?" he asked, calmly sliding the knife underneath the skin of the apple, letting it fall to the floor in ribbons.

Maya said nothing but held his gaze defiantly.

"We both know I've never had a damn thing to worry about from you," Slick continued after a sharp, mean laugh. "You tried taking Anna from me legally then *illegally*, and you failed both times."

"How?" Maya spat.

"How did I find her?" Slick casually popped out the core of the apple. "Well… I got a little lucky. You see, I got eyes everywhere. When I put up a one-hundred-K reward, those eyes got *reeeeaal* chatty. One trail led to the driver that shuttled Anna to a lonely little house way out in Speerville, Kansas."

I clenched my jaw and glanced at the floor a moment, reflecting on all the people Slick had murdered to get Anna out of that safe house. The radio said it had been a bloodbath. It wasn't a state- or federal-funded operation, so any kind of reasonable security force wasn't involved at all. All those battered women and their children had no one to call for help.

No one even found the bodies until a full day after it happened.

"When are you going to learn, you little traitorous bitch?" Slick pointed the knife at Maya and sneered. "Anna is *my* property. *I OWN HER.*"

Maya bit her tongue, probably not wanting to let on that the real Steel Veins were actively on the hunt for Anna. If Remy was half as cunning as the rumors said he was, he'd find Anna in no time.

"What really disgusts me about you, Maya, isn't that you tried to take my property from me. Stupid fuckers try that all the time." Slick chuckled sardonically. "No. What really disgusts me is that you *failed*." He walked across the room and grabbed Maya roughly by her cheeks, eyes boiling with hatred. He lowered his face to hers and screamed, *"Merritts don't fucking fail!"*

He let her go only to backhand her to the floor. I called out in protest and received a heavy right hand to the stomach by one of his men restraining me. It knocked the wind out of me to the point that breathing was an active chore.

"I know about the safe-deposit box." Slick stood up and let the bloated silence suffocate the room as he walked slowly around her. After over a full minute, he finally continued. "When my little girl disappeared, I tore her room apart, looking for signs of where she went. That's when I found a letter from the bank. Apparently they sent a few. So what did your mom and your poor, dead Uncle Robbie put in there, huh?"

"I don't know!" Maya retorted, wincing through the pain and the split lip. "It might not be anything but baby photos."

"But it might be something." He carved off a chunk of the apple and ate it. It was an intimidation tactic and a good one too. He wanted us to see just how relaxed and in control he was. That he held all the advantages here. "And that's why I want you to go get it."

"What? The bank is closing, and you still want me to get it?"

"When a bank closes, unclaimed property goes to the state. I don't want 'might be nothing' to turn into 'a pain in my ass.'"

"No," Maya flatly stated. "I won't do anything for you."

Slick put down the knife and apple then ripped off a paper towel from a nearby roll, cleaning his hands and mouth. He studied her quietly and sighed. Then he drew out his gun and shot me in the thigh.

"Hendrix!" Maya screamed.

I grunted and fell sideways to the floor, refusing to cry out to give him the satisfaction. The pain was searing, but I was no stranger to being shot, so I, at least, knew what to expect. Fortunately the bullet must have passed right through my leg, which meant I might be able to avoid going to a hospital and the inevitable police bust for violating my parole... but that was only if I made it out of this alive.

"Seems you two have grown attached to each other. That's nice. I'll tell you right now, though, you shouldn't get involved with bikers. They're bad news," Slick teased then raised the gun to fire again.

"Stop it!" Maya stepped in front of me.

"You think I'm fooling around?" Slick arched an eyebrow when she wouldn't step aside to give him a clear shot. He glanced beyond her to his guy and cocked his head to have her dragged, kicking and screaming, off to the side. Now Slick had the line of sight on me that he wanted. There was nothing in arm's reach for me to grab. I couldn't move faster than he could fire, and he was a damn good shot to begin with.

"Okay! You win! I'll go!" She broke away from the biker's grip.

"I know." Slick relaxed his gun and motioned her away with it. "Because Merritts don't fucking lose."

She stubbornly resisted, not wanting to leave me and her aunt and probably fearing that she would never see us alive again.

"It's all right." I controlled my breathing and barked the words through the pain. I had to convince her to leave. There was no point in pissing her father off if she was going to be forced out anyway. "Do what he says."

Maya worriedly exhaled. Yes, she really was afraid that Slick might shoot me again. I knew better. He was too smart to kill off his hostages until he had what he wanted.

After he got that box, though, he was too smart to leave any witnesses alive.

"Go with her." Slick motioned to one of his minions. "If it looks like she's doing anything aside from getting that box, you call me."

"Copy," the enforcer agreed and forced Maya toward the door.

"Wait. You won't be able to get that box without this!" Slick reminded her just before the front door opened. Maya faced him, bemused, and he shoved a folded document into her stomach until she reluctantly took it and unfolded it. "Your mom, the clever bitch she was, apparently had paperwork drawn up giving you power of attorney over her estate when you reached the age of twenty-one."

"She must've known even then what a pile of shit you were," Maya sneered, glancing up from the letter.

"And how'd that end for her?" Slick roughly grabbed the corner of her mouth tightly with his burly fingers, drawing her close to him so his eyes were all that she saw. "If you so much as cough suspiciously, I'll put your boyfriend down like a dog. You hear me?"

Maya slowly nodded, her steely-eyed gaze never leaving him. She wasn't afraid of him anymore, but she was worried about what might happen to me and her aunt.

"Good. Get 'er outta here." Slick turned and strolled back into the kitchen.

Maya flashed me a concerned look on her way out. I smiled, trying to ease her fears. It was best she focused on getting that box. On the drive here, she had expressed concern that Robbie never told her the pin number that would unlock it. It wasn't something I could help her with, but I had faith in her that she'd figure it out.

Somehow....

Once Maya was gone, the strategy of the Broken Veins that remained was to guard us or trash the place. Slick opened the fridge and knocked a bunch of stuff onto the floor while another Broken Vein smashed Aunt Gina's flat-screen TV over his knee and flipped over her vintage kitchen table, making this mess look like a robbery gone wrong. Aunt Gina winced with each loud crash, but she breathed forcefully and glared at Slick with utter contempt. That was when I noticed that her struggling was loosening her binds. *She might be able to slip her hands free soon.*

*Wait,* I silently mouthed the word to her when she discovered me watching her efforts.

At the moment, Slick's two remaining men were too spread out, so if they caught her anywhere but the chair, they would gun her down before she could do anything useful. If we were to survive and stop this asshole from hurting Maya, we had to work together. Aunt Gina imperceptibly nodded back at me. It was hard to know for certain if she was on board, but I hoped she'd figure out what I was up to and would follow my lead.

Slick kept a vigilant eye on both of us as his guy went to the other rooms to spread the devastation and steal any valuables. Almost an hour later, the phone in Slick's pocket rang, and he answered. "Go ahead." Slick whistled for his guy in the other room to come back into the kitchen. "Good.

Run into any trouble?... Okay. C'mon back." He then hung up. "Wrex, wrap that shit up. They're on their way—"

"Bruce Merritt," I interrupted Slick, letting the words linger in the air. I wanted him to know that I knew exactly who he was. I wanted all their attention on me. I slumped against the wall and played up my leg wound so that I made myself appear weakened, suffering the effects of serious blood loss.

He smugly sauntered over, raised his eyebrows, and spread his hands out in an expression that said *well?*

"I gotta know, man... did you have your brother Robbie killed because you knew you couldn't control him or because he could fuck your wife better than you could?" I watched his fair-skinned face flush scarlet with anger. So that's where Maya got that adorable trait from.

"Do you have any idea who the fuck you're talking to?" Wrex entered the room and was astonished that I would dare insult the president of the newly established Broken Veins.

"Robbie told me this story about his brother. How when Brucie here was a kid, he used to rub peanut butter all over his dick just so that the dog would lick it off!" I laughed painfully, ignoring this peon's question, while I exaggerated the difficulty in getting the words out. Truthfully, my leg *was* in rough shape, but for this to work, I really had to sell it.

I had no idea if it was true, but I wasn't about to let honesty get in my way. After all, I was talking to Slick's guys, not him. It was a great story, and it seemed to be doing exactly what I'd hoped it would. Slick fumed at my insolence and swiftly rewarded me with a punch to the jaw. The blow dropped me to the floor, and I wasn't faking my struggle to sit back up. I must have struck a nerve.

"It's a much better story knowing that he was talking about you," I sputtered, offering him a bloody grin.

Slick punched me again, only this time even harder. He grabbed my hair and jerked me up, jamming the muzzle of his gun right between my eyes. "My brother is dead because *I said so!* What do you think I'd do to some jerkoff I don't even know?"

"You could ask your guys to check the refrigerator for some peanut butter. All this rough play has got my cock rock-hard."

He thrust the gun even harder against my skull, striving to intimidate me, but I knew he wasn't going to kill me… at least not until Maya returned.

I covertly glanced beyond him and discovered Aunt Gina had slipped one of her hands free, but it wasn't time yet. Fortunately, neither of them were paying any attention to her efforts because I wanted all eyes on me. Slick's second minion was still too far away, while Wrex was hanging back, watching his boss beat the shit out of me. I needed him closer. I subtly shook my head, hoping she'd hold off just a little longer.

We were only getting one chance at this.

One of my teeth was loose enough that I was able to dig it out with my tongue and catch it between my teeth. Bloody drool oozed from my mouth into my beard as I smiled at Slick and spat the toothy projectile directly into his eye.

Slick howled and jerked away, stuffing his gun into his belt before scooping the gore from his face. Then, half blind and fed up, he screamed his rage and relentlessly kicked me. I doubled over to shield myself as much as possible, but it would never be enough, especially with my hands bound behind my back. My body rocked with each heavy blow from his steel-toed boots, and there was no doubt in my mind that he had cracked a few ribs.

"Hey, ponytail!" I coughed up the words while fighting down waves of excruciating pain that strangled my body. He even got a few well-aimed kicks to my head, and steel-toed boots were no joke. I was on the verge of blacking out, but I couldn't let up. "You wanna show peanut butter dick here how it's done? This is—" I cleared my throat, hocked up phlegm and coagulated blood, took a breath, and continued. "This is getting embarrassing."

"Wrex! Get him up!" Slick shouted as his control invariably disintegrated.

Wrex finally squeezed past Aunt Gina, grabbed my dead weight, and forced me into a kneeling position. My body ached, varying from dull numbing in my limbs to sharp stabbings in my chest whenever I breathed. Now I nodded toward Aunt Gina, only hoping she had it in her to do what was necessary when the time came, otherwise we were both fucked.

"I wanted Maya to see this, but she'll just have to find your body instead." Slick unsheathed his gun from his pants waistline.

"Please, please don't do this, Slick! I'm so sorry!" I

thrashed and pleaded loudly, making a show out of it. It must have worked because they didn't notice Aunt Gina grabbing Slick's apple-carving knife off the counter and cutting her leg bonds free.

"Die with some fucking dignity, Jesus Christ!" Slick was obviously disgusted at my pitiful groveling. He quickly checked the magazine on his gun to make sure that it was loaded then aimed it at my chest, nodding to Wrex who edged aside. "In the end, that's all we really have."

*Any time now, Aunt Gina! Stab the motherfucker!* Unfortunately, she was struggling with the rope. *Shit!* She wouldn't make it in time, and he was just out of my reach. I'd never be able to stop him. Well, it had been a good plan. Too bad it didn't work.

My last thought was of Maya.

# Chapter 12
## MAYA

"Looks like you made it in the nick of time," responded the cheerful, blonde lady when I told her that I was here for my safe-deposit box. Glancing up at me from some paperwork on her desk, she gasped at my cleaned-up but freshly swollen lip. Aside from that, I still had a number of injuries from the past few days. "Oh dear! Your face! Are you all right?"

"Oh? Yeah...." I glanced at the biker who stood a few feet away and was analyzing every word I said. "I, uh, I'm an amateur boxer. Just had a fight last night. You should see the other girl."

"Oh. Okay...." The blonde rose from behind her desk in her open cubicle and shook our hands tentatively, more out of habit than desire. Her face quickly returned to its default of all bright and practiced smiles.

I handed her the power of attorney paperwork and my driver's license while explaining the situation as best I could without implicating any foul play. It was a bit of storytelling gymnastics about me being her own personal assistant as she was quite the recluse, but I got her caught up well enough to get her to take me to the vault.

"Just meet me right by that door, and I'll show you to your box." The bank officer strode off to inform her manager that she would be taking someone to the vault, which appeared to be company policy.

Slick's biker trailed me like a shadow as I headed over to wait for her. He had been forced to leave his gun in the rental car so he would not draw additional attention, but he made it crystal clear to me that if he had to pull out his phone regarding anything suspicious, people would die.

"Do you have a box as well, sir?" the animated lady kindly asked the Broken Vein when she returned.

"Uh, no, but I'm her husband, so I'll head in with her," he replied gruffly.

"Oh, I am so sorry. Only customers with boxes can enter the vault. Bank policy, you know." The lady squinted and shrugged in an overly apologetic gesture, then immediately brightened back up when she asked me for my license again. I fished it out of my pocket and handed it to her. Once again, she carefully reread my demographics, but I suspected she might have accidentally forgotten my name already. "Right this way, please, Mrs. Merritt."

I followed her through the office door and down the short hallway to the giant, rounded, metal door. It was open, pressed against the adjoining wall, and it was absolutely massive. Its rings and gears must have weighed more than my car. I'd never seen one like this in person, and I was immediately reminded of the many bank heist movies I've watched in the past. The small room beyond it was lined floor-to-ceiling with removable metal drawers with a small table in the middle. A concrete-and-iron tomb for untold riches.

The smartly dressed woman approached one of the many drawers on the sidewall and inserted its master key in the lock. With a series of clockwise and counterclockwise turns, she unlocked the drawer revealing the locked safe-deposit box inside. She grabbed the thick handle and pulled the long yet flattened safe-deposit box out of its shelf. Placing it on the viewing table, she gestured me over. "Don't worry. I won't hover." She giggled, having mastered the art of being overly bubbly while falling just shy of being patronizing. "We at SeaCoast Bank value our customers' privacy."

I glanced up at the room's cameras that were set into the walls and were hardly noticeable but, of course, were still there. *Privacy, right...* Not that I cared. In fact, I wanted less privacy.

I wished I could explain the situation to the bank official, but beyond her, all the way down the hallway and standing in the doorway, the Broken Vein watched me like a hawk. He wouldn't be able to hear what we were saying, but he would see the lady's reaction and know that I'd told her something terrifying. It was best that I kept the conversation as short as possible with her.

"When you've finished, just come right out and see me, and we'll box your contents. No rush. We're open for another hour." She was nice enough, but she also seemed like she was the type of person who enjoyed the tap-tap of her heels on the tile floor far too much. A showman with a stage but not much real substance to offer.

Whatever was in the safe-deposit box was heavy. I shook it slightly but couldn't get a gauge as to what could be hiding inside. I scolded myself for stalling and placed it back on the table. No more delays. Hendrix and Aunt Gina were depending on me to open this damn box, a box that I had no idea what the code was....

I positioned the box to the side of the table that was out of sight of the biker in the hallway as I wanted as much solitude from him as I could get. I needed to concentrate if I had any hope of unlocking this.

I tried to think like my mother. What could the combination be? What would she use? I tried all the birthdays I could remember. Mine and Anna's first. They didn't work, but I knew those would be too obvious. Even Slick, when pressed, could remember our birthdays… well, maybe. It had to be something else. I tried anniversaries and other important dates. The first and last four digits of our social security numbers, the first four of our zip codes, phone numbers, licenses, everything!

I took a step away from my nemesis, brimming with frustration.

The four-digit combination lock stared back at me, peering into my very soul as if to taunt me. If I survived long enough to ever sleep again, that brass-colored, number-printed, metal box would haunt my fucking dreams.

My hand grazed Robbie's pocket watch in my pocket that I had forgotten I still had on me. The epiphany erupted from my brain like a geyser. This had to be the key!

I tore it out of my pants pocket. It was a miracle that Slick's goon had let me keep it after he had frisked me. Well, I guess he was more interested in guns, knives, or cell phones.

I opened the watch and noticed the time had stopped. Had it somehow broken in the scuffle? Then I remembered Hendrix telling me that it looked like it had been damaged a long time ago. I peeled off the picture of my mom and sister. There had to be a code behind the picture—*there had to be!* It made so much sense that I could already see the handwritten digits in my mind. Why the hell else would Robbie carry a broken watch around?

When I finagled the picture out and those four desperately needed digits weren't there, I nearly screamed. *Where the fuck was it!* Why not just keep the picture in his wallet? None of this made any fucking sense.

Dread set in. I wouldn't be able to open it. I'd have to go back empty-handed. The anxiety was becoming too much to bear as the hyperventilation started. I thought of Hendrix shot in the head, lying on the ground, bleeding out all over my aunt's carpeting. All I could hear was the sound of my own heart frantically beating. All this was my fault, all of it! My hands trembled uncontrollably. This was all too much.

*The knob was broken off the pocket watch.* That one fact stuck out in my mind like a needle piercing through the mounting self-pity and panic. Why *would* Robbie keep it?

*Figure this out, Maya. You can do it.* It was my mother's voice I heard in my head this time. I calmed down and forced myself to think. *What was I missing?*

From what Hendrix told me, Robbie was ex-Army and was the type of person who hated being idle. He didn't strike me as the sentimental type. Sure, keep the picture, but the broken watch? He wouldn't have bothered.

I rolled it around in my hands. What was so special about this plain, metal, pocket watch? I'd never heard of the manufacturer, and if anything, it looked a little cheap. I started trying to figure what numbers correlated with what abbreviated letters for acronyms related to the words on its face. I also came up with a few number combinations for the periodic elements the watch was made of, but they didn't work when I tried them. Was I going about this the wrong way? It had to be something personal.

I propped my elbows on the table and stared at the broken timepiece. If he liked it so much, why wouldn't he have fixed it? Then I took a hard look at the time. It was stopped at...

The hands of the clock were set at 11:43. Wasn't that the time Anna was born? Then it hit me like a freight train as everything fell into place.

Oh my God. Uncle Robbie wasn't just Mom's lover....

In a stupor, I tried the number. *Click.* The locking mechanism released immediately. Holy fucking shit! It worked.

I slowly pulled back the lid and fumbled through the safe-deposit box's contents. It was all there, everything I hoped for. Records, pictures, descriptions of events. It was a wellspring of evidence. No wonder Slick wanted this so badly. This information was so damning, not just for him but for his whole chapter, maybe even the whole club. With this, I could take them apart.

Underneath everything, I discovered what was to be something of a love letter that read:

Amanda,

I hope to God you've been burning these. Bruce cannot know what we have planned. He's a fucking weasel, but the reach of the Steel Veins is some serious shit. I think we've got enough dirt on him that we'll be okay. Just make sure you put everything in a safe place, and no matter what, you can't tell me where. If things go bad... I don't want them to be able to get that info out of me.

I saw the girls the other day. Prettiest damn things in the world. They look just like you. I think about Anna all the time. I think about how we brought something that beautiful into the world. I never knew my heart could get so big... or hurt so damn much! Soon, I'll get to see my daughter grow up rsthand.

Maya's getting so big now too. She's so beautiful! It's the only good thing my brother has ever done. You're always saying that everything happens for a reason. Well, baby, maybe Maya was that reason. She's worth all of it, and I can't wait to get to know her when all of this is over.

It's almost over, baby. Just a few more weeks, and I'll have everything lined up, and you, me, and the girls can get far away from that shitbag and the Steel Veins. I just need a little more time.

I'm not very good at putting my feelings down on paper. But if that's the only way that we can talk right now, then I'll keep writing. Please be careful. I love you.

Always yours.
Robert

"P.S. Sorry about all the cursing. I know you hate it.

I carefully set the letter down. I must have started to cry at some point. That note was a lot to take in. Robbie was Anna's father? I guess I did know the truth but forced myself not to see it. There was no mistaking that Anna has Robbie's dimple on the same side of her face as his.

I imagined just how different my life would've been if their plan had worked. Growing up with a father who actually cared about me and my sister? Jesus, Anna would only have been a half sister, but that didn't matter to me. With Mom and Robbie, we'd have had a *real* family.

But their plan didn't work. They both wound up dead.

Now that monster, Slick, was threatening everything else that I held dear. I would die before I allowed him to hurt anyone else I loved. What I needed was a plan. I had to leave the bank a message somehow.

I quickly scanned the area, but, of course, there was nothing to write on or within this vault. I glanced up at the cameras and slowly mouthed as clearly as possible what the situation was, that I needed help, and what Aunt Gina's address was. It was all being recorded, but they might not check it until after the bank closed, if at all. By then, it would be too late.

No, I needed to leave a physical message as well, and for that, I needed something sharp enough to carve into the table. Unfortunately nothing in the box could help me, and I couldn't ask for a pen, or the biker would call Slick. I had to find a way to leave the message in here, but how?

I picked up the shabby pocket watch. This small chunk of cheap metal had been invaluable to me so far, and now it had one final thing to offer me. I snapped the watch cover off and tried to carve a message, but the table was too hard.

I sighed, turned my hand over, and looked at my palm. "Fuck...." There was only one other way to do this, yet it made me a little queasy just thinking about it. But I had no choice. I took a deep breath, pushed passed my hesitancy, then stabbed my palm with the jagged edge of the watch cover.

Blood beaded onto my hand, but it wouldn't be enough. I drew another deep breath and jabbed my hand again. My fingers twitched, but now the blood was flowing freely. I scrawled my aunt's address and the words *HELP ME*. I must have overdone it with the cut because the blood had yet to clot. I couldn't go out like this as the biker would immediately know that something had happened. I slipped one of my shoes off and grabbed a sock. It was kinda gross, but it was all I had at the moment. Fortunately, I was wearing ankle socks today, so I'd be able to hide it in my clenched fist easily enough. I just hoped the thin fabric would be sufficient to stop the bleeding.

Being that Slick wouldn't know how many documents were in the box originally, I took half that was there and shoved the other half back in the hole in the wall where my box belonged. Just in case something were to happen to them or to me, I'd made sure to leave enough incriminating evidence behind for the police to put that son of a bitch away for a long time.

The Broken Vein was waiting for me when I exited the vault empty-handed. He gave me a skeptical, searching look, which I ignored. Then he followed me over to see the same bank officer that had been helping me. I thanked her and asked her to wrap up everything in my box, which I left on the table in the vault. She removed a flattened cardboard form from her desk and folded it together into a box that was approximately the same size as my safe-deposit box. Then she hustled off, her heels tip-tapping down the hallway.

When she returned, her smile was slightly tarnished and she looked a little rattled, but nothing could shake her polished demeanor, and, of course, she was still as pleasant as ever. The bank officer handed me the box, and I could feel that it was still half full, so she'd only boxed up what was on the table and not what was in the hole. So far, so good.

"Thank you, Mrs. Merritt, for your patronage, and on behalf SeaCoast Bank, we're pleased to have been able to assist you. You two have a wonderful day," she stated, quickly returning to her practiced, bubbly cadence.

I thanked her again before the biker draped an arm over my shoulder and ushered me outside. On our way out, I saw the lady's happy, helpful façade fall away as she called the bank manager over to her cubicle. Now I could only hope that they would notify the police in time.

Once we were inside the rental, he grilled me on why it took so long. I explained to him that it wasn't my box to begin with and that it was my mother's, and that I had a lot of trouble figuring out the pin number—all of which was true. "You saw that I didn't talk to anyone inside," I retorted unhappily.

He regarded me skeptically for a second then pulled out his phone to call Slick.

"Wait! I told you the truth. I—"

But apparently, he totally ignored me. "We got it," the Broken Vein spoke into his smartphone. "All set, bro." He slid the gun out from underneath the seat and placed it on his lap, the muzzle uncomfortably facing me. The creep studied my face carefully. I thought he was deciding how to answer a question that Slick asked. "No, everything's fine." The biker then hung up.

*Oh, thank God!*

He narrowed his eyes at me and started the car. It was a clear warning that I'd better not have fucked around or the consequences would be severe.

We made the short drive in silence with his one hand on his gun the whole time. When we arrived at my aunt's house, the biker slid his black gloves back on, retrieved the cardboard box, then bodily shoved me toward the front door. It made sense that he'd want to be behind me in case I ran.

I opened the front door to find the house completely trashed and Hendrix on his knees, about to be executed. He had been severely beaten, bleeding all over the place, and now was groveling. I'd seen Hendrix stare down the wrong end of a gun before, but he never groveled. He had to be up to something.

Slick, the executioner, was standing a few feet away, his gun pointed at Hendrix, while the other biker simply crossed his arms and casually looked on. Behind them was Aunt Gina, who was frantically cutting her leg restraints with a knife, somehow completely overlooked.

*That was the play. Hendrix was buying Aunt Gina time to get free.*

"Perfect timing." Slick's voice was thick with triumph. "I wanted you to see—"

"Slick! Behind—" my biker chaperone yelled, having seen Aunt Gina clear as day.

I knew that if I was going to act, it had to be right now. I couldn't let that psycho win. I spun on my heels and slammed the door behind me shut, locking my biker shadow outside. There was loud but muffled cursing through the door when I felt the doorknob connect with a part of him that I hoped was extremely sensitive to pain.

"The fuck are you—" Slick's momentary confusion gave

Aunt Gina the few more seconds she needed to be fully free.

Aunt Gina screamed through the gag, which she hadn't yet bothered to take off, and buried the paring knife into Slick's back. He shrieked and whirled around, bitch-slapping her to the floor. Then, to my horror, he shot Aunt Gina three times in the chest.

I screamed at her, leaning back against the front door. The biker outside apparently wasn't hurt as badly as I had hoped, and the wood around the locked deadbolt cracked apart as he kicked it in. The force of the blow sent me careening into the adjacent doorway of the coat closet. I slumped to the ground but was able to kick the door shut again before he could get back inside. That was when I heard the sirens in the distance. The bank lady *had* called the police! Hope swelled within me. We might just make it!

Bullets punched through the door, zinging right above me. The Broken Vein outside must have heard the approaching sirens and decided that killing me was the only way in. I, however, wedged myself against the closet doorframe and the bottom of the front door itself.

Slick flailed for the knife that was jutting from the musculature of his back, making him look like a life-sized, wind-up toy. Decades-old anger drove Aunt Gina's hand, but she wasn't a murderer. She had stabbed him out of unwilling necessity, which led to Slick's wound being painful but not deadly. He would survive.

The other Broken Vein inside the house drew his gun but foolishly left Hendrix unattended to help his president. Hendrix seized the opportunity and somehow sprang up like a striking rattlesnake. He had appeared positively death-like when I first saw him, but now he was filled with energy and vigor. How much of that was playing up his wounds for show and how much was just pure adrenalin?

It didn't matter because Hendrix was ready for a throw down. He grabbed the back of the passing biker's head and rammed it into the nearest wall with such brutal strength that the biker's face smashed right through the drywall between the studs. The Broken Vein's unconscious body hung limply, suspended awkwardly by just his head and neck.

The sirens wailed in front of the house as several cars screeched to a halt. The biker outside crashed against the door once more, desperate to get in. I braced myself with everything I had left. The metal hinges strained and twisted, and deep cracks spread along the wood grain, threatening to snap it in half, but somehow it still held. He wasn't getting in.

There was yelling outside, back and forth from both the police and the stranded biker. Then more shooting, so I rolled away, knowing I didn't need to hold the door shut any longer.

Slick whimpered as he finally extracted the knife out of his back and dropped it to the floor. Hendrix glanced at me with a concerned expression, making sure I was all right, before he hurled himself back at Slick.

But the Broken Veins' president was much too quick, stepping backward and firing two shots into Hendrix.

"No!" I screamed as if the words could somehow deflect bullets. They didn't. Hendrix crumpled to the floor like a sack of potatoes, and my heart crumpled with him.

My aunt and now Hendrix too? It was soul crushing. I shifted my gaze up to my father, the man who had taken everything from me. Sorrow, self-loathing, depression—all were just tiny islands in my ocean of vengeance.

*He had to pay for this!*

Slick kicked Hendrix's body over to check the entry wounds as he was always deadly thorough. Seeing that Hendrix wasn't dead yet, he lined up one last shot that would finish the job.

Like most of my life, my father didn't notice me. He didn't notice that I had picked up the unconscious biker's pistol. He didn't notice that I had carefully aimed, but he sure as hell noticed me when the wrist that held his gun exploded.

Slick screamed, stumbling back to stare at me with both shock and anger.

*Do you see me now, Dad?*

His hand, now only loosely attached to his arm by a few ligaments, flopped lazily, while the wrist spurted blood onto the ground and the gun splattered into the ever-growing pool.

"You fucking cunt!" Much to my surprise, he refused to quit and wasn't giving in to the pain. With his other hand, he picked the gun up and brought it around to shoot me. Again, I was faster. I fired, this time catching him square in the knee. Broken bits of cartilage and bony shrapnel sprayed out through the brand-new hole in his pants.

Slick staggered backward, tripping over some of the

wreckage from their trashing of Aunt Gina's place earlier. His injured leg buckled; then, with a series of sickening pops, it bent the wrong way completely, causing him to crash to the floor in a crumpled heap. Slick lay there, whining and moaning.

"Hendrix!" I rushed over to him. By now, he had lost a lot more blood and was in rough shape, but the only life-threatening wound that I could see was the one just above his left pec, and he had placed pressure on it already.

My father missed.

"Do it! *Kill me!*" Slick yelled at me through labored breathing. We heard the police cautiously approaching the house. They'd be here any minute. It was all over for him, and he knew it. I stood over him anyway. I needed to see that even monsters got what they deserved.

"Why did you kill Mom? Was it because you found out about her and Robbie, or was it because you knew that Anna wasn't yours?" I didn't have a way of recording our conversation. There would be no way to prove any of what he said right now in court, and Slick knew that too. I didn't care. I just needed to hear it from him. I needed this closure.

"I didn't give a fuck about your mom. She was just some chink whore that I married to keep up appearances. I killed her because my brother needed to know his place!" Struggling against the tremendous amount of pain, Slick used all of his concentration to just form the words. "I put your mom on her knees and made Robbie watch as I blew her fucking brains out. Then I warned him that I'd do the same thing to his daughter if I ever so much as heard his name mentioned again. He needed to disappear and live knowing that everything that happened was all on him. That he was nothing but a worm beneath my boot heel!"

He was goading me on. My arm shook. I really wanted to kill him. He deserved it. The gun I held was pointed at his head. My finger tightened around the trigger. It would be the easiest thing in the world to end his life, to kill the monster that had caused me so much hurt over the years. I could take vengeance for Mom, Hendrix, Aunt Gina, Robbie, Miles, and probably countless others as well. And all I had to say to the cops was that it was in self-defense.

"Do it!" he snarled at me, drooling through clenched teeth and grimacing against the pain. "I'm owed too many favors! I won't be in prison long, and when I get out, I'm coming for you! Be the tough Merritt girl I always knew you could be."

It was a bluff, all that talk about not staying in prison. With all the evidence I had against him, if I testified in court, he was fucked and he knew it. He wanted me to kill him. Death was his only way out of a lifetime of mental torment in a tiny, windowless cell.

"No. You get to rot in jail knowing you lost." I kicked his gun away instead. Then I tossed my gun aside as well as I didn't need it any longer. I would hopefully never need it again. "Bruce Merritt *failed!*"

Slick's expression darkened once he realized there would be no easy out for him. "Even without me, the Broken Veins are still out there and growing every day. They're going to come for you, cunt. I'll make sure of it. You, Anna,

Hendrix—you're all as good as dead, you—"

I kicked him as hard as I could in the face, which wasn't enough to do any permanent damage, but it mercifully knocked him out. I then sat beside Hendrix and waited for the cops to make their way inside.

"Great speech... I wanted to clap, but I thought I might die." His free hand slid over mine, and he managed a weak smile. "The good news is that I'm hurt too badly to go directly back to jail." His strained chuckle became a horrible wheeze.

"Don't you dare joke about this, you idiot!" Tears streamed down my face. I was racked with remorse over his wounds but was relieved that he was alive. "I, too, worried about you. After all this, you're not allowed to die on me now."

"Don't worry. I'm not going anywhere. I don't care what it takes, but I'm never going to lose you again. That's a promise." Hendrix squeezed my hand, then in extreme pain, cocked his head over to the side. "Go check on your Aunt Gina. I saw her chest moving. I think she's still alive."

# Chapter 13
## HENDRIX

There was a soft knock on my hospital room door.

"Can I come in?" Maya's silky voice greeted me, and I spied her peeking around the doorsill, wearing a black business suit with a white blouse underneath. It was quite the change from stolen lost-and-found clothes. But Maya looked great in, and especially out of, anything she wore.

"Of course. I'd get up, but...." I raised my arm to the length that the handcuff would allow. "I've never been much of a jewelry guy, but at least they didn't give me a matching set."

"Bracelets aren't a good look for you. Now an earring, that's a different story." She brushed the hair from her eyes and smiled. It had only been a few weeks, but I missed the hell out of that smile.

"How's your aunt?"

"It's going to be a long road, but she's recovering. She told me to send you her thanks." Maya sashayed over to my bedside, her heels clicking on the laminate flooring. "You've been on my mind a lot lately."

"I'd have called, but you never gave me your number. I was hoping I'd get to see you before they transferred me."

"That's part of why I'm here. Your charges are in the process of being dropped. I wanted to be the one to tell you that in person."

"You're joking! A twenty-year sentence doesn't evaporate that easily."

"No joke, Hendrix. The gun you had under the seat of the rental car was picked up by the Broken Vein that brought me to the bank. With both sets of prints on there, they couldn't prove who used it to do the slayings in the casket warehouse. And with him killed while shooting at the police, obviously they couldn't get a statement from him. All they really have you on is skipping town while on parole."

Maya unlocked my cuff. Now was my first taste of freedom since I had been shot. "Between my witness statements of what happened with the Broken Veins and the Coffin Eaters, plus everything my mom had stashed away, I practically had the ATF bending over backward for me. Negotiating your release took a little work, but that was easy within the scope of things."

I rubbed my chafing wrist. "Sounds too good to be true. These kinds of things don't usually happen to guys like me."

"It doesn't hurt that I *am* a lawyer, even if I'm a freshman, at that." She winked at me and smiled. "Also Star contacted me and told me the Steel Veins MC would be willing to cooperate with the investigation on the one condition that you were cleared of any charges."

"Well, I'll be damned...." Now I'd have to go meet Remy

and Star and thank them in person.

"After this and what they'd done for Anna…" Maya scoffed, shaking her head. "I never thought I'd be saying this, but I guess I was wrong about the Steel Veins."

Apparently, hours after I had originally talked to Star, Remy had brought the full weight of his MC down on the St. Louis chapter of the Broken Veins. He rescued Anna and kept her safe until Maya could get to her. Then he went back and utterly destroyed Slick's chapter, going so far as razing the clubhouse to the ground.

"You and me both," I agree with a disbelieving chuckle. This whole mess started because Tex wanted to sell out Maya to Slick's chapter of the Steel Veins back before they broke off into the splinter faction, the Broken Veins. Who the hell could've foreseen that the Steel Veins would be the ones to actually save the day?

"I'm sorry I couldn't get here sooner," Maya concluded.

I scooted to the edge of the bed and forced myself to stand. The various tubes I was hooked up to pulled taut, and pain crackled up my leg from the slowly healing bullet wound in my thigh. I fought through the pain, but I stumbled a little though Maya caught me before I could take a tumble. I gazed into her beautiful reddish-brown eyes. "You're here now."

"Get back into bed, crazy," she weakly protested. "You're still injured!"

"Not yet." I slipped a hand behind her head and kissed her. I needed that far more than painkillers or whatever else these doctors and nurses were giving me. I was dying without it. We parted lips, but I couldn't let her go just yet. I hugged her and breathed her in enough to fill my wounded soul. Lilacs. She still smelled of lilacs.

"How's your heart?" Maya whispered, her chest fluttering a little at my closeness.

"Better now. It missed you."

"Hendrix...." She swallowed hard. I knew she missed me, too, but I could feel her hesitancy. Something weighed heavily on her.

I leaned back to get a better look at her. "If you're trying not to get attached, it's a bit late for that."

She sighed. "It's not that. I just...."

I awkwardly sat down on the edge of the bed, and she followed suit. "What did they want from you for my freedom?" My voice took on a darker tone. That's what this was about. Nothing from the government ever came without strings attached.

"It's one of San Francisco's assistant district attorneys. She, uh… she *hates* the fact that you're getting out of all this with just a slap on the wrist." She let her gaze sink to the floor. "Topeka wanted first bite at Slick, but she was successful in keeping Slick within her jurisdiction because of the incident at Aunt Gina's house, plus Mom's incriminating paperwork. So being the vindictive bitch that she is, she told me that she's dropping me from her witness list because I have done nothing to contribute to her case other than retrieve Mom's safe-deposit box's contents. I can't even testify to my part in the chain of evidence because that's being done by that damn bank officer since she states she watched me the entire time, and her statement is backed up by the bank's security cameras within the vault. And now I found out that my testimony about what happened at Aunt Gina's place will not be used because there's plenty of good stuff from yours and Aunt Gina's statements."

"What about the DA?" I asked, growing more and more worried. "You basically handed them their fucking case on a platter."

"I talked to the DA until I lost my voice, but he's still supporting her." Maya's lips pulled into a tight line, and the red flecks in her brown eyes seemed to flare angrily. "Apparently, he's up for re-election soon, and this case is going to boost his popularity. Imagine him taking down a dangerous MC in order to protect the good citizens of San Francisco. Whoopee.... I've already gone on the internet and raised hell about it, but I'm not winning much in terms of supporters for my cause, probably because I'm the MC's president's daughter, so there goes my credibility."

"They fucked you." I let my head sag as I slowly realized where this was headed.

"Yeah." Maya let out a frustrated burst of air. The look on her face told me she was still having trouble believing how everything went down. "In the end, my repeated requests for witness protection have all been denied. Me and Anna both."

And there it was.

The Federal Witness Protection Program would mean a new name, a new social security number, and a new identity. It would mean a new, anonymous life courtesy of the United States government for those testifying against large networks of organized crime syndicates.

With Slick still alive and the Broken Veins rapidly growing, Maya and Anna wouldn't be safe on their own. If they couldn't get into witness protection, they'd be sitting ducks for any Slick loyalist who wanted revenge.

"But it's okay." Maya attempted to smile through her frown. "I found an expat asylum program that we qualify for in Denmark, so I'm selling everything I own and taking Anna out of the country."

"Jesus…." I let the news slowly register. I wasn't positive, but I was pretty sure the asylum program wouldn't give them a new identity. It would certainly be more difficult for Slick to get to them, but it sure as hell wouldn't be impossible. "Do you know anyone there that can watch your back?"

Maya shook her head. She started to choke up a little but stayed strong. "So I guess that's the other part of this visit. I'm here to say goodbye."

The thought of losing Maya hurt a lot worse than any bullet wound. My body would mend, but…

"I don't like this, Maya. You and Anna won't be safe." The words burned like acid in my mouth. Slick might spend his life behind bars, but who knew how many friends that bastard had that were still out there? MC grudges lasted a lifetime. Maya and Anna would always need protection. "What about your career?"

"What career? It's a different legal system there. I'll probably have to start all over." Maya shrugged, looking away long enough to change the subject. "What will you do now that you have your freedom?"

"I'll figure something out. I've always been pretty good with my hands." I let some mischievousness creep into my face to help lighten the mood.

She glanced at me and couldn't help but smirk back. "That is true."

Looking at her too long made my façade fall away immediately. I was fooling myself to think the levity could last with so much heartache ahead of both of us. I shook my head. "All I've wanted since I got out was my freedom, but at some point in our trip to Cali, I realized that freedom wasn't enough." I gently turned her chin to look at me. "These last few weeks without you have been hell."

"Don't, please. I can't...." Her eyes were racked with so much pain. She turned away, but I caught her chin again and gently led it back toward me.

"What I really wanted wasn't freedom, Maya. I wanted something to believe in. Someone to believe in. That person is you, and I can't let anything take you from me again."

"Hendrix, we don't have a choice. This asylum program is our only option." Her pained expression worsened as she cleared her throat. It took her a minute to regain enough composure to continue. "We don't like it, but it looks like distance is the only thing that'll save us now."

"No, it's not." I exhaled hard, slowly gathering courage. "Stay with me, and I'll protect you. Always."

The shock of the request had taken Maya aback so much that she blurted out an exasperated yelp. She knew I was serious but probably wondered how I could possibly be so confident in the face of all these odds. "You're the toughest man I've ever met. I have no doubt of what you're capable of, but, Hendrix… we're talking about an army!"

"So let's get an army to watch our backs too." I reflected back upon Star's offer.

"What are you talking about?"

"Join the Steel Veins with me."

"What? Hendrix!"

"Hear me out! Hear me out!" I raised my hands and patted the air. "All the schooling you did, passing the bar exams, all that insanely hard work. Don't let Slick's shadow make you throw that away. Stay with me, and you won't have to start over again."

"I don't know." Maya considered it but was still racked with uncertainty. This was a huge life-changing decision. "Remy and Star did treat Anna really well after rescuing her, but it's going to be a while before you're healed up enough to even leave the hospital. I worry that I can't keep Anna safe if we stay here and wait for you."

"You're right. It's probably going to be a few months before I've recuperated enough to go out to wherever the hell this asylum dumps you. And during that time, you'll be completely unprotected." I paused, grimacing at the thought of my Maya being out there on her own. "I can't let that happen. I believe in us too much, and I'll be damned if I let anything on Earth tear us apart again. At least stay with Remy and Star in Leslie until I'm healthy enough to come after you."

"Hendrix, that's asking a lot from people we don't know. Anna and I would have to move into their clubhouse or a safehouse—one that was actually safe." Maya was no doubt thinking of what happened at the last safehouse Anna went to. "What could I really offer them for that kind of protection? I don't have much money."

"You're kidding, right?" I chuckled incredulously. Her naïveté was endearing. "With all the bullshit swirling around the Steel Veins, I'm sure they'll need a lawyer like you more than ever."

"Dealing with ruthless bikers might actually be a step up from the sleazy partners at the two legal firms I've worked at," Maya joked darkly, her disposition softening for a moment before abruptly hardening again. Now she frowned with a heavy sigh as a look of hopelessness washed over her. "Hendrix, that offer from Star was for you, not me or Anna. What are we to them?"

"Family," I defended, grunting with exertion as I forced myself out of bed once again. The pain was so excruciating that it brought me to my knees. Maya shot over to help me, but I stopped her with an outstretched hand. Gazing up at her overly concerned face, I did the craziest thing I had ever considered. "I love you, Maya. I always will. Marry me."

Her almond eyes became as big as saucers as she was stunned into silence.

"I-I can't hold this position very long. What do you say?"

"Yes! *YES!*" She yelled it so loud that the guard opened the door to see if everything was all right. She apologized to him for the outburst and waved him off.

"I have one more question for you," I said, the agony of what I was stupid enough to do quickly setting in.

"What? Anything!" Her smile and eyes were brighter than I had ever seen in so long.

"Can you help me up?"

She laughed and assisted me back onto the bed. After a long—and careful—hug and burying me in kisses, we spent a little while discussing timeframes and details. I assured her that having one of the biggest MCs in the country watching over us was the most protected we'd ever be.

We joked and said that marriage would be the only way to see if the relationship could work out, but I thought deep down, we knew that didn't matter anymore. We had already survived so much together, it was hard to think of anything that could shake that foundation.

We talked about Maya's future and how much good she could do with a massive organization like the Steel Veins having her back. She really liked the idea of getting into advocacy work. If anyone could reshape the underground railroad for domestic violence victims, it was her. Maya's experience and expertise with abuse, abandonment, and survival coupled with her vast legal knowledge and researching talents made her the best possible person to help families that desperately needed help. She might not have been able to save her mother, but she could sure as hell save many other mothers out there. And when I was healthier, I would help Maya's practice in any way I could.

It felt amazing for us to gaze at the starry horizon and see so much future ahead of us now.

I was looking forward to meeting her little sister, Anna. Technically, Maya and I would be her legal guardians until she turned eighteen. That alone was pretty heavy, but I knew right away it was a good decision. Probably the best one I had ever made. I had finally found what I had been searching for.

I think Maya did too.

## Epilogue
### HENDRIX

"Welcome home," Star said, opening the door and stepping out to meet us. Her glasses caught the afternoon light just right so that I couldn't tell if the knowing amusement in her smirk reached her eyes or not.

"You're shitting me, right?" I asked, looking past her into the living room. "What is this, a nine-bedroom?"

Pulling up we saw the stone-sided, two-story monster with enormous ceilings, eight-foot-tall windows, two-car garage, and a sea of bright green lawn, and Anna joked that we definitely had the wrong address. How could we not? With neither of us actually working yet, this house was far nicer than anything Maya or I could afford.

"Three," Star stated matter-of-factly before turning and waving us in after her. "C'mon, I'll show you around. We've got all the essentials in already—beds, major appliances, kitchen equipment, couches, tables, and all that, but the rest like the TV and everything else will be here later in the week."

"Star, this...." Maya slowly shook her head in disbelief as she set her bag down in the cavernous living room. She glanced back at me, and I could tell we were both on the same page. This was all way too much. When Star and Remy said they were going to set us up with something to get us back on our feet, we were expecting a shitty little apartment somewhere in town for a few months, not a fucking mansion.

"Is exactly what we talked about. Road to Hope needs a headquarters. and you all need a place to stay. No brainer." Star was unyielding and spoke with the certainty of her position within the Steel Veins. Her husband, Remy, was the club's president and face of the organization, but it was no secret that they ran things like equal partners.

"Do most nonprofits have hot tubs in the bathroom?" Anna asked, peeking into the room to our right. "Also, I call the master bedroom!"

"Like hell, you little monster." Maya wore a playful smirk and shoved her sister.

In the long weeks I spent recovering from the fight with Slick, Maya, Star, and another new member's ol' lady, Elisha, created a nonprofit subsidiary company through the Steel Veins called Road to Hope that would be focused on helping abused spouses and children escape bad situations. Between Star's resources, Maya's legal knowledge, and Elisha's entrepreneurial and bounty hunting experience, the NPO was going to be a force for real change. It was also going to put the Steel Veins at odds with dangerous one-percenter clubs like the Broken Veins, but after everything they put Maya through, I thought she welcomed the chance to get back at that shitty MC. Maya already had a big target on her back from her father, so she'd decided she was going to lean into it instead of trying to run from it. If they wanted her dead, she'd damn well give them a reason to. Road to Hope was publicly a way to legitimize the Steel Veins as a nonprofit and help people but was also a way to secretly dismantle the Broken Veins and clubs like them.

That was where I came in.

After long talks with Remy, we'd decided that both Maya and this new organization were going to need extra protection, especially being that Slick had a lot of friends who would be looking for payback. That was going to be my job—keep Maya and Anna safe and lead the team when the court systems failed and we needed to make house calls in person.

Star took Maya into their new office and began talking logistics as to what was going to be delivered when and what their next steps were for the NPO. I threw an arm around Anna, and together we checked out the rest of the house and grounds to give them their space.

"What do you think?" I asked when we got up to the second floor to check out Anna's bedroom. "Is it rebellious teen approved?"

Anna was anything but rebellious. The whole ordeal with her scumbag father had torn her up inside, especially after hearing how close her sister had been to being killed. She was an introverted mess when Maya took custody of her and couldn't bring herself to meet me for a long time just because I was a biker.

I suggested we get ice cream and go play mini golf together for our first meeting. No motorcycles or vests with patches, just a large man who couldn't sink a golf ball to save his life. I'd worn these terribly ugly, but funny and disarming, bright orange and white diamond patterned golf pants I found at a thrift store and by the end of the day had Anna smiling. It took a few really soft visits like that for Anna to get comfortable enough around me to start opening up.

Even still, having Anna eventually move from one MC right to another took a lot of convincing from her sister. We were doing what we could to take it slow with her, only introducing her to one or two Steel Veins at a time, always without their vests to show her that these men weren't anything like Slick's crew. It was going to be a process, but she was making progress.

"Can we get a tree planted closer to the window?" she asked, having opened the window and surveying the view. "It's going to be hard to sneak out if I have to climb down the side of the house." Anna turned back to me, wearing her best administrative look that she no doubt picked up from watching her sister work. "It's kind of a safety issue."

"Hmm, what are you thinking then?" I asked, crossing my arms and looking intently at the proportions of the window. "Zipline, water slide, or bat pole?"

"Let's do all three, just to be sure." Anna sat on the bed, flopped onto her back, and sighed. The bed was new and neatly made with perhaps a few too many pillows. It looked out of place in the nearly empty room. Anna would eventually blanket the place in posters or even paint the walls and otherwise fill it with personality, but until then it was all so plain and sterile. It drove home the feeling that this wasn't home, at least not yet.

"How're you doing, little rock star?" I asked. The full-sized bed would've been too small for me if I wanted to lay next to her, so I just sat in the middle and did a half turn to look at her. "Stressed?"

"Yeah. It's all... I don't know. It's all so much." Anna put her hands over her face and groaned.

"You got dealt a real shitty hand, and that's coming from someone who's been to prison. More than once." I chuckled, shaking my head. "But you're a smart kid. I heard that they weren't even holding you back a grade because of how well you tested at the new school."

Anna groaned, not convinced yet.

"And," I added, "you're not alone. I've seen how hard your sister is willing to fight for you. She's a beast!"

"She is." Anna lowered her hands and cracked a smile. "You're pretty tough, too, I guess."

"Between me, her, and the small army that makes up the Steel Veins, I promise you nobody will mess with you."

"I'm sure the boys at school won't be intimidated at all by that." Anna raised an eyebrow at me.

I laughed. That never even occurred to me. I was so worried about her safety I didn't even think some of her concerns might be normal kid stuff. I really had a lot to learn about this whole parenting thing.

"Hey, I promise I won't come to the door with a shotgun when a boy picks you up on a date." I paused thoughtfully. "You're sister, however...." I let the sentence drift, offering only a shrug and an exaggerated gesture to show I wasn't all that certain.

Anna laughed this time and sat up, then she gave me a hug.

"Thanks. For everything. I'm really glad you're around," she said, squeezing harder.

"Me too," I replied softly. "I'll try not to screw things up too much. Just a little. Ya know, to keep things interesting."

After a little more joking around and Anna painstakingly explaining how she was going to decorate her new room, we headed back downstairs.

"Enough business!" I hollered from the stairs. "You've got a hungry teenager here."

"Hey!" Anna elbowed me in the ribs for using her as an excuse.

"Okay, okay. And a hungry adult man. And we demand...." I looked at Anna expectantly.

"Chinese food!" Anna declared. "The angry mob has spoken."

"All right," Star said, smiling as she finished typing out a text on her phone. "I know a place nearby. You settle in and get unpacked, and I'll go pick it up."

Maya laughed darkly, but there was no mirth in her tone. Her and Anna's expression dimmed slightly. It was a stark reminder of how little we all had, and while we had the help and generosity of the club, we were basically starting our whole lives over again. When Slick first found out that Maya was trying to get custody of Anna, he'd sent people to torch her apartment in case she had any evidence against him, and the police had never let Anna go back home to get her things because it was too much of a safety risk. Neither she nor Anna had anything more than a duffle bag with some sundries and a few changes of clothes. After my stay in the hospital, I barely even had that. Needless to say, there wasn't much to unpack.

"Ah, I'm sorry," Star said, seeing the pain on Maya's and Anna's face. She quickly added, "Hey, tomorrow's a big day. As the first official workday of RTH, we'll need to go meet the Leslie community. We're going to partner up with a lot of the local shop owners in town, and it would be rude not to pick up a few things along the way." Star winked at the girls, and it seemed to lift their spirits a little.

I walked Star out to her car to thank her again for all her hospitality.

"Remy wants you at the clubhouse tomorrow. A few bikes are coming in around 9:00 a.m. All the prospects who don't have one will need to pick one out." She opened her door then paused to crack a smile at me. "I suggest you get there an hour early."

"Prospect?" I asked. The Steel Veins had the longest and most intense initiation process of any club in the country. It was mandatory to do a full year as a hang around before you could be sponsored and join the club as a lowly prospect. A year or two after that, you could be voted in as a full-patch member. I hadn't even started as a hang around yet, and they were putting me through as a prospect? It was nice to hear, but it didn't make any damn sense. "I haven't put in my time yet."

"Remy was impressed at how you handled yourself with Slick's MC." Star got into the car and started it up. Through the open window, she added, "He brought you up to the board and made a case as to how you've already proven yourself. The rest of the guys agreed. Welcome to the Steel Veins, Hendrix."

"Thanks," I said, taken aback at the news. I expected to have to fight tooth and nail to prove myself. I guess all the shit I went through with the Coffin Eaters, the pain, the death, all of it wasn't for nothing in the end. "Who's my sponsor?"

"Who do you think?" Star laughed. "So you'd better not screw up and let him down!"

*The national president himself is my sponsor!*

I watched her drive off, momentarily too dumbstruck to even move. My whole life changed when Maya showed up at our club's door looking for her uncle. It was crazy to think about where I was now... prospect in an honorable club, engaged to his niece, legal guardian to his daughter... Out of all the old C.E. members, I missed that old bastard the most.

*I promise to take good care of your family, man.* It struck me that they weren't just his family anymore. *My family,* I thought, smiling wide.

Goddamn, that was a warm feeling.

"Now there's a hell of a smile." Maya's touch on my arm gently brought me out of my thoughts. "Everything all right?"

"Yeah, you know—" I glanced back at our new home, catching Anna in the window making faces at us, then back to my beautiful fiancée. "—for the first time in a long time, I think so."

She said nothing and just gave me one of her knowing smiles.

"You knew, didn't you?" I asked, scooping her up into a big hug, lifting her small frame several feet off the ground. Of course she knew. Maya and Star talked all the time, and even if they didn't, she was still the smartest person I'd ever met. It would've only been a matter of time until she figured it out. "You are just the worst, you know that?"

"What! How am I the worst?" She laughed and draped her arms around me.

"The national president." I gave her a flat look, then spun her around in quick circles. "That's a big fucking deal and you didn't tell me."

"Okay, okay, okay!" She whined for me to stop. When I began to lower her to the ground, she stopped me again and gave me a playfully stern stare. "I didn't tell you to put me down. Yeah, you caught me. She told me earlier today. What can I say? I wanted to see the look on your face when she gave you the news."

"You are a first-class punk." I let the words linger in the air as I held the woman I loved in my arms. I couldn't help but think back to the years I spent in prison for a club doomed to die, never dreaming in a million years that I'd be watching the sun set over our new home—*our new life.*

This truly was far better than a thug like me ever deserved, but I sure as hell wasn't going to look a gift horse in the mouth. I glanced back at Maya, mere inches away; the bright warm tones of the dying light bathed her and made her look like she had a faint glow radiating from her already beautiful features.

*Yeah*, I thought, burying my face into her neck. The scent of her made my heart skip a beat, and when she squeezed me tighter, I felt a warmth fill my whole body. I didn't need to be the baddest motherfucker on the block. Knowing I had her made me *the luckiest motherfucker in the world.*

# About the Author

Jackson Kane is a professional stuntman, athlete, romance author, and above all else, a hopeless romantic. From American Ninja Warrior, to some of your favorite films, Jackson brings a unique writing style forged from countless harrowing adventures.

He's a lover of travel, his fans, his romance author peers, dulce de leche, and all things beautifully weird and interesting. He invites you to relax, have a whiskey sour and let him thrill and excite you in a way no other author can. Jackson will show you what the world looks like through the eyes of a genuine *Bad Boy*. Come with him, and…

**DARE TO READ DANGEROUSLY**

Become one of Jackson's Nerdy Rebel Readers

In Jackson's fan group, you'll have access to contests,
cover reveals, exclusive content, and secret videos.
You'll have private access into the world of a BAD BOY
male author.
His Rebels ALWAYS see it first!

**<u>Stalk Jackson Properly</u>**

(for his stunt work, American Ninja Warrior training and being a goof)
WWW.FACEBOOK.COM/JACKSONKANEROMANCE
WWW.FACEBOOK.COM/GROUPS/1734782496770518/
HTTP://BIT.LY/JACKSONKANEMAIL
WWW.GOODREADS.COM/AUTHOR/SHOW/15308326.JACKSON_KANE
WWW.JACKSONKANEROMANCE.COM

# About the Publisher

Hot Tree Publishing opened its doors in 2015 with an aspiration to bring quality fiction to the world of readers. With the initial focus on romance and a wide spread of romance subgenres, Hot Tree Publishing have since opened their first imprint, Tangled Tree Publishing, specializing in crime, mystery, suspense, and thriller.

Firmly seated in the industry as a leading editing provider to independent authors and small publishing houses, Hot Tree Publishing is the sister company to Hot Tree Editing, founded in 2012. Having established in-house editing and promotions, plus having a well-respected market presence, Hot Tree Publishing endeavors to be a leader in bringing quality stories to the world of readers.

Interested in discovering more amazing reads brought to you by Hot Tree Publishing? Head over to the website for information:

WWW.HOTTREEPUBLISHING.COM

www.ingramcontent.com/pod-product-compliance
Lightning Source LLC
Chambersburg PA
CBHW061102190726
48286CB00006B/1847